LESS OF THE SAME

LESS OF THE SAME

★★★★★

C.G. JOHNSON FRSA

Dedicated to my wife,
Raffaella Johnson

Time

Time the great creator,
a painter through and through.
Infinity it's pallet.
The probability is you.

Gravitons are galaxies,
That Higgs Boson sits upon.
Life is just a moment,
When truth is lost or won.

The deepest darkest secrets,
Lie within our dreams.
No waking hour can reveal,
What nothing really means.

Explaining nothing, is the question,
the answer is the truth,
But we are merely mortal,
and dreams are no man's proof.

A poem by Colin Johnson

Contents

Chapter One

The Placement

A gentle cry came from beneath the rubble, not loud or insistent, but unmistakably that of a baby. Joan, a young pretty lady just out of nursing college, looked over at her husband, Michael. He'd also heard the cry and, without hesitation, ran towards the collapsed building on Aleppo Street.

It was early morning and there were only a few people around, most of whom Michael recognised. There were a few other men around with guns slung casually over their shoulders, whom Michael didn't recognise. They probably belonged to one of the many factions that had risen against Assad, he thought.

He looked around, but no one else appeared to have heard the baby. Michael scrambled in the dirt, passing stones back to Joan as she looked on anxiously. Suddenly, Michael slowed his efforts and gently removed the last few rocks from around what was obviously a child. Being careful not to pull on its small joints, he lifted it away from its erstwhile tomb. It was a boy, covered in dust from head to toe, giving the impression, to anyone watching from a distance, that Michael had mistakenly rescued a child's doll. Close up, though, he was obviously a perfectly formed, beautiful baby boy, alive and breathing. Michael gently handed him to Joan, who cradled him as if she had held him since birth. She really is a natural born nurse, thought Michael, looking over at her. She was framed by the bomb-damaged buildings that stood behind her, and he found himself wishing they were anywhere but here. Joan turned to get up and leave. As she did so, the baby erupted into a ferocious screaming fit, forcing her to turn back towards Michael. On doing so, the baby stopped crying immediately. Joan wondered whether he'd been injured, and perhaps her movements had hurt him, but when she backed away from Michael, he screamed again, kicking his little legs into her arms. Joan decided to pass the baby to Michael.

"It looks like he doesn't want to leave you," she said, handing the baby gently to him. Sure enough, this seemed to work, until Michael stepped away from the demolished house. The baby's screams erupted again.

"Do you think his mother is still in there?" asked Joan.

"Well, if she is," began Michael, "I don't hold out much hope for her. This building fell two days ago. This baby's survival is a miracle in itself."

"We have to look," Joan insisted.

"Joan, do you expect me to move the whole house, piece by piece?"

"No," replied Joan, "but we should listen for a while."

"Okay," replied Michael, nodding. He knew better than to argue with his young wife when her face took on that determined expression. They sat down by the rubble and called out to others for help, whilst looking around for the brave rescue workers, known as the 'White Helmets', named for the white safety helmets they wore. But they must have been elsewhere that day. A lady brought over a bottle of milk and a damp cloth, which, allowing for the shortages from the war, was remarkable for the beleaguered city of Aleppo in 2016.

Michael called for quiet and they waited, but nothing stirred. Sitting in the hot, dusty rubble, not a sound emanated from what could once have been a living, thriving home, where a family had grown together for many years. They had probably baked bread, planned lives and received guests, he thought. Now, strangers, people who had never visited their home, or even met the family, were deciding their fate. Not because the family had threatened or offended them, but, perhaps, because they themselves lacked the imagination, or maybe the will, to deal with the problems they'd faced in any other way. Michael had no way of knowing that the bomb that had destroyed the home had been manufactured five years before the war had even begun. Ironically, its original purpose had been to protect the home and the family it had ultimately and perversely destroyed.

Fifteen minutes went by before Michael looked at Joan. She nodded to him in response. Just as he was about to walk away, he spotted an unusual shape in the dust. Carefully kneeling down, he brushed the dirt from the object. As soon as he made physical contact with the small round lump in the rubble, he realised it was a baby's head. It was only by chance that they had not stepped on it. He shivered at the thought. Carefully, he extracted the baby to chants of "Allahu Akbar", God is Great, from the watching crowd. He stood up and walked back along the pile of rubble, following Joan. The baby boy was now peaceful, even smiling, in her arms.

They found a place to sit. Michael carefully wiped the dirt off the baby girl so he could try to feed her. He needn't have worried; she took to the milk-soaked rag straightaway. As the crowd started to disperse, Michael called to them, asking if they knew who had lived in the house, but they all just shrugged. There was little left of the street and most of the people around were just passing through. Joan looked at Michael and smiled.

"Congratulations, Michael, it looks like we've just started a family, and thankfully without the birth pains." Outwardly, Joan laughed, but inside, she was worried. Michael smiled. He felt he knew her very well, despite the short time they had been married, and he could sense she was scared.

"Well, it certainly cuts through the … should we? can we afford it? … conversation!"

Joan reached over with her free hand and held his. "It's the will of Allah," she said, and he nodded.

The four of them headed back to their house, one of the few left standing in their street. On arriving home, they sat for a while, just looking at each other. Joan's expression conveyed the need for an answer, but Michael had none. He was not usually the 'forceful, take charge kind of guy', which is probably why Joan had been attracted to him in the first place. As a child, she had hated watching her mother being bossed around by her father. Occasionally, her mother had stood her ground, but she knew she had to pick her moments. From Joan's perspective, at the time, this wasn't a relationship, although she had still loved her father. Although, she could not accept that marriage had to be that way.

Michael had been a breath of fresh air to her. They had first met at nursing school in London. Even after he dropped out to look after his family, or rather, was forced to care for them through peer pressure from his brothers, she had stuck with him, despite her parents' objections, or maybe because of them. They got married and, although they had a few settling-in arguments, they had turned into a functioning couple, a couple who, for the most part, were happy; at least as happy as was possible in the middle of a war. Now, she really needed him to be her rock, for the first time in their marriage. Michael also realised that he had to man up.

"Joan, it's simple. We'll ask around. Someone must know something and we can take it from there."

"Okay, Michael. You're right. I'll be fine. I just need to put things into perspective, which is not easy."

Joan looked down at the babies and smiled. Michael kissed her ear in a way she understood.

"It would help us both relax."

"Alright," she said with an understanding smile. "But first

we need to figure out how to feed them, and then …"

She stopped abruptly, realising for the first time just how much they had taken on in the middle of one of the most brutal wars in history. The realisation made her start to cry.

"This is not good. There are no hospitals left to take them to. The children's clinics closed years ago. If they need medical attention, surgery or whatever, I'm pretty sure it's beyond Syria's, and our, capability right now."

Joan looked downtrodden. Her mind wandered to the war raging around her, and what she'd been forced to witness. Having seen so many atrocities, she thought that this one should have been just another one of them. However, despite it all, this one tragedy had, somehow, become their responsibility. Other tragedies surrounding them were down to others to manage, but, from this moment onwards, this problem was theirs alone, and they both knew it. However, if you'd asked them at the time, neither could have explained why or how they knew that life for them had just become a lot more complicated.

"We need to feed them," she announced awkwardly.

"Yes, but how?" Michael asked, biting his tongue for being so negative.

Joan shrugged and stared affectionately at the babies. They were both wrapped up next to each other on the old sofa, the one her auntie had given them, which they both hated. That's it, she thought to herself, she would just have to rely on her instincts. Right now, her instincts told her it was time to feed the babies, so that's what she set about doing. Normally, a trip to the shop on the corner would have been the next step, but, as it had been blown up and was no more than a pile of smelly rubble now, she knew that option was out. In fact, all the shops had either been bombed or looted. The owners were either dead, or had fled to save their lives. Their only hope was a food drop, which, if they were lucky, may happen any day. At least, that was the word on the street. There was some aid remaining, although she was unsure how that had managed to get through. She'd not heard of any new ones being attempted. Aleppo had become the home of the damned, she thought.

At first, they argued over who would go, but, as usual, they settled on going together. Deep down, neither could face returning to a pile of rubble, knowing the other was under it. If they were going to die, they'd both decided that they would rather be together when it happened.

Joan raised the question.

"What we shall call the babies, Michael?"

The naming process took longer than they anticipated, and, following a lot of bargaining, they settled on Adnan for the boy, meaning pleasure, and Adara for the girl, meaning beautiful. Both agreed that there were more pressing matters that required their attention. With that important function accomplished, they gathered some things and set off.

Chapter Two

Air Support

The Russian jets cruised, unopposed, across the blue Syrian sky. Every now and then, their radios chattered messages, conveying orders, which were immediately confirmed by the young pilots. The jets' wings left a thin, white whisper of vapour, which widened as they hurtled forward. From the ground, they were just specks in the sky, the roar of their engines only reaching the ground long after they had gone.

One of the pilots, a man called Serge, was a family man. Like all pilots across the world, he was immensely proud of his accomplishments, particularly the fact that he'd become a fighter pilot for his country, in his case, mother Russia. He had completed ten successful sorties into Syria. Each one had involved bombing specific terrorist targets, either ISIS or anti-Assad forces, usually the latter. He was confident he was making a difference. He was also proud that Russia, in his opinion, was again playing its proper role in the world: once again a leading figure in international affairs. Although his superiors didn't encourage him to think too deeply, or to linger on the subject of politics, he had been assured by those he trusted in his command, that he was doing the right thing, and he had accepted that whole-heartedly. These thoughts didn't occupy much of his time, though. Like all pilots in war, reliance on his orders was everything.

The ancient country was still beautiful, despite the war. Serge was enjoying the view; if you climbed high enough in the sky, he thought, you lost focus on the destruction. Suddenly, the radio crackled and new orders came through.

A convoy heading towards Aleppo was designated as their next target. They swung their elegant, gravity-defying metal towards the road, the vapour trails leaving a pattern in the sky. Even the vultures had come to recognise this pattern and it was becoming a regular food bell for them. The vultures rarely missed a potential meal, so they began to head towards new ominous signs in the sky.

Jack Summers had been working on the refuge bins for most of his life. He had retired at sixty and found that sitting around the house was not going to be enough for him. He had no hobbies, having never felt the need to take one up, so now he had the time, but not the inclination. Jack was five feet eleven, with a face like a walnut. However, it was a face loved by all who knew him.

He had raised three children, making sure they all had a good education. His daughter, his youngest, had provided him with his first grandchild, which had made him happier than his wildest dreams. The little girl seemed to glow whenever he held her. The rush of emotion he experienced seemed so unique to him, he could not have described it, even if his life had depended on it. So, it was with some regret that he had left his home to drive an aid convoy truck to Aleppo.

He had previously offered to do some volunteer work in a warehouse for Food Aid, but soon realised that the main skill he had to offer was driving.

All the family, bar his sister, had tried to dissuade him from volunteering, but he had laughed them all off. It wasn't that he didn't understand the dangers, it was more that he felt that it was the right thing to do. This same attitude had kept his marriage together for forty-one years, until, tragically, his wife passed after battling breast cancer. Somehow, after this experience, the fear of death seemed less important to him, so he found himself trundling along the Halb-ldilb road from Dar

Ta Izza. He'd begun by taking a short stopover in Turkey, where he had picked up the convoy of the fifteen trucks. The truck drivers were from all over the world: America, France and many more that he simply couldn't identify. Luckily for him, the organisers spoke English. He had also teamed up with the Americans and one Canadian. They, too, were retired and had families and stories to swap. Jack was only too happy to oblige. Out came his wallet and, as they shared a beer in the Turkish bar, everyone was treated to a photo of his granddaughter. She had been named Maria after her grandmother, who had tragically died the same year she was born.

The road was mainly dust, not like in the UK at all, he thought. He had visited Marmaris in Turkey some years previously, and loved every minute he was there. Especially the sea front, which led down to the roundabout where the road led back on itself. From there, you could walk through the covered market. The front itself had been lined with Turkish boats: the smaller ones set up for fishing, the larger ones designed for cruising. He loved the walk, although he never did take up on the captains and crews insistent offers to book a trip. They, in return, never gave up trying to persuade him.

He touched his glasses. They reminded him of the opticians that sat along the front of Marmaris. He'd reluctantly entered the high-class shop, sceptical that they would not be up to UK standards, and had been pleasantly surprised. The glasses were better than the ones offered at home, and were half the price. The opticians, to this day, still sent him a Christmas card. He had soon realised that a lot of his fears were misplaced, and he grew to love Turkey and its people on his brief visit.

He shook himself back to the present. That had been a holiday, this was different. He had seen bodies left lying along the road and children walking around aimlessly, with blank expressions, as if they were in a Steven King movie. Only, this was much worse. Even as this thought crossed his mind, he knew the description was grossly insufficient to describe the real horror. He knew that when he returned home, he would not be able to find a way to describe the horror he had seen here, even if he wanted to. You had to visit hell to really know it, he thought. It couldn't be described. A person would only have to look into those children's eyes, and that person would never be the same again. He shuddered at the thought of his family ever having to witness something like this. It would never happen if he could help it, he thought, hitting the steering wheel.

The convoy began picking up speed, so he concentrated on keeping a constant gap between himself and the truck in front, as he'd been asked to do. He had been told that the cab radio would issue instructions on when to stop, which came through in multiple languages. Luckily for Jack, English was usually the first language used over the mic. This time, though, it was Arabic. To Jack, it was just a string of noises, but he did recognise one thing in the voice, and that was panic.

Serge swung his jet around and lined up on his target. All his training clicked in perfectly. The state-of-the-art guidance system locked onto the convoy, electronically linking in with the plane's normal flight systems, which were mostly flying the plane anyway. Like in all modern jets, the fly-by-wire system was installed in all the Russian jets. The computer checked the pilot's movements and then adjusted to optimise the pilot's desired action. The subsequent effect was that, when the weapons joined together with the flight computer and the pilot, they produced an efficient trinity of death. Its sole purpose was to remove from the world all those your country had decided to terminate.

The green dots on the HD screen lined up and turned red. Serge followed the many instructions he had been given over the last three years of training. Playing out his part in the deadly dance, he pushed the red button.

Chapter Three

Hide and Seek

Joan and Michael weaved their way through the streets, passing vast numbers of people, and collected whatever they could from the rubble. A lady to their right was desperately pulling at a table cloth that was held firm by the rubble of her home. Her husband was standing over her and pleading for her to leave it behind, but she was having none of it. Instead, she was crying, praying and screaming about something to do with its value and the time it took to make. She had lost everything and wanted to keep the last thing she had managed to hold onto with her old, gnarled fingers. Joan looked away. Somehow, the scene was worse than the death that surrounded her.

Such was the fate of the people of Aleppo. It was hard to comprehend that most of the shells that had killed these people had been paid for from their own taxes, Joan thought. Surely this was the final absurdity in Syria. She longed for the day when wise men and women would once again rule the world; people without a personal agenda. Her daydreams were short-lived as she heard the familiar drone of jets high over the city. She pulled Michael to one side and into an alley. Some of the alley's walls were still standing, but this would not save them from a direct hit. She hoped they would at least shield them from some of the shrapnel. This time, no bombs came, although, she could hear explosions several miles to the south. Thankfully, she thought, they were well away from them.

Crouched in the corner of that alley, she held Michael's hand. With the other hand, she held one baby close to her breast, while Michael carried the other in a basket held in front of him.

"Michael," she began. "I know we have spoken about this, but I don't think I can go on this way. We have to leave, not just this city, but the country. This war will not end well for anyone, and I fear we won't make it. I love our city as much as you do, but ..."

Joan started to cry. It was obviously not a means of getting her way. Michael could clearly see that his wife had reached her limit. He was a good husband and knew what he had to do. Wrapping his thin but strong wiry arms around her, he softly whispered, "We will start to pack today."

The two made their way back through the depressing carnage they once called home. They felt the usual relief, as was typical nowadays, when they realised their house was still standing. They quickly opened the door and went inside.

After a cup of tea and a constructive discussion, the only place they felt they had a chance of getting food, was at a collection point that had been put together by locals and the White hats, as they had become known. Their white safety helmets were ever present after the bombs stopped, digging people out and risking their own lives. They were the real heroes of Aleppo, thought Michael as he took another look around his home for anything that could prove useful. This house had been a gift from Joan's parents. But it was now in the possession of the coward, Bashar Al-Assad. A man who was living in denial and luxury in the capital with his English wife, while his people were being slaughtered.

Michael tried to focus on their immediate problems. He could hear the babies crying but, unusually, their cries were more a gentle weep, a reminder of their presence, rather than their insistent screams. The sound of their pitiful weeping disturbed Michael. He found himself returning to thoughts of their survival, which was not his usual comfort zone. He was far from it, so he looked around, desperately trying to see if he could find anything useful, or even potentially edible. He and the other residents of Aleppo had long given up on being picky. Food had been superseded by sustenance; if it kept you alive, you ate it, with the noted exception of cannibalism, and who knew how long before that became a necessity. He shuddered at the thought.

It was several blocks of rubble and misery before they got to the collection point. Somehow, Michael thought, this never got easier. Joan was right, this would either drive them both insane, or kill them. There was no upside to staying. Joan spotted a few friends and called to them. They greeted each other emotionally as no one had ever expected to meet again.

The three men and two women were also on the hunt for food. They became visibly upset when they recounted their journey so far. The centre they were heading for, they said between sobs, was now just a crater in the ground. It had been hit by a bomb the day before, taking with it five aid workers and countless families waiting for food. No one would ever know how many died there, they said. They all simply disappeared. One of Joan's friends was particularly emotional as she described the scene. "They had gone," she explained, "to 'another place' before the sound of the bomb had even finished echoing around the streets." Joan hugged her. Hugs were all they had left of value to give. The bombs had taken everything else.

Mohamed, a good friend of Michael's, spotted the bundle Joan carried and asked if they had found food.

"No, but they are edible," Michael joked, trying to lighten the mood.

Joan smiled as she pulled back the cover to reveal the baby's head; Michael did the same. Together, they looked around at the smiling faces, and when the babies joined in with their smiles, it melted the hearts of all around them far quicker than any bomb could have.

A crowd gathered around, all eager to see something

positive amidst the mess surrounding them. Afaf, Joan's distant cousin, asked curiously, "Where did they come from?"

"Well, it was like this ..." and Joan went on to explain what happened, finishing with "... and, well, here we are."

"Where are the parents?" asked Afaf.

Joan looked sadly at Afaf. He immediately understood and went no further. There was no one who lived there who needed to know the details, not in this city, not any more.

Joan changed the subject, pointing out that the babies were hungry. Instantly, small packages that had been stuffed inside clothes, came out. The little their friends had, they shared. It could have been Dhu al-Hijjah, the last four days of Ramadan, she thought. That's how it felt to her at least, had it not been for the time and location.

Joan looked around. She wouldn't immediately be able to place where she was. Around her was pure devastation, not one building had been spared. They told their friends of their plans, who simply nodded with understanding.

"When are you going?" Mohamed asked.

Michael answered. "Today. We must go today. If we leave it to tomorrow, there's a chance we could change our minds. That is, if we live that long. Please let the others know that I'm not running from this fight. Although, between us, I'm not sure we, or Assad, can win this one. Right now, we are just pieces on someone else's board game. The players aren't on the board; they're not the ones dying. Their hands just appear from time to time."

The others nodded and talked amongst themselves while Joan fed the babies some milk using a scarf. It wasn't as hygienic as she would have liked, but it was the best she could think of. Their friends came up with reasons for why they themselves couldn't leave: old parents and businesses they'd built up; all good reasons, but none of them sounded sure. Joan just hoped they would be safe, although she feared the worse for them all.

They reluctantly parted, with tears all around. Joan and Michael headed back to their home to pack. It took them an hour to return, which was much longer than they'd expected as they were traveling against the crowd, who, it seemed, had also chosen to call it a day and leave.

They opened the front door to find a stranger standing in the hall. Michael took a step forward, but Joan stopped him. Quietly, she asked the stranger what he wanted. In response, the intruder moved towards her and raised his hand to hit her. Then, seeing the babies, he seemed shocked and somehow lost his footing. Straightening himself, he turned to run. As he did, he turned his head. His eyes showed confusion before he ran off towards the rear of the building to escape through the back porch that led on to the alley.

Michael grabbed Joan. "What were you thinking? He could have killed us all."

Joan just looked at him.

"I'm sorry, Michael. I just thought it was the best thing to do, I can't explain it."

Shaken, they both went through to the back of the house and secured the rear door, although this seemed pointless under the circumstances. Joan looked around.

"What do you pack when there's a chance you may never come home?" she asked Michael, rhetorically.

He just shrugged and then smiled. "I'm taking the only thing that matters to me."

He kissed her on the cheek.

They packed lightly, just taking what they could fit into one large rucksack, which Michael would carry, and a smaller one that Joan would carry. They would take turns in carrying the babies, swapping them around as they went along, mostly to allow each to bond with both children. They were both very fit, and it also gave the babies the opportunity to get used to them both.

They left late that afternoon. It had been tempting for them to delay their departure to later in the day, as an excuse to stay. But they both agreed that it was now or never. They had decided to head for Latakia, hoping to get a boat to Cyprus and on from there to Europe, but it was a loose plan with no goals beyond that. Their main objective was survival, or at least time, until they could return to their home in Aleppo. Walking away they didn't look back, they just headed in the direction of the M5 that led away from Aleppo, hoping to get a lift or purchase some form of transport with the little savings they had.

Chapter Four

Bite the Hand

Jack slowed the ten-ton truck. Its tyres scraped on the dusty tarmac and the brakes let out little squeaks, like mice being stepped on. He wasn't too bothered. It would, he thought, at least give him a chance to stretch his legs and relieve himself.

He pushed the heavy door open and jumped out. He had barely touched the floor with his feet when he was propelled upwards and thrown twenty feet into the sand dunes that lined the road. The noise made his right ear bleed and he was knocked unconscious for three minutes. When he came to, he felt a sharp pain in his head. He tried to rise but his back almost gave way. Almost blind without his glasses, which had shot off somewhere into the desert, he reached out to the only solid object he could make out. It moved as he grabbed it for support. Looking down, he saw the Canadian driver below him. Jack pulled his hand away. The driver was barely alive and was trying to speak, but he died before he could; his lower half had been pulverised by the bombs.

Jack pulled himself up again and looked around. Smoke was everywhere, which didn't help. But it was clear that the convoy had been attacked from the air very effectively, as no more than three trucks were left on the road, and one of those was on fire.

He was frozen at the sight. Nothing moved. Twenty people were in that convoy, he thought, or thereabouts; someone must still be alive. He made his way through the acrid smoke, which creeped into his lungs. He vomited, partly from the smoke and partly from shock. Walking over to what was left of his truck, which was on its side, he could see his bag hanging from the door. He reached up with a piece of metal and unhooked it, catching it as it fell. Scrambling around inside the bag, he searched for one of the water bottles he was now very glad he had packed. The water helped clear his throat and improved his breathing. He even wasted some of it to wash the dirt from his face.

Jack turned and walked back to see if others were alive. He called out, immediately regretting the effort as the strain caused his lungs to rebel and he vomited again. Nervousness made Jack recall an experience from his younger days, when he'd first ventured into the foolish pastime of drinking to excess. His mother had commented that he could have made vomiting an Olympic sport. He laughed at the memory, and that hurt, too.

He was almost at the back of the convoy, or at least what was left of it, when he spotted a man of about thirty-five bending over a young woman. Approaching the man, Jack could see that he was gesturing to him. He spoke clearly but, unfortunately, in Arabic. Jack responded in English and the man made a gesture of understanding, which was much clearer than communicating in Arabic. He threw up his arms.

The man then smiled, an intelligent, caring smile, which was apparent despite his half-grown beard.

"Ali," he offered, holding out his hand. Jack reciprocated the introduction and smiled in return.

"Jack. You're like the boxer," he said, mimicking the moves of a boxer.

Ali looked concerned, but then laughed.

"Yes, float like a butterfly," he said in broken English.

Ali pointed over to where a girl lay, obviously in a serious condition. They both kneeled by her. At first, she seemed fine, but when they went to help her up, she screamed. Jack had done some first aid, but that was over fifty years ago in scouts, and the badge he took never covered screaming Syrian women lying in the desert.

He cursed his nervous inner humour, and glanced at Ali. Ali turned to the girl and said a few words, moving to loosen her clothes. She immediately protested, saying something in Arabic that Jack didn't catch. He looked at Ali, who gestured towards him, and then the girl, who Jack guessed was about sixteen. The girl clearly preferred him to exam her. Looking at Ali nervously, he asked, in English, "Why does she want me? You speak the language, don't you?"

No response. He raised his voice slightly, but insistently, and repeated the question. "You speak Arabic?"

Ali seemed to understand and made a gesture: he ran his index finger down his face. Jack recognised this as the universal expression of 'old'.

"Oh!" he said and smiled at the girl. "You think I'm safer than the young buck. Okay, I can live with that."

Ali pointed to the left and said something that Jack was sure meant, "I'll be over there."

Jack loosened the girl's clothes. She was wearing a cloak or sari, which was the best Jack could describe it. She was a little malnourished and as he shifted her clothes, it was evident she was bleeding. He quickly located the wound. A piece of metal, probably shrapnel, stuck out just below her ribs. Jack sighed out loud, then managed a weak smile when he noticed the girl looking up at him. Life had not really prepared him for this, but something inside told him that the right thing to do was to push on. He grabbed Ali's attention by throwing a small stone. Then, using his best impressions, and with the aid of charades, he asked Ali to build a stretcher. Ali, luckily, was good at this game, because Jack sucked at it.

Jack was better at administering first aid. He found medical kits lying all over the place, as those were one of the things they were moving to Aleppo. Bandages were plentiful, but they had to open two boxes to find one unbroken bottle of antiseptic. Another held antibiotics. He twisted one of the bandages in a circle around the shrapnel, then placed another bandage over it. Lifting her gently, he shifted some of the sand beneath her so he could extend the bandage all the way around her torso. They gave her a double dose of antibiotics and formed a small tent to keep the sun off her while they made a stretcher. This took a while, but soon it was ready.

Jack pointed to the two intact trucks left on the road. Ali got the message and quickly ran up to the first one. As he opened the door, the driver, a middle-aged French women fell towards him, still hanging by her seatbelt. Ali fell back, stunned at first. Then, taking a deep breath, he climbed up and released the seatbelt, pulling the body past him as he went in. He looked down to find the keys still in the ignition, but in the off position. The driver must have just pulled over. As she was further back in the convoy, she would have stopped later than Jack. It was too late though, as it turned out. Ali turned the key and the powerful Peugeot diesels played a welcome, non-musical tune.

Jack and Ali carefully lifted the girl onto the make-shift stretcher. To take her mind off the pain, Jack asked her her name, with the usual, "Me Jack, you?", half expecting her to say Jill, but she said "Jalila" instead. Close enough, he thought to himself.

They moved her closer to the van, then opened its rear doors to clear some of the contents inside. What they saw made them laugh: stretchers, dozens of stretchers. They cleared them out and replaced them with some medical and food supplies. With Ali driving, and Jack in the back to care for Jalila, they headed off towards Aleppo.

Serge had just pushed the button; the missiles flew off so fast, it was as if they couldn't wait to explode. They tore down from the sky. Serge shifted his gaze to the full HD monitors, where he observed the convoy making its way towards the M5 from the A road 60. The images were so clear, he could even make out the UN blue badges on the top and sides of the trucks. His heart missed a beat, but only one before the missiles hit. The screen turned to sand and dust. He took control of the plane and, like an automaton, went through the procedure of heading home to base.

The radio spoke to him like a far-off voice from the grave, requesting him to report in, so he did:

"Mission successful. Permission to return to base?"

"Permission denied. Secondary target. Coordinates being sent now," came the humourless voice.

Serge was familiar with this kind of response and was normally enthusiastic in this situation, but bombing the UN trucks had unhinged him a little. Why would they ask him to blow up an aid convoy? Surely that had been an error? A horrible mistake? His government wouldn't do that. He clicked the transmitter, then stopped himself. What if they did? You didn't question orders. But, surely it was okay to pass back information? He would mention it on his return at the briefing he decided, and flicked the switch back. Serge checked the new coordinates and locked them into his computer. He was feeling better already.

Chapter Five

Comrades in Hell

Michael carried the baby boy and the large backpack. Joan was feeling weak from lack of food and clean water, but she pushed on. They were approaching from the left of the International School in Aleppo, in Aadhamyye, which meant they were only about two miles from the M5 motorway, where they hoped to find transport to Latakia.

Prior to the war, this journey would have taken no more than half an hour on a local bus. Today, it had taken them five hours on foot. Every other block, they had to climb over rubble and avoid desperate people, who would likely rob them of what little they had. So far, they had been incredibly lucky. Even the bombing had stopped. Although near exhaustion, they felt they were incredibly fortunate. They knew, only too well, that things could have easily been a lot worse; they had witnessed far worse with their own eyes.

Along the road ahead of them, a string of cars had been abandoned. The owners were either dead or had been unable to find fuel. Michael tried a couple of them, but he had no idea how to hot-wire a car. The ones where the keys were hidden under the sun visor or wheel arch, were empty. Joan looked over at him, gesturing for him to come closer.

"We need to rest, Michael," she pleaded. "Can we find an empty house or somewhere to get out of the sun for a while?"

"Okay," Michael agreed. "Let's do that."

He, too, had had enough for the day. It seemed hotter than usual, so he looked around. It wasn't hard to find a place to shelter in. Soon they were lying on a bed, which was surprisingly clean and dust free, despite the fact that the house it belonged to had suffered a direct hit and had been surgically removed from the block.

Joan changed and fed the babies, then checked their food levels. She realised their supplies would not last long, despite their friends' generosity, but tried not to dwell on their situation. At least they were out of Aleppo, or almost, she thought. Michael lay down and fell asleep immediately. Joan gazed at him and smiled. She had been lucky to have met him. Although her parents were traditional in many things, once they had met Michael, they were happy to forego arranging her marriage. They had liked him from the start, which wasn't hard. He had a smile that could charm a snake, but in a nice way. Michael was just one of those men women knew they could trust from the very first moment. It was as if they had been given the perspective of a man who was somehow kinder and more honest. She knew Michael had his faults, but one of his virtues was trust. That summed him up, she thought, 'trust'. If Michael said he would do something important, he would. Come to think of it, her thoughts continued, he was not so great at remembering the less important things, like shopping and appointments with friends; he was dreadful with these. But, on things like their marriage, the babies and the war, he was as solid as a rock. This is what her parents had seen, as had anyone who met him. He was simply a good man, which, she thought, was an accurate reflection of him. She looked down at his sleeping form and smiled. He was not handsome as such, but he was cute, although she would never tell him that. His enormous eyelashes were the envy of many women he met. He was wiry and fit, and, on a good day, he liked to think he was six feet tall.

Joan tucked a blanket around both babies and placed them next to her. She fell asleep instantly, as did the babies. They would all would dream in peace for a few hours.

Michael was the first to awake to the sound of gunfire. It was close and he reluctantly woke Joan. The sound was so familiar now: the steady rat-tat of the Kalashnikov, Russia's contribution to humanity, which, he thought, would have been a little harsh had it not been for the bombs falling like rain around them. They deserved his anger; they deserved the world's anger.

They cautiously set off a while later, having left a note of thanks to the owners of the empty house. They also said a short prayer for their absent hosts' wellbeing before leaving.

The road was quiet, far too quiet. Michael had seen this before. Although he had been recruited into the Syrian freedom fighters, he had not yet fired a shot in anger, and he doubted whether they would miss him. They had soon realised that killing just wasn't in him. He was no coward, but he held his gun out in front of him as you would a soiled nappy, or a rat you found in your backyard. This probably explained why he'd left the gun in the hallway at home. Joan had noticed, but said nothing; they were soul mates and she understood.

The quiet, though, was unnerving them both. It could mean a sniper or even snipers, were in operation here. They looked nervously at each other, and then Joan spoke. "What choice do we have? I suggest we walk normally and openly. Hopefully, if there is someone watching us, they will see we are no threat and will have no reason to shoot us."

Neither of them believed the last part of that argument, but they both agreed on the first. They had no choice, thought Michael. They walked at a normal pace toward the M5, desperately trying not to look dangerous. With Joan carrying one baby, and Michael carrying the other baby in one arm, with his other around Joan, trying to shield them as much as possible, they certainly looked harmless. A shot fired out, making them jump, but it was some way over to their right in another street. This went on for the next hour, until they finally spotted the roundabout leading to the motorway. Twenty minutes later, they reached it. Now that they were mostly out of the range of potential snipers, they sat down in the shade near another group of travellers, who looked equally relieved to be there. Michael approached two of the men, who eyed him with suspicion. One glanced at his rifle. Leaning against the wall next to him, Michael opened his arms, offering the time-honoured greeting, "Assalamu Alaykum wa Rahmatullaahi wa barakato. (Peace and mercy and blessings of God be upon you)."

"Wa alaykum assalam. (And peace is with you also)."

Although they were still a little tense, Michael's smile worked its magic. Not before long, they were all sitting together and exchanging stories, which was relaxing for them all. The news, however, wasn't good. They hadn't heard about the aid convoy's troubles, but they did say that it was way overdue. Michael felt it was still his best bet. He left the pair, exchanged goodbyes, and walked back to where Joan was sitting and feeding the babies with some of the little food they had that was suitable for them. Joan was amazed at how the easily the babies had accepted the mashed-up food, mixed with the remaining milk they had. She had always believed that babies only had milk. Under normal circumstances, she would have looked for a nursing mother, one who may have been willing to share her milk, but they were harder to find now.

Michael and Jean agreed that it was best to rest and wait with the others. They chatted away on lighter subjects, such as where they would consider settling down until the war was over. Joan had joked about the Bahamas; Michael said he preferred the Seychelles. They settled on Bognor Regis. The sun was starting to set. Its incredible beauty that normally signalled a peaceful night, was now ominous.

A night in the open could bring its own dangers for the refugees and they were nervous.

Chapter Six

Computer Glitch

Jack held Jalila's hand and gently spoke to her. She couldn't understand the meaning of his words, but he could see that it comforted the young girl. He told her about his granddaughter and his wife. Throughout his story, Jalila smiled at him, unless they hit bumps in the road, when she winced. Jack winced in sympathy, but tried not to show it.

The roads were smoother now that they were on the M5 leading to Aleppo. Although Ali was familiar with the truck he was now driving, as it was identical to the one he had driven before the convoy had been attacked, everything else had changed for him. The aid convoy had now become a desperate dash for survival.

"Why?" he asked, looking upwards. "Why would anyone attack a convoy carrying food and medical supplies for civilians?"

The sun shone down on them as relentlessly and mercilessly as their attackers had been, but he received no response to his questions, only more heat and more dust. Was that the answer? he wondered. "Might is right?" No, he concluded, he didn't believe that. But there seemed to be no other plausible explanation. The strong always seemed to get their way.

In rooms far away, the end game for Syria was being planned. In a cold and cynical manner, the leaders worked out the best strategy, possibly believing they were acting in their country's best interests. For Assad, it meant retaining his power; for Russia, it meant naval or air bases; to America, well they said it was to destroy ISIS or Daesh, another name for the

Islamic State, but as noble a reason that was, who knew what their true motives were.

Assad, supported by Russia, had, it seems, decided that the rules of war no longer applied. Chemicals were being used to terrify and maim children publicly, for the world to see. They had demonstrated that they cared little for the UN. They could, after all, veto any vote, an especially popular act amongst desperate, scared leaders, and Assad was definitely one of them. Bombing hospitals and schools, and demoralising and crippling the community, all played a part in their 'no rules' war. With Russia's backing, and armed with his new-found freedom to cross US laid red lines with impunity, Assad knew full well he was safe. The UN and America simply spouted platitudes, with loose, false teeth. Obama's red line had been worn out, it had been crossed that often. What had been a new, black hope for a better world, now stood barely able to cover his ineptitude with his practised speeches. That was the trouble with bluffing against a country led by a sociopath, whose country's favourite pastime was chess.

Ali knew the road well. He had made this journey several times before the conflict began, but, as he approached the roundabout that overlooked the city of Aleppo, his breath left him. He slowed the truck and stopped, staring at the devastation. He had, had no idea that it was this bad; it was as if a giant had repeatedly smashed its fists down on the city. Jack shouted to him over the noise of the engines. Unable to hear Jack, Ali turned them off.

Jack repeated the question. "Why are we stopping?"

Ali pulled back the partition that separated the front from the back of the truck, and waved for Jack to come forward. Joining Ali at the front of the truck, Jack saw why he'd stopped. Jack's imaginative mind conjured up the scene with Charlton Heston at the end of *Planet of the Apes*, where Heston shouts at the destroyed Statue of Liberty. People like me aren't meant to see this, he thought, not outside of the news channels like the BBC. His concentration returned to the scene.

"Well, Jack," he said to himself, "this is why you came. Even if you had no idea what you'd find." He stayed with Ali for a while, taking in the devastating view. Having seen enough, Ali returned to the cab and started up the engine. Jack went back to the girl.

They moved slowly towards the roundabout, where several people had gathered. The people had obviously seen them coming and had started to rise up from the floor and head towards them.

Serge, in his Russian jet, had been called off his second target and had resumed patrol as ordered.

His mind was now free to drift to his family. He kept a picture of them on his instrument panel. In his mind, he was back in his home in Russia, with his beautiful wife and children, playing by the nearby lake, where he took them to feed the ducks.

His daughter, Tanya, particularly loved the ducks. She was only eight and very much a daddy's girl. He was putty in her hands; he couldn't say no to her. This, of course, infuriated his wife, who complained that she had to live with Tanya when he went off for months on end. He had laughed. What harm could he do, he thought, she was the sweetest kid in the world.

An incoming message interrupted his thoughts. A new target came over the radio. He cleared his thoughts and checked his position. The target was not far away. This won't take long, he thought, and checked the programming for the new target as it was fed into the computer, then pulled back on the throttle.

Chapter Seven

Like Souls

The heat had risen to its peak. The sun was only doing what it did every day in Syria, and it did it well. Heat and fear were a bad combination, though. The people around Michael and Joan had plenty of both; they were restless. On top of that, they were hungry. Spotting the UN aid truck, they headed straight for it. Michael and Joan joined them, grabbing the babies as they moved. They, too, were desperate and hungry. But, as they moved towards the truck, it stopped dead. It was still a distance away, too far to chase after it in the relentless heat, so the crowd stalled, preferring to wait and see what it did next. A few minutes later, the truck started moving again. It's not moving fast, but at least it's heading towards us, thought Michael.

The truck driver got out and waved his hands in the air, urging them to go back. He was shouting in Arabic, but it might as well have been Chinese. The crowd rushed to the back of the truck and threw back the heavy tarpaulin, which threw up a cloud of dust into the air, temporally obscuring their view of the inside. When it cleared, the crowd visibly shrank back. Instead of the food and water they were expecting, they saw stretchers stacked to the roof, and Jack and Jalila.

The dejected crowd dispersed. One or two talked with Ali, who imparted another familiar story of madness. Afterwards, they embraced Ali in a true brotherhood fashion, as only Muslim men do, oblivious to the western coldness. Handshakes were not for them, just a full embrace and a kiss with feeling. There were no homosexual intents, just brotherhood between men without shame.

Michael and Joan approached Jack and spoke to him. Jack was surprised and relieved to meet people who spoke English. They spoke it surprisingly well and explained that they had both visited England five years previously, before they were married. They had, in fact, met each other on a medical student exchange course when they'd been studying nursing at St Thomas' Hospital in Westminster.

Jack was glad to hear they had medical training. Out here, they were as useful as consultant surgeons. Jack started to recount the events of the morning; they just nodded with heavy hearts, their faces conveying their understanding and sorrow.

Joan climbed into the truck, handing the baby girl to Michael. Under normal circumstances, he'd have easily borne the weight, but in his weak state, he visibly struggled, so Jack offered to help. Joan nodded her approval to Michael before turning to speak to Jalila, who nodded and responded. Jack couldn't make out what they were saying, but Joan asked him to leave them while she examined Jalila. Jack got down from the truck with the baby girl, and then closed the tarpaulin a little, leaving just enough of a gap for light to enter so Joan could see.

Michael looked Jack up and down and liked him straight away. Jack had that effect on people, he was modest to a fault. Michael thought he looked like a real gentleman. Somehow, if you lived your life as one, as he suspected Jack had, it showed all over your face like a badge of honour. The opposite was also true. He shivered when he pictured Assad's weak-chinned face and beady eyes; his features said it all.

Michael and Jack wandered off into the shade where Jack offered Michael some water. Michael immediately sat down and gave the babies some, before getting up to go to the truck. Jack held his shoulder and quietly said, "It's okay, Jalila has plenty in the truck. She will share. We have some food, too.

Michael understood the injured girl's need for privacy and peace so he nodded and sat down.

The plane did not come equipped with audio cd's, so Serge had smuggled his own on board. He was listening to some Russian rock, by a band called Chaif. He looked out of the cockpit and sang along to the music. It really got his adrenalin going. When he was a boy, this was what he had dreamed of: flying jets at mac three, and returning as a hero of the new Russia. Life couldn't get better than this, he thought.

Glancing at his instruments, he turned off the music. As much as he wanted to keep it on, he was professional enough to know it would be a distraction. He lined the plane up and switched the attack computer on. His order, this time, was to drop incendiary bombs on a group of suspected terrorists who were unloading weapons from a vehicle. A drone had confirmed the activity, but did not have enough fuel to carry out an attack. So it was down to him, and the three other jets he was flying with.

There were ten seconds to drop when he checked his screen. He could just see the target, a single truck with small groups of people milling around. He felt his heart beating faster, the adrenalin pumping through his veins. I really love this job, he thought, with just four seconds to go. The UN logo on the truck became clear. He wondered whether they were western arms traffickers. Two seconds … his visuals turned from green to red, then flashed hypnotically … one second.

He flicked the switch forward on his aptly-named joystick and waited, but nothing happened. It was too late to try again, so he passed the message on to the other three jets and banked away.

Jack heard the jets and shouted for everyone to take cover. Looking around, he noticed that he and Michael were not the only ones not running for cover.

Michael made for the truck, handing the babies to Jack as he did so, although, he knew he was too late. As he neared the truck, he expected to be vaporised where he stood, as had so many before him. At least they would go together, he thought. He opened the rear flap on the truck and looked straight at Joan. She had been focused on Jalila and was unaware of the impending attack.

"Joan, I love you," is all he said before the bombs exploded, throwing him to one side. The searing heat from the incendiaries blew across the road, despite the distance from the impact. Then, with a whoosh, air rushed in to replace the used oxygen from the bomb. Further explosions could be heard, but further away. Michael felt strong hands lift him up from where he'd fallen. Looking up, he saw Jack giving him one of his best smiles.

"They missed."

Michael took his hand and got up, dusting himself off as he did so.

"They don't do that often," Michael said, and smiled back. Then his face changed to one of deep concern.

"The babies?"

"They're fine," answered Jack. "I was at the front of the truck. The blast missed me and the kids. I put them over there."

Jack pointed to the floor where he'd placed them, just out of Michael's view. He picked the girl up and handed her to Michael before picking up the boy. It was then that Michael realised how close he had become to the babies in the short time that he and Joan had had them. Those few seconds just gone had felt like hours. He knew he would never be his young carefree self again. Responsibility had found him, and he now accepted it without regret.

Holding back the tarpaulin, Joan said, "Jalila needs a hospital. I can't help her here."

"Well, we have two choices, return to the city or carry on to Latakia, hoping we meet someone who can help us along the way," said Michael, without a great deal of conviction in his voice. Neither option seemed good to him.

Joan spoke with authority, "I don't think we should go back to the city. Even if we make it to the hospital alive, which is doubtful, they may not be able to help us there. They're overwhelmed as it is."

Jack waited for her to finish, then he spoke.

"I feel like a spare wheel here. I volunteered to drive one of these UN trucks to help your people, so I'll take you wherever you want to go."

Michael held his shoulder and thanked him, then turned to Joan.

"So, that's it, we go to Latakia," Michael declared.

Jack sighed. "That's a bloody relief, I didn't fancy driving into that." He pointed towards the city that currently looked like ancient Rome before they dug it up.

Back in the Russian jets, Serge and the other three pilots chatted amongst themselves, trying to work out what had happened. Their best guess was that a jamming device had affected their weapons systems, and that's what they reported to base.

Serge knew this would go right to the top.

Everyone piled into the truck. The babies were put in the front with Michael. With Jack driving to give Ali a break, they set off.

By now, the crowd had lost interest as news of the attack on the convoy spread amongst them. Their hopes of food had been dashed so they wandered, depressed and hopeless, back to their city. Their progression was not for safety, this was their home; broken, smashed, but still their home.

The truck continued along the relatively good road, the M5, which would soon turn into the 60, bringing with it the dust clouds.

After a while, they came upon the wreck that was once the aid convoy. It had been picked clean. The petrol had been syphoned from every truck and all the supplies looted. Luckily, Ali and Jack had taken spare petrol canisters and a good amount of food and water before they had left. With foresight, they had hidden the stolen possessions behind some stretchers in the back of the truck, which had worked as none of the crowd back in Aleppo had even bothered to search the truck. They'd settled with a cursory glance into the back. Seeing the injured Jalila lying by the stretchers had slowed them down. After all, who would want to scramble over a wounded girl for no good reason.

They slowed down a little as they passed the carnage, which had become a temporary morgue for the good people who died there. Each person in the truck prayed, in their own way, for the souls they had just passed.

Jack changed gears; the big diesel took a second breath, coughing before settling back to its usual comforting rhythm.

"Michael," Jack began. "If it's okay to ask, can you explain what I am in the middle of here? I'm a simple working man, from a simple working background." Jack smiled as he spoke, trying to keep his voice down as the babies were asleep. "To tell you the truth," he continued, "I'm a bit lost. I know I must sound stupid to you. You see, of course I know there's a war on, and that Assad is trying to hang onto power, but it seems, having spoken to the other drivers, God bless their souls, that there is a lot more to it than that."

Michael hesitated, hanging his head a little to one side, as if in deep thought. Then he looked over at the older man and spoke. "Imagine you were living with an evil landlord, who only looked after his favourite tenants in the block. Everyone else could go to hell; no plumbing, no electricity, evictions, you get the idea. Then one day, the disregarded tenants decided to stand up to him. A fight starts between them and the landlord, including all his favourite tenants. This is where it gets complicated, because the disregarded tenants formed different groups. The neighbours got involved and felt that they ought to sort it all out as they lived on the same street. Eager for revenge on the landlord, they wanted their side to win so they would have an easier time. If that wasn't enough, the local hooligans thought they would also jump in and take over the whole block, if there was a chance."

Michael looked over at Jack.

"Is that any clearer, Jack?"

Jack smiled. "A little," he said.

"So, who are the hooligans, the Russians?"

"No," replied Michael, "they're the neighbours."

"Then, the Americans and the rest of Europe?"

"No, the hooligans are Daesh or ISIS, you could say."

"Oh!" answered Jack. "I don't think I've come across them yet."

"You don't want to," replied Michael. "They are evil in a way that is hard to imagine. When they take over a town, everyone becomes their slave, especially if you're not their …" he hesitated, "… brand of Muslim, like the Yazidi. You see the Yazidi believe in a lot of things from many religions, including Christianity, Judaism, as well as Islam. So Daesh decided they are just the spoils of war. The men are killed and the women taken as sex slaves and raped. Even the Daesh wives go along with it. They make children and execute prisoners, dozens at a time. We do not want to run into them."

Jack nodded, he was quite worldly, but the things he was hearing sickened him. Somehow, he thought, the news affected you differently. Hearing these things on the TV at home, when you're comfortable on the sofa with your family, was completely different. He remembered thinking, just a few months back, when he picked up the remote and the news had come on: "I don't want to see that horrible stuff on the TV every night." He'd switched channels to watch *Only Fools and Horses*.

Now, sat in the truck, with the heat and the dirt, and the very real possibility of being stopped by ISIS at any moment, he felt ashamed for the first time in a while. He had always thought of himself as a good man, one who tried his best. Then again, he thought, how good can a man be. If mere geography could pacify his conscience, how much distance, he postulated, would it take before you felt compelled to act to stop an atrocity. He wondered, was it enough to be far enough away not to hear the screams?

They both sat in silence for the next hour. Michael hoped he hadn't upset Jack. Then again, he did ask. He looked over to the usual happy face he had recently taken comfort from. The happiness had been replaced by sadness. He hoped the old Jack would return soon, he liked him.

Jack swerved and the truck jumped. He quickly corrected it. Michael had seen the bomb crater and held the babies tight in anticipation of the jolt, but Jack hadn't. The resulting jolt had thrown everyone around in the back. Jack pulled the truck over and angrily jumped out. Michael followed, carrying the children. He was about to speak to Jack when they both heard a commotion coming from the back of the truck. They ran to see what had happened and found Joan weeping, with Jalila in her arms.

"Oh no. No, please God, no!" Jack exclaimed.

Joan saw his reaction and gently placed Jalila down. She jumped down from the truck. "It wasn't you," she pleaded to Jack. "She died before the truck swerved."

Jack looked at her, desperate to read the truth in her words and face. What he saw was genuine, which gave him some comfort. Then he remembered the poor girl. She had been so quiet, despite the terrible pain she must have been in. He sat down on a wall belonging to the village they had stopped by, and lowered his head in prayer.

Michael handed the babies to Ali and helped Joan move Jalila from the truck. They placed her in a shady spot and covered her up with an old scarf he'd found in the truck. Ironically, when he shook it to get the dust off, before placing it over Jalila, he noticed its beauty. It was possibly made of silk and was covered in embroidered butterflies in all colours. Jalila looked like a Muslim woman resting, modestly covering her face.

They all felt the loss, despite the carnage around them. Jack remembered his thoughts from a few minutes earlier. Distance really did matter. Michael was comforting Joan, who at least had her training to fall back on. But it only helped a little. The doctors' words in England were a distant memory now. Here in Syria, on a hot road, she was little better off than the rest of them.

Michael and Jack wandered off to one side to talk. The others took the opportunity to feed the children and eat and drink a little themselves, not that anyone felt particularly hungry.

Michael and Jack talked about the journey. Neither wanted to dwell on negative thoughts, but Jack calculated that they had about another four hours to go. He suggested they put the rest of the diesel in the tank, it would save them having to stop along the way. They returned to the truck to unload the last few jerry cans containing the fuel. Suddenly, the ground ahead of them erupted into small explosions as automatic gunfire bounced around them. It had only been a short burst, but it seemed longer to Jack. The owner of the rifle appeared with several others and approached them. Most of the leader's face was covered by a scarf, but Jack could see that his eyes were black as night and he stood well over six feet tall.

"Get on the floor," he barked in Arabic.

Jack just followed the others and got down on the ground. It was pretty obvious what the man had ordered.

It had been an hour and the heat was unbearable. They had been tied up and placed with their backs to the wall. The babies had been taken into a nearby house with Joan. The men didn't seem to want anything to do with them, which was a relief to Michael and Joan. Now, though, Michael was scared for them all. His imagination was playing tricks with him. What were those men doing in the house with Joan? He wanted to call out to her, but knew this might bring the wrath of their captors down on them. Depending on whom they were, that could be the last thing he, or any of them, did. So he sat and waited, trying to ignore the flies and mosquitos feeding off his face.

Chapter Eight

The Coast

Ellie Frost had worked with the UN for ten years, and had been promoted to Field Logistics manager. She wasn't beautiful, but she was pretty in her own way; fit but not shapely in the Vogue sense. She was taking a well-deserved break on a beach in Latakia. The waves gently lapped the shore, and, she thought, she could easily have been on a Greek island, which is where her mind wandered to. Ironically, there was one facing her, if she fancied an eighty-mile swim.

Ellie was a tough manager. She'd seen a lot in her ten years. All the naïvety had been knocked out of her many years ago, back when she had witnessed corruption, bribery and illegality on a massive scale; and that was inside the UN and the charities she had worked for and with. Unfortunately, sometimes it was the only way to get things done. At first, she had fought it, even been shocked by it, but when she'd seen the starving children, she realised they had no other choice but to pay off the corrupt local government officials, and the police. If that was the only way to get aid through, then that's what you do, Ellie had told herself. It's not pretty, but if it's all you can do, then you just have to do it. The alternative was to fight city hall while people died.

She picked herself up and dusted off the sand.

"Back to work," she said to herself, starting back towards the warehouse building that the UN had occupied near the port.

It had been an old custom's warehouse when Syria was still a trading nation. Now, its only trade was the aid that was coming in from all over the world. The problem was, it rarely went any further.

Ellie had met her match; she couldn't very well bribe Vladimir Putin, but, given the chance, she would have tried. Ellie was frustrated, and it was showing as she walked back into the warehouse. She entered through the little door that was housed within a massive door, the ones you had to step over. Once inside, she cast her eyes over the vast area. The aid they'd received so far had just filled a small corner of the warehouse. Although, it still represented over two hundred tons of aid. The air inside was several degrees cooler than the boiling temperatures she had just come from. She shivered but enjoyed the feeling of the cool air on her skin. The temperature inside was as warm as an English summer.

Ellie shouted at a man driving a forklift. "Gary, what on earth are you doing?"

Poor Gary had no idea what he'd done, but he did know he was going to find out.

"You have just piled tinned condensed milk on top of the snap-up tents. They are not called that so you can enjoy the snapping sound they make when you stack a ton of sickly-sweet milk on top of them. It's not a bloody giant bubble wrap for your entertainment."

Gary flushed red. Then, as he always did, he looked indignantly at Ellie and said, "If they had been properly labelled on the side, as they should have been, I wouldn't have made that mistake. I think I mentioned this to you a week ago."

Ellie counted to five in her head. Ten was out of the question. "And …" she said with as much control as she could manage, "… what did I tell you?"

Not waiting for an answer, she continued, "I told you to check carefully, anyway, because mistakes at the other end will always happen."

"So," said Gary, still on his high horse. "It's suddenly my fault if the other end gets it wrong?"

Ellie felt like she was not getting anywhere, and just replied, "It's not suddenly your fault. There's nothing sudden about it. My guess is, it's been happening all your life. It's like a steam roller, it may be slow, but it will still run you over if you don't move."

Gary was speechless, that went right over his head, so he just muttered some inaudible profanity and spun the forklift away.

He is good with that machine, thought Ellie, probably the best she had seen. Pity he didn't come with an instruction manual, she smiled to herself. No one could unload like Gary, you just had to make sure a lot of thinking was not required.

Ellie went to her office, a little porta cabin raised up on two old containers with a makeshift set of stairs that ran up the side. She climbed the stairs, trying to ignore the ominous creaking. If the stairs could withstand the giant Arab warehouse manager who used to be here, she was safe. The office was purposefully sparse. Ellie knew she might be given a five-minute warning, or less, to vacate at any time, or 'bug out', as the Americans liked to call it. Bugs would be the only thing left, she thought.

The phone rang. It was one of those connected to an outside bell, so that a manager could hear it from anywhere in the warehouse. It had obviously been put in long before the advent of cell phones. Ellie rushed to answer as she feared for her eardrums.

"Ellie Frost, UN," she answered efficiently. She never knew who would be on the other side: generals, politicians, overpaid heads of charities; the only constant was that it was never good news. This time was no exception, only, it was personal.

The voice at the end of the phone was familiar, it was her boss, a man she had known from her early days. He was a good friend and she trusted him.

"Hi, Bob, what's the latest act of inhumanity to man?"

Bob was quiet for a moment, so she prompted him. "Bob, what is it?"

"It's the convoy," he said in a choked voice. "It's been hit."

Ellie sat down on the filthy cushion of an old chair, one she always tried to avoid sitting on. She preferred to sit on the wooden one that was reserved for workers receiving a grilling. It wasn't comfy on purpose, but Ellie was pretty sure she would need another tetanus shot for sitting on the cushioned chair. Somehow, this didn't matter anymore. She sat back and tried to absorb what Bob was saying.

"Why?" she asked. "Why and who?"

Bob's voice came back a little steadier. "We don't know yet. Everyone is denying responsibility, but it can only be Assad or the Russians. They're saying it was a ground attack, but it wasn't, it was called in, but the signal was cut off ..."

Ellie interrupted. "Survivors?" was all she said.

Bob answered. "We don't know. There is word of a truck getting though, but nothing's been confirmed, yet."

"I have to go there," Ellie insisted.

"No, Ellie, there isn't anything you can do."

"I'm going anyway, Bob, and don't try to stop me."

Bob knew it was hopeless arguing with her. He could have put his foot down, but that would have put him in an awkward situation later. So he backed down.

"Okay, but you take Mike with you."

Ellie started to protest, but she also knew when to back off. Mike was an ex-marine and had been a useful go-between when they were dealing with the military in the past. He spoke fluent jarhead.

"Alright. Any other conditions?"

"No," answered Bob. "Just be safe."

"I will," she reassured him and hung up. Then, realising what she was sitting on, she quickly jumped up.

Mike was ex-military. He was in his early forties and had taken a job as a security consultant with the UN, which had recently morphed into the role of Ellie's bodyguard. He was enjoying a beer, sitting at the only bar left open, when he was surprised to see Ellie walk in. She didn't drink that often.

"What's up?" he asked in a welcoming fashion. His handsome but rugged face broke into a smile.

Ellie moved quickly towards the bar.

"The convoy's been hit."

"How badly?" asked Mike, now very serious.

"Bad," she replied. "There may be some survivors as there's been word of a truck getting through. They're also saying it was an air attack."

"Bastards," Mike stated. "What new low shit is this? It was an aid convoy. Everyone knew its timetable. This was no accident!"

Ellie nodded in agreement.

"The Russians and Assad don't give a crap. Sadly, there are no rules in the mad house when the staff goes on strike."

Mike agreed.

"I'm going out to find them. Coming?"

"Like I would miss a road trip," Mike half-joked. He stopped short of smiling as he knew how important this was to Ellie.

"You know," said Mike, stretching his legs as far as they would go in the Land Rover, "I was thinking, earlier, that this bombing, if that's what it is, has just become a new world low. You know, call Guinness and get it registered, but then I admonished myself for being that naïve. People have been doing things to each other, just as bad or worse, for hundreds of years. The difference is that we now get to see it in HD."

Ellie abruptly stopped the truck.

"I know what you're saying is true, but right now, I would give real money to have sight of one or two of those images. So I could examine them closely, to see if they are dead or alive."

Mike understood.

"So, let's focus on the task ahead, or we may be the next

statistic out here. And that's not something I'm planning, okay?" Not waiting for a response, she carried on, "Mike, I know you know what I mean. It's just that, sometimes, I think you have your head in the clouds. I need you here with me. There's no battalion backing us up. There's just you and me. If that doesn't scare you, then make it scare you, because it should."

She paused. She knew he was a good man, but he had a habit of drifting off topic, and that could prove fatal in a war zone. UN work was different to the military. You had to have a non-official degree in diplomacy and eating shit.

Mike nodded again and sighed.

"I'm here," he said with a grin. "Lead the way, boss."

Ellie smiled at Mike, then gunned the engine. They were on their way.

Chapter Nine

The Enemy of My Enemy

Jack looked across at his fellow captives, Michael and Ali. They were muttering something to each other in Arabic. Noticing Jack staring at them, Michael spoke to him, "We could be here for some time. This is not going to get easier, so you should prepare yourself." His face showed no emotion as he spoke, just acceptance of his fate. Jack was furious.

"You can think that way," he said, "but if that's the way the shit's going down, I'm going down fighting."

Michael nodded; he had to admire this old man's grit. He had witnessed a mock form of this bravado in England, while he was at medical college and hearing opinions in a pub, brave talking from the bottom of a beer glass, spurting of opinions to friends of what they would do to terrorists if they were left alone in a room alone for half an hour with them. Although, no one ever added the fact that terrorists had machine guns.

He knew he was now hearing the true bravado, and it scared him. Jack could get them all killed if he tried something. Situations like this, which for him was new and unique, equipped Michael with a new sense of fear. The kind of fear that left you feeling helpless. Michael had not felt this since his childhood. Only then, the fear was only of the wrath of a parent, this was more visceral. This was like lying on your back, staring up at a lion as it effortlessly pinned you down with one paw, its saliva dripping on your face.

Their suspected long wait never occurred, and neither of the three thought it was necessarily a good thing. Their captors exited the building. The last one out, a short, older man, guided

Joan out with one hand. His other hand casually cradled a sniper rifle. Joan cradled both babies and looked tired, but not afraid.

The taller man with the dark eyes beckoned to another of his group, then purposefully headed towards Jack. He pulled Jack from the wall, spinning him around as he did so, then bent down and cut the ropes. Jack rubbed his wrists. The tall man beckoned for Jack to stand up. Jack slowly complied but only succeeding in falling back again. The man reached down to help him up. Seizing the opportunity, Jack reached for the man's gun and pushed him forward. He raised the gun, fully prepared to fire, but the tall man and Joan screamed out to him.

"No, Jack. They're not what you think."

As was typical in any stressful situation, people often reverted to their native language, which is what Joan did. Luckily, Jack gaged the situation accurately and lowered the rifle.

The tall man jumped up and reclaimed the gun from Jack's inexperienced hands, shoving him gently but effectively to one side in the process.

"Jack," Joan pleaded in English, "they're freedom fighters. They're against Assad and on our side. They needed to be certain of our own status."

Night fell quickly, but no one in the group noticed the sun disappearing. Somehow, the dark was more welcoming than usual. They settled around a small fire, which they'd put together, sheltered with corrugated iron. Cutting a flat piece of iron and placing a similar piece at a forty-five degree angle to direct the smoke, they managed to mask the light from the flames, which could have easily given them away, making them a target for any aircraft above.

The fire was comforting, thought Jack. He had helped light it after drinking a good two litres of water at the firm insistence of the tall man, whose name was still not forthcoming. For that matter, none of the fighters had volunteered their names, but Jack and the others understood why and hadn't pushed to find out.

Lighting the fire seemed almost spiritual: the small flames casting shadows across the desert whenever anyone stood up. Its sudden appearance made it seem like a giant was walking behind that person, along the base of the sand dunes. Their voices were hushed and they spoke in Arabic. Jack found the language hypnotic and marvelled at its easy flow. He now understood why storytelling was a revered gift across desert regions all over the world. Although he couldn't understand what they were saying, he was more than happy to sit and listen to the tales, coaxed out of a gifted imagination and shared across the flames. They were told in such an intriguing tone. Mixed with the mystical smell of the spices used on the meat they were cooking, and the non-alcoholic heated cranberry drink, Jack was sure he would always keep these memories.

In the morning, they awoke to find that blankets had mysteriously been laid over them. The babies, who were the reason they'd awoke, were crying to be fed. Although, they were now in baskets that looked almost new, equipped with their own mosquito nets and matching sheets.

"Where on earth did they get these?" asked Jack, genuinely shocked.

"We're not in the third world," Michael answered, a little indignantly. "Someone in the village probably donated them. They're similar to the one my sister has."

Jack looked mortified.

"I'm really sorry, that's not what I meant," he said, looking genuinely sorry for unintentionally insulting their country,

"It's okay," said Joan, stepping in. "I know what you meant." She threw a look at Michael, who stayed silent. Some things are universal, thought Jack, remembering the thousands of moments his wife had managed to shut him up with one look. He turned from the others as tears flowed a little at the memory,

Looking around, they realised they were alone. The freedom fighters had all gone. A few villagers went about their business, but the freedom fighters had definitely left. Presumably so that no one would know which way they went. Jack knew these chaps had a good chance of winning, despite the odds against them, and he hoped they would.

The others prayed to the east. Jack prayed, too, in his own way. He was beginning to enjoy the ritual, one he had ceased to do. This wasn't just an obligation or a routine; it was more a beautiful time of the day. No minarets or Oman's called them to prayer; they just came together and prayed. There was sincerity about the whole event and it didn't make Jack question his faith. He was a Christian and, from what he understood, which wasn't a lot, there were similarities between the religions anyway, which was good enough for him. It did, however, make him feel a little guilty and self-centred.

A small meeting was held, but the overwhelming majority believed it was still better to head to the coast. So they jumped in the truck, now fully fuelled, and set off. This time Ali drove. Jack sat in the back with Joan and the babies and couldn't help but feel that he'd been demoted, which, in truth, he had.

The road was still the same, as would be expected, but the changing scenery was not welcoming. It would have been a rubberneck's dream, however. Every mile or so, there was an accident of one sort or another. But 'accident' was completely the wrong word in this case. They passed cars riddled with bullets and full of bodies. Jack's mind was slowly breaking up, not that he or anyone else fully realised the subtle changes they would carry with them for the rest of their lives. They all masked the effects from each other and themselves, through joking and making inappropriate comments. All of which seemed politically correct, or at least acceptable, under the circumstances. In reality, they definitely weren't acceptable.

The lasting effect of their trip and experiences would, if they survived, be dished up by the mind at a time when it hoped there was a chance of survival amidst the unimaginable and unthinkable; hope being the operative word.

One of the convoy drivers who'd returned to England had told Jack a story. It was about two children he had given sweets to in a village, where they had stopped to refuel. The driver had offered sweets to a group of children, but only two of the youngest had accepted. This confused the driver, until they stopped at the same village on their way back, where they found the two young children had been hanged by the roadside as an example to the others. The lesson was simple: do not take anything from what was considered an infidel. Jack had not been able to get the story out of his head and, now that he was here in the middle of the war, he was sure the story was true. Though, at the time it sounded unbelievable to any human who desired to remain one. Now he had his own stories and nightmares to tell.

The ride was smoother than he expected. Ali had successfully avoided potholes. Jack spent the time speaking to Joan. They chatted about her time in London. In return, he told her about his family and shared memories of his deceased wife. Joan reciprocated by telling him of her family back in Aleppo, and how beautiful the city had been. Jack finally lay back, apologising to Joan for being old, and fell asleep. Joan watched him and the babies as they slept. She focussed on their similarities: they itched at their faces, almost in unison, and even farted at the same time, which she couldn't help laughing over.

The babies had held up well. It was obvious to Joan that they had escaped unharmed from their ordeal in Aleppo. She used this rare moment of peace to think about her future. A few years earlier, she had it all planned: nursing college, followed by marriage. Actually, she thought, marriage had sneaked up on her. She'd planned on building her career, buying a nice house, and then, children. Well, things had turned out slightly different, concluded the part of her brain that helped her cope. College first, marriage, war, get bombed, have someone else's children and then emigrate. So much for planning she laughed to herself, but the farts had been funnier.

Chapter Ten

Land Rovers Are Great, Aren't They?

Ellie looked over at Mike. He had made himself comfortable against the window and was dropping off to sleep. She had taken an instant liking to Mike from the moment they'd met. He had a rough but charming smile that seemed to cheer her up every time she saw him. He'd served in the marines, which, alone, wouldn't have endeared him to her. Not that she didn't hold marines in the highest regard, quite the opposite in fact. It was just that she evaluated people as individuals, not as a group.

Ellie's mind wandered. She was worried about the convoy, although she was fairly sure she should be preparing herself for bad news. Of everything that might have been hit, Ellie had not expected the convoy to be targeted. Everyone involved had agreed to let it pass. It made no sense; why not just disagree in the first place. It was as if Russia were using Syria as a training ground, a live fire exercise with real people. The thought brought on a rush of fear through her whole body. If mad people could climb to power so effectively, and surround themselves with similarly afflicted thinkers, or people too weak to counter them, then Syria was just the beginning. When a mind was capable of playing with a country's army, as if they were toy soldiers and plastic people, that mind would surely not be content with dealing with domestic, day-to-day politics when the war was over. Where would that mind look next to feed its desire for another, adrenalin-fuelled power trip? He felt cold at the thought.

The road had been surprising clear. Ellie had long since learned not to focus on the evidence of war that was strewn around the country. She had plenty of pictures in her mind for an involuntary show when she got home. Sleeping tablets and vouchers for psychiatrists should have been issued as benefits for her job.

Villages passed by and luckily the sky remained clear. A lone Land Rover, even with UN badges on it, especially with what had happened recently, could potentially be a target. "That's right, cheer yourself up, girl," she muttered to herself. She picked up the radio and pushed the transmit button, calling through on her designated frequency to let Bob know they were on their way. Her attempts were met with silence. She tried again, but there was nothing. She admonished herself for not checking that everything was working before leaving. She really didn't want to go back now. She leaned over Mike and grabbed another bag. Rummaging around, she found what she was looking for, a Sat Phone. It was very expensive to use, but the UN were paying, so she dialled the numbers. Just then, she hit a massive pothole, throwing the Land Rover into the air at an angle. It came down, bounced twice and, with a quick movement of the steering wheel, straightened. Ellie sighed. Land Rovers are great, she thought as she searched for the phone she had let go of. Mike, now fully awake, commented as he handed it back with the antenna broken.

"I'm pretty sure that's six points off your licence and a hundred pound fine."

Ellie wasn't smiling.

"Oh, come on," Mike said, trying to make light of the incident.

"We still have the radio."

Her expression shut down that line of thinking.

"We don't?" Mike asked.

"Broken, it's useless. An ex-radio," Ellie said, remembering her Monty Python.

"Oh." It was Mike's turn to be serious. He placed his jacket on the window as a pillow and went back to sleep. It was what it was. He knew she wouldn't turn back, even if they should have.

There were parts of Syria that hadn't changed. They could have been any place in northern Africa, which, in no way whatsoever, resembled Ellis's home town. Ellie was born in the north of England and had left school at the tender age of fifteen, not because she disliked school, on the contrary, she loved it, but it was just what girls did in her school. Most went off to work in the local shoe factory, not two miles from the school. That is, of course, if they weren't pregnant, which, admittedly, was less frequent back then

Boys, if they were lucky, ended up in the docks, on the dole, or in prison. This, Ellie thought, was probably an over simplification, but it accurately portrayed the choices they had, and it applied to the majority of children in her town.

There were good things, too. She let her mind wander back to her childhood days as the heat-hazed road became a screen for her memories. She thought of ex-boyfriends, who were mostly married off now, with kids of their own. She smiled to herself as she thought of James, the butcher's son, having children. That was hard for her to comprehend. He had been so shy the first time he had tried to kiss her. They had been in a field overlooking the town, a place they'd walked to several times as friends, looking for butterflies or, for that matter, anything interesting to break the awkward silences.

James hadn't been much of a talker, partly because he was a well-fed youngster, something his peers often reminded him of, peers who were differently afflicted. They teased him to compensate for their own insecurities; a ritual they performed at his school on a regular basis. Their chants were as unoriginal as the school uniform, and seemingly as obligatory. This had had the effect of prematurely wearing down James's self-esteem and confidence, which was in short supply anyway, even before he'd begun his school years.

On the field, they stopped and, with fate's light touch, their angelic heads turned at the same time. Their eyes met. James moved slowly and nervously towards her. His heart was beating like a marathon runner, his mind was driven on by feelings he didn't understand. Seeing those beautiful eyes and lips, knowing that he was about to join with them, and then tripping on a vine and, with the precision of a Glasgow hooligan, he smashed his forehead into Ellie's nose, efficiently and painfully breaking it. The trip to the hospital and explanations to her father and brother had put him off girls for another year. Ellie had tried to comfort him and explain that it wasn't his fault, but they both realised that romance had passed them by.

Ellie's daydreams ended abruptly when she spotted a vehicle coming towards them. She slowed the car to get a better look. It looked like a truck, but Ellie waited until it reached a bend to get a better view. At the same time, she woke Mike up, who jumped up, rubbing his eyes.

"What is it?" Mike asked, still half-asleep.

"It's a truck," Ellie replied. Then excitedly said, "It's a UN truck. Mike it's UN. It must have turned around and come back."

She pulled the Land Rover to a stop and jumped out to flag the truck down. The truck occupants had seen her and were slowing down to stop near them.

Ellie approached the truck as she spotted Ali jumping down from the cab. She recognised him as one of the drivers from the aid convoy from when she had supervised part of the loading back in Latakia. Most of the trucks were loaded in Turkey, but some items had been shipped direct and that's where she came in. Ali spoke to her and Ellie replied. She spoke a little Arabic, enough to get by; she had to in her job. Ali was very pleased to see her.

"Hello, it's nice to see you again. Were you looking for us?"

"Us?" enquired Ellie anxiously.

"Yes, there are six of us, including two babies and the couple we picked up outside Aleppo."

Ellie quickly did the math and moved to the back of the truck. The math did not leave her with much hope, but hope was hope, she thought. Ellie pulled back the tarpaulin and immediately covered her face as she cried.

Chapter Eleven

Traffickers

Aaqaa's name meant 'master or owner', and he was proud of it. The meaning, however, he may have misinterpreted. He seemed to think that it meant being superior to others, or at least that's how he acted. Abd-al-Hakim was his partner, or business associate, as they over-kindly referred to themselves.

Both had both been running an electrical shop for eight years before the trouble began. Most of the money generated came from selling fake electrical goods and components to unsuspecting travellers. It had proved to be a very lucrative enterprise, especially when mixed with a good deal of money laundering from drugs. So, they hadn't been very happy when the war had ruined their business, as one was useless without the other. There weren't enough people who wanted new camera batteries or lenses, or even keyrings with camels on them. So, they'd looked around for other opportunities. The unscrupulous pair found that smuggling people across to Greece was even more profitable than their previous business.

They transformed the back of their shop into a factory, turning out cheap grey inflatables, which were hardly suitable for playing on the beach on a good day, let alone on the angry Mediterranean. Add to this the fact that the inflatables had been re-designed. They'd extended the inflatables to be five times longer than the original schematics allowed, which they had downloaded from the web. Now, stocked with second-hand cheap outboards, which only had to pass one check, they started up. They would only get as far as being out of sight of the beach before seizing up; they were the perfect death traps.

The cost to the refugee traveller was equivalent to taking a ten-day, all inclusive, cruise on a luxury liner, for one person. Even if you considered the free burial at sea, which was the only benefit, the travellers would unwittingly take up on their short journey

For Aaqaa and Abd-al-Hakim, which ironically translated to "servant of the wise", it had become a routine. Initially, seeing babies being carried onto the flimsy rubber boats bothered them a little. However, their corrupted minds soon justified the unjustifiable.

Later on, they and others would be giving similar arguments in an international court: "I had my own family to care for"; "I thought the boats were safe"; "I had no idea what was happening", these were amongst the dozens of varying pathetic excuses that would burn the ears of incredulous listeners all over the world. They would only be overshadowed, a little, by the crimes committed by Assad and Russia, or any other state that believed that dropping bombs on starving children and civilians would somehow help them more than dropping aid would.

Aaqaa kissed his three children goodbye and, smiling, he jumped into his Toyota Land Cruiser.

He smoothly pulled the giant car from his street and patted the nine-millimetre Beretta in his shoulder holster, in the same way one would check they hadn't forgotten their wallet or phone. This was all part of his life, although he rarely had occasion to use it as the people he now conducted business with were terrified before they even got to him.

It was a short drive to the shop. The warehouse he owned was at the back and he could have easily walked, but he wrongly believed that it enhanced his status with the workers who re-designed the death boats. He needed all the help he could get with this, as he had very little, if any, management skills. He usually substituted his deficiency with yelling or aggression, which, he found, worked quite well with the uneducated men, boys and women who worked for him.

He, of course, underpaid them. He made them work long hours and deprived them of sleep, which ensured they didn't have the will to fight him.

They all were required to live above the shop, packed into two rooms. An outside toilet behind the warehouse was provided for their use, which was continually backed up from over use. The resulting stench from the raw sewage soon led to illnesses, not that Aaqaa cared. He owned two other premises, and, in war, workers were not hard to find.

However, he soon realised the terrible toll this business took on workers. The mixture of glue and lack of ventilation usually meant that the workers were off their heads half the time. In such cases, Aaqaa simply threw them out on the street until they could prove they were able to do the job again. Some even worked to pay for their own escape at the end of their employment, ironically. They built the very craft that would ultimately kill their own families.

Today was a big day. They were due to launch five boats that evening, which meant a lot of organising, paying off the local police, who still required discretion from them despite the bribes. The boats were almost finished but the glue should have been given another day to cure and set. Aaqaa had decided that, due to expected poor weather conditions, the humanitarian thing for him do was to get them on the water as soon as possible. His psychotic denial system was working overtime that day.

Abd-al-Hakim's role was more complicated. Getting five boats sorted was one thing, dealing with two hundred scared 'passengers' was another. The fathers constantly moaned about the cost. He was also being constantly asked the same questions, time and time again, from people seeking reassurances.

He would be glad when the day was finished, he thought to himself. Another frightened father asked,

"Is it safe?" Abd-al-Hakim answered with a practised reassuring smile, "We know what we're doing. We have been helping people for a long time and no one has died on our boats. We received dozens of thank you cards from Cyprus."

"Here," he'd continue, pulling out a few they'd made themselves earlier for exactly this purpose.

"It may seem expensive, but what price would you put on your life?" was another standard response.

Bouncers would mingle with the crowds, pretending to be passengers themselves, and inject positive stories and impart their personal reasons for why they were happy to go. This was effective in filtering out the most belligerent protestor, who would conveniently disappear, never to be seen again.

Then there were those who had no money. Those who begged to be taken from the war-torn lands. They offered anything, no matter how extreme: sex with wives or worse. Abd-al-Hakim didn't take them up on these offers anymore, after a big bust up with Aaqaa about it being a business. Aaqaa had been right though he thought.

The night drew in and Abd-al-Hakim witnessed the well-oiled routine of the bendy, oversized boats being lifted to the water. In the moonlight, at first glance at least, they looked like "brand new inflatables", as described.

Soon he had his cargo following him like a silent pied piper through the alley, across the road and onto the beach, lit only by a half-moon and the red neon lights from a bar on the front, which refused to quit flickering; an unheeded warning to the victims it bid farewell to as they excitedly boarded the boats.

As the boats began to fill, low, muffled protests about the number of people per boat could be heard, but such was the efficiency of the perilous loading that they were underway before their protests could make any difference. Huddling together as the wind and cold night air took hold, they moved out.

Over the noise of the engines, the last thing those left on shore heard were the cries of children. As nature intended the shrill cry of a baby travels a long way. However, in this case, they would also echo through time, forever replayed in the minds of those left listening on the beach. For now, though, they walked back to the road, another shipment gone. They had more money in their pockets than they knew what to do with. The two men were happy, for now.

Chapter Twelve

War

Ellie pulled her hands from her face to reveal a big smile.

"Thank god," she said.

"I would never have forgiven myself, neither would the family."

Jack climbed down as fast as he could, which was pretty slowly, and hugged his sister. He knew only too well how she would be worrying, but with phone signals and landlines down, and with all that was going on, he had no way of contacting her. He took her to the cab of the truck, out of the way of the sand, and began explaining exactly what had happened to him over the past few days.

Ellie had been the inspiration he had needed to volunteer. He fully understood why she felt responsible for him, even though he was the older brother. He told his story while Ellie held his hand, squeezing harder and harder as he spoke. When he reached the part about the attack and Jalila's injuries, tears formed in his eyes when he spoke of her fate. Ellie could tell it had affected him badly. He was not used to the relentless death that she had witnessed. Ellie worried about what it would be like when she finally went home for good. She had heard so many stories of people who were so brave in the face of death and horror, who somehow couldn't cope with the stark contrast of peaceful streets and normal life. This, Ellie thought, was waiting for her back home, and now, because of her, it waited for her brother, too.

Jack and Ellie left the cab and walked back to where Mike was waiting. He had briefly met Jack when the convoy had rolled in from Turkey. Ellie had been keen to introduce her big brother. Mike, like most people, took to Jack straight away. Jack had also taken to Mike, but there was something about him that he couldn't figure out. There was a distance in his eyes that Jack hadn't seen before, and it had shaken him a little, even scared him, although he had no idea why.

The group's consensus was to return to the coast, so Mike turned the Land Rover around. After a couple of turns of the engine, they were off.

The Land Rover led the convoy. With Mike at the wheel, they set off on the short journey back to Latakia. Ellie rode in the back of the truck and listened to Joan and Michael's incredible story. Looking at the babies, then at Jack, Ellie shook her head.

"Some story. Those two babies are so lucky to have you," she said, smiling at Joan and Michael. In every war, she had heard fantastic stories, but this one was pretty good she mused to herself.

Jack then looked at her seriously.

"Ellie," he said, reaching out to take her hand, "I can't leave them here. The war will swallow them, I know we can't save everyone, but these two, I have to try."

Ellie had been worried that Jack would get too personally involved, even before he had left England. Now her fears were confirmed, but, again, she felt responsible. She knew him well; she knew what he was thinking.

"Jack," she began, then turned to face Joan and Michael. "I am a neutral here, I can't help you. I could tell you that I could make phone calls, try to pull a few strings, but this was made clear to me from the start. The refugee crisis is at breaking point, no one will give me permission to potentially make it worse."

"What?" interrupted Jack. "I can give them a home. I have

more money than I need to live on. They wouldn't be a burden to anyone." Ellie looked over at him and he fell quiet. Ellie did too. She loved her brother, mostly for who he was, a rare commodity, a good man, he would literally give you the shirt of his back. She had witnessed this all through her life. Some called him a soft touch, but she knew better, he was no fool. But if you were in real trouble and lucky enough to cross paths with Jack, you would quickly learn what she already knew. He was a rock you could rest on and catch your breath. For this reason, Ellie chose her words carefully.

"Jack, this can't happen." Looking back at Michael and Joan, she spoke with sincerity:

"And don't you even think of trying to cross to Greece. Bodies are floating up on the beach daily. It's heart-breaking. I will try to get some money together, to get you passage somewhere the Daesh are unlikely to go.

"That's the best I can do."

Michael nodded and Joan just hung her head. She had been hoping to get to England. She loved the people there and they both had many friends in London. This news hit her hard.

The coast was in sight now, but for some reason, Mike pulled the Land Rover over. He jumped out and climbed onto its roof. As he raised a pair of binoculars, the rest got out to stretch their legs. It was then they saw what Mike had seen. Latakia was on fire in several places, including the docks.

Mike jumped down. His mood was deadly serious. Instead of shouting, he firmly told everyone what to do, and nobody argued. His voice carried an air of confidence, which they all needed. The truck was quickly placed alongside a single building housing, which looked like straw, and the Land Rover was placed by its side. Mike stripped the sheet someone had placed over the straw and threw it over the car, then began to anchor it down. Next, he took oil from the truck and poured it over the sheet, spreading it around with his hands. When he had finished, he threw the straw, and dirt over the plastic sheet. When the others had worked out what he was doing, they joined in. Soon the car and its sidekick were gone. Mike beckoned for them all to get in the truck; they obediently followed his instructions.

Catching their breath in the hot dusty truck, they all turned and looked at Mike. It was obvious that they thought he knew what to do. He did, but it wouldn't comfort them, Mike thought to himself, but then decided to trust that they could handle it. Taking a deep breath, he began, "I can't be absolutely sure, but I thought I saw black flags flying down there."

They all looked at each other, knowing that, if Daesh or so called ISIS, as the west knows them, were there, any thoughts of getting into the town were dashed. These were, singularly, the most evil group on the planet. Nothing you were, or believed in, would save you. In some cases, even if you went to join them, you would not be certain of a welcome.

They killed and tortured every age, sex and religion without mercy. Their followers were drunk on their own doctrine, literally power mad, they acted as if they had a licence to be evil.

Mike continued.

"Okay, now that's been absorbed, here are our choices: one, we can hide and hope they won't find us; two, we can fight; three, we can move and evade, and hope to contact or bump into help. Can anyone think of a forth?" he asked sincerely.

Allowing time for another to speak, no one said anything for about two minutes, which seemed like ten to anyone there in that truck.

Then Jack spoke.

"How long, Mike, before the opposition? Or before the west try to clear them out, do you have any idea?"

"Good question," said Mike. "I think I know where you're going with this. The truth is, I don't know, but an early assault would make sense, before they can entrench. But it won't be a major concern for the outside forces to stop them."

"Look at Aleppo," Jack interrupted, almost apologetically.

"Michael, what do you think? It is your country."

Michael fidgeted around a bit. He wasn't very opinionated, but Jack was right.

"Okay," he said. "I think that, either the Kurdish army, or one of the factions, will try to take Latakia, probably tonight. They won't want to wait, as Mike said. Although, they may wait for day break."

"Why daybreak?" asked Jack.

"Most people are half-asleep then. They will have been up all night, till half-light in the morning. It's called the killing hour."

Mike nodded; he was familiar with the tactic.

"So," Mike began, "shall we wait for tonight? We're all too tired to push on, especially with the babies, who, I must say, are remarkably quiet."

Jack nodded in agreement. For a man who had, in the past, given up countless nights of sleep, thoughts of rest was like gold dust.

Jack looked around; they were all nodding.

"With your permission, Ellie, I would like to get a closer look at the town, to see for myself what comes down in the morning."

She looked at him, trying to form an answer. In any other situation, she would have taken charge, but she knew why Bob had wanted Mike to come along. This was his world now and she knew she would be better off trusting him.

"Alright, Mike, but be back here early. If you're not back by mid-day, we'll head down the coast to see if we can sneak through to Turkey." Mike nodded and slid out the back of the truck.

Michael watched him through a hole in the tarp. Mike went to the back seat of the Land Rover and took out a rifle case and bag. He slung the bag over his shoulders and grabbed two bottles of water. One he downed in one go, the other he carried. In his other hand, he carried the rifle. Michael wiped his eyes and when he looked again, Mike had gone.

The night was cold. Mike tried to concentrate on his surroundings. He had got to within a few hundred yards of the town and settled on the second highest of two hills. He avoided the highest hill, knowing it was too obvious a choice. If the ISIS commander turned out to be any good and set guards around his perimeters, even bad ones, they would have spotted him. He decided to try and get a couple of hours' sleep. Although risky, he wanted to be fresh enough to be useful if things got hairy.

As a younger man, he used to wake up on cue, but now he overslept. The sound of gunfire did the trick. He was fully awake in a second. Slowly and gently, he rubbed his eyes then looked around for any change in the area around him. Shots were fired again, but this time it was sustained gunfire coming from the town. Mike concentrated. The town was ahead of him but the return gunfire was coming from the right. He was just far back enough to not be caught in the middle.

"Okay, Mike," he sighed to himself, "let's have look." He rolled over and peered through the Scorpion scope attached to his Barrett No. 3, 50 calibre sniper rifle. He soon picked up the shooters. They were firing from the top of a building, about four hundred yards away. Mike had no intention of giving his position away before he knew the size of the force. They hadn't taken the town with three men, he thought. Then he saw others running in the alley ways, all dressed in black, moving quickly with a purpose.

He decided to observe for a while, but didn't have to wait long. The rooftop where the men had been, exploded. Like with the last brick in Jenga, the wooden brick game you played at home, the building fell. No one was walking from that, he thought.

More gunfire erupted at street level. Mike could make out others dressed in white, in the alleys. They were combing through, block by block; a very familiar sight to Mike from when he was last in action, but it had been a while. Then, from his left, he heard the sound of a single shot. He couldn't pinpoint its exact location, but he knew where the shot went. The target was an Arab dressed in a cream Arab outfit. He'd been hiding behind a tree in the square. Mike had followed his movements just a few seconds earlier. Now, Mike watched as the man jumped, as if electrocuted, falling motionless in the dirt several yards from the tree. Mike recognised the signature of the shooters gun. Someone out there also had a 50 calibre, and that was bad news for him.

He moved to a better angle to see, but was only too aware that a better angle for him meant a better angle for the shooter out there, too. He could only hope his adversary was concentrating on the town, not his hill. His only cover where he was, was his gillie suit, basically a net made into a poncho that was appropriate camouflage for the area. In this case, a sand dune or rock, and neither would stop a 50 calibre.

Mike waited. Another shot rang out, although he couldn't see who was at the receiving end. He did spot a slight flash though, and dust flying about seven hundred yards to his left. The good news was that he didn't have to move. The bad news was that the guy could shoot. He made himself comfortable, settling back behind the scope. He turned the top screw nine clicks up, while keeping an eye on the brush, then moved two clicks clockwise on the side. He was used to having a spotter, but he would manage he told himself. The scope's telescopic lens rushed the scenery forward. What had been hazy dust covered hills, became defined rocks and bushes. He slowly shifted his view to where he saw the movement, but there was nothing there. He then scanned the area immediately around the spot, looking for somewhere his adversary might pick, somewhere not obvious, but effective cover. His brain started to over think, what if I'm overestimating him?

He couldn't see anything. He told himself to calm down and not overthink. The day was warming up with the sun doing what it had always done, burning all things exposed to it, that also meant Mike. He hadn't planned to be there for long, but to move now would be suicidal. He admonished himself for his lack of concentration, and realised why the marines trained so often. You get rusty, he thought.

The landscape gave nothing back. Mike recalled his training: you have the advantage, he doesn't know you're here, but it's a good bet that he's still looking. So, patience, Mike. An hour, then another, went by. Even the town had quietened down, bar the odd handgun shot. The rebels must be keeping their heads down. Clever bastards, he thought, grinning.

He hated ISIS and all they stood for. From a bush only four hundred yards away, came another shot. This time the shooter was within sight. Mike was just in time to see a lithe body rise to kneeling position, and then move with astonishing agility to the right, before dropping down behind a rock. Mike had him. He steadied the reticule and adjusted it back eight clicks and one anti-clockwise. The hairs were now lined up on the rock. Mike waited, checking the air. At this close range, the 50 calibre wouldn't deviate very much, especially in these conditions.

He waited. The rock, seemingly, grew a tumour on one side, but nothing else moved. Mike thanked the Lord he hadn't fired earlier. He would have been dead, for sure. He lined up on the centre of the lump and squeezed the trigger smoothly. Not for a second had his target anticipated the shot. The heavy bullet flew, hitting its mark in under a second; the results were instantaneous. The sandy lump turned red and the snipers head flew off the gillie suit, leaving a headless corpse slumped over the giant rifle in a deadly pose. Mike breathed again, but took his time to check the area. Snipers sometimes worked in pairs. Confident the sniper was acting alone, he started to move backwards, only to feel cold steel pushing into his neck. An Arabic speaker invited him to stand slowly, which he did. Turning slowly, he was confronted by a very tall Arab with black eyes. Although the man had his face covered, Mike could swear he was smiling. No, the bugger's laughing at me, Mike realised.

His captor guided him back to his truck. Mike wondered why he had not been tied up. They were about fifty yards away from the truck when he saw the others walking confidently towards his escort, smiling. It was obvious they all knew each other.

"Okay," he said by way of greeting,

"the joke seems to be on me. Who is this guy?"

"He's one of the few remaining from the First Division of Aleppo," Joan said, adjusting her mask. She was holding one of the babies, Michael had the other.

Mike walked up to her and spoke to the baby, muttering something about being pleased to see her, but it was really an excuse to steal a sniff from her head. He found it more intoxicating that he'd thought. More than the smell of homemade bread from his mother's kitchen.

Everyone else caught up. Ellie gently manoeuvred Mike away from the others before confronting him.

"Do you want to tell me what the hell it is you're doing, bringing that ...?" she pointed to the rifle.

The rebel captor had returned it to him and he carried it casually on his back.

"We are meant to be observers, not combatants. I can understand it being difficult to make the transition, but you risk everyone's lives and status, here and elsewhere. Not only in the UN, but also the charities. You're not a UN soldier, and this will turn us all into legitimate targets if we're found out." Ellie continued, looking Mike right in his eyes,

"Okay, you're right," Mike said genuinely, nodding in agreement. He had known the risks when he took the job and was fully aware of the rules. He could carry a small weapon for personal protection, and to protect the likes of Ellie, but there were strict rules about using it. The 50 calibre didn't qualify though. She was right, he was way out of line. They walked back to the others and Ellie patted his back. It was hard for her not to show her admiration for Mike.

They sat down and ate some cold food while Mike spoke of his observations. The rebels were clearing out the streets in the town, but the ISIS force had been small and the town had not been guarded heavily enough. The town's resistance had been almost nil. Luckily, the rebels had been nearby, enabling them to mount a quick counter attack. They conveyed their admiration for Mike, through Joan. They had walked right passed the truck and the Land Rover in the night, only realising that Mike was there when he opened fire. By then, luckily for Mike, it was obvious which side he was on, as the rebels had been sneaking up to the sniper when Mike fired. They were fairly sure he saved some of their lives and wanted to thank him. One by one, they approached Mike and hugged him, like a long-lost brother, before kissing him, something Mike, although aware of, could not get used to. Their sincerity impressed him, though. It was similar to what he'd experienced with the Marines he'd fought with, and it felt good to feel it again.

Ali approached Jack and shook his hand. He was dressed

differently, and now carried a gun. Jack held his hand firmly, knowing and understanding the young man's decision. If Jack hadn't come to Syria, he would have thought Ali was mad. Now he understood the young man's need to protect his country. Ali walked off. Jack knew he would never see him again.

The group decided to wait an hour, to be on the safe side, then made their way into town. When they informed the rebel leader of their plans, he warned them that their intelligence had reported a large contingent of ISIS heading towards the town. Although they were meeting resistance from the rebels, they couldn't guarantee their safety. This started a debate, which lasted for half an hour. Jack and Ellie wanted to go to the town and try to get word to UN headquarters, hoping to get airlifted out. Mike and the others wanted to wait. Before their discussion was resolved, the tall rebel leader approached the group. Although some of them did not speak the language, it was evident to everyone, from Michael and Joan's reaction, that it was bad news. Joan translated.

"ISIS," she began, shakily, "are now approaching from three directions. It seems like they are determined to take the town."

Silence fell over the group as fear set in. It was everywhere, even in the air they breathed. Mike, sensing the atmosphere, spoke to them.

"We have no other choice now, we have to go into the town."

"Why?" interrupted Michael. "A minute ago, you wanted to bypass the town. Why don't we try to go past them?"

Mike sat down and took a while to answer.

"If we try that, and we could," he started, acknowledging Michael's contribution with a nod, "it would be a classical mistake. We must not underestimate ISIS. They would almost certainly spot us coming from the town, the same town their brothers were just killed in. There would be no mercy."

Michael spoke again, a little insistent this time.

"What if we travel at night?"

Mike acknowledged him with another nod. He knew the importance of not shutting anyone out; a rebellion in their midst could cause deaths, or worse.

"Again," he began, slowly, "we would be underestimating one of the richest terror groups in the world. It's quite likely that they have thermal imaging capabilities or night vision binoculars. It would be easier for them to spot us at night than during the day."

"So what? We wait for them to come to us?"

This time Ellie answered.

"If we can get to a phone, or radio, I can call for help."

"Is that help for us all?" Joan asked, looking accusingly at Ellie.

"I'll see what I can do," Ellie replied. Joan did not look convinced.

The sun was rising and, not for the first time, it played its part in moving a decision forward. It was if the group knew that their choices weren't going to improve with the increasing level of heat. Mike's suggestion seemed the best one, although no one seemed happy with the outcome. They shuffled back to the vehicles. Mike pulled the tarpaulin that covered them and rolled it up before throwing it into the back of the large truck. Goodbyes were said to some of the rebels, but the tall, dark-eyed man and another man travelled with them to give a them a little more security on their way through town.

They made their way down to the coast without incident and the sea air lifted their spirits somewhat. It had been a long time since Michael and Joan had been to the sea. It always felt right, somehow. It brought a sense of positivity, thought Joan. It probably linked back to their childhood days at the beach. But Joan knew it was more than just that. She knew it was a potential escape from the madness.

They moved through the town. It almost seemed like nothing had happened here, bar the few new bullet holes in buildings that only a local would spot. Otherwise, things were returning to normal. The town's folk obviously didn't know what was coming. If they did, the town's heart would have been moving to different beat.

They pulled up outside the newly acquisitioned UN warehouse. Mike and the two rebels checked the building and declared it clear. Entering through the small door, they immediately felt the welcoming drop in temperature. Ellie quickly made for her office. Everything was as she had left it. She picked up the phone, but it was dead. Moving behind her desk, she lifted the mic for the radio, which crackled into life, sounding like frying bacon, and just as welcome.

Ellie quickly voiced her call sign and waited. A familiar voice came back. It was her friend and boss, Bob,

"It's great to hear your voice," she said.

"Yours too," replied Bob, obviously pleased to hear from her. Ellie quickly told him of their encounters and experiences, ending with a request for a helicopter to get them out.

"I'm sorry, Ellie. It's not going to happen any time soon. The whole area is an active war zone, and it's just too much of a risk. You understand, I hope? Your position is just too hot right now.

"Yes," came her response, but she didn't understand. She was angry with how she was feeling; she knew better. He was right, but right didn't matter when it was you in the shit, she thought.

"What do you suggest, Bob?" she asked, hoping for alternative support.

"I really don't know." His response was tinged with frustration.

With growing anger, Ellie went on the attack, her nerves getting the better of her.

"Nothing, Bob? You have nothing?"

"Wait a minute, Ellie. There are things you can do, but my guess is, you have already thought of them. You can either stay and hope that that works out, or go, and hope for the same. I'm sorry, but that's just how it is at the moment."

"So, we just become a bloody headline, then?"

"I certainly hope not," Bob said in a firm but caring voice. He was willing to give her all the space she needed, to be the trooper he knew she was.

"I'll stay in touch, Bob. As long as I can. Over and out." She replaced the handset.

Ellie walked slowly down the makeshift steps. The others watched her descend. It was evident from her face that it wasn't going to be good news, and they weren't disappointed.

"What now?" Jack enquired, looking at his younger sister. The situation felt a little strange for him. He was always the one advising her.

"Well," Ellie begun, looking less than confident, "I say, we get the hell out of Dodge, and quick."

"How and to where? Both seem like appropriate questions," added Mike.

"Well, if this were a chess board, back, left and right are covered. That leaves us with forward," Michael offered, lifting his hands as a gesture of finality.

"Great, who can't swim?" asked Jack, half-smiling.

Mike looked around to see if anyone else wanted to speak, then moved forward to face them all.

"I have been frequenting a local bar, one of the only ones left, so it's fair to say that everything that happens in Latakia is broadcast there. One thing I did hear, which, at the time, I wished I hadn't heard, was a rumour about a couple of guys making rubber boats to smuggle refugees to Cyprus." He paused and looked around.

"Well, it's something," Jack hesitantly offered.

"Not necessarily," Mike replied. "The word is, these boats are basically crap, no good," he simplified for Michael and Joan, seeing their confused faces.

"Great, does anyone have another suggestion?" Ellie asked the group.

They looked around at each other, but no one spoke. Not one of them wanted to bump into ISIS.

"Okay, I suggest Michael and I go and have a chat with these boat guys, and see what our options are. Okay?" Mike looked around at everyone's faces and was met with silence. Only Ellie nodded, which Mike took as a unanimous acceptance as the others seemed to be following her lead.

Chapter Thirteen

Passage

The streets were starting to get dark as the two men worked their way through the back alleys. Mike led the way as he had some idea of where they heading, but not the exact place. He played it by ear and Michael just followed, not really sure why he was there, other than to act as a translator. But he was fairly sure that Mike knew a little Arabic.

Through the darkness of the night came the haunting tones of a violin, playing the Violin Concerto "In Memory of an Angel" by Alban Berg, not that either man was aware of the composer. The notes floated through the air, giving the sense they had been transported to a Hollywood set with musical backing. It didn't improve their mood. Instead, it brought on a sense of foreboding. The tones seemed to be warning them of doom that potentially lay around every corner. Had they been in a graveyard, this would have been the perfect musical accompaniment. Neither wanted to voice their feelings, until Mike smiled and Michael let out an inappropriately loud laugh. They stopped for a moment to compose themselves, then carried on, just as the music reached a crescendo before suddenly stopping, leaving the streets empty and lifeless once more.

Mike turned into a larger street where empty shops, now boarded up, lined its sides. A few useless vehicles, their tyres removed, were begging to be towed away. They had been abandoned, never to be claimed, and were now just targets for children's stones and games.

They walked quietly, with Mike checking the roofs and alleys in every direction, but everything was quiet. Further along, the street curved towards the sea, and in the distance, a small light lit up a single strip across the street. The sound of people talking and metal on metal could be heard. Mike looked over at Michael and nodded, as if to say, "that's it".

The shop was closed so they made their way to the back via an alley, but on reaching the corner, they heard shouting and angry voices. Mike couldn't make out what was being said, but Michael could and went to push past Mike. The bigger man stopped him and held him back.

"What is it?" Mike whispered.

"They're threatening to kill a child," Michael translated, with fire in his eyes.

"Okay, but we do it my way, alright?"

Michael nodded.

Mike pulled out a woman's compact mirror from his back pocket. Noticing Michael's face, he placed his finger over his lips to prevent another of Michael's outbursts. He opened the mirror and carefully moved it passed the bricks and around the corner. He could see two men standing over a boy about eleven. A gun was pointing at the child's head, in close proximity, while another man, presumably the father, looked on in anguish.

Mike had seen enough and replaced the mirror in his top pocket. He slipped his revolver from its holster and slowly pulled back its action to load a round. He then smoothly moved around the corner, his gun aimed.

In English, he shouted for the two men to put their guns down, which they did, almost immediately. Mike recognised one of the men from the bar by the docks, and motioned for them to step back into the workshop. They both complied. Michael walked over to the frightened boy and helped him to his feet before following Mike and the men into the rear of the shop.

The first thing they noticed was the smell of the glue and chemicals. They'd smelt it outside, but inside it was intoxicating.

It felt like the first puff of a cigarette when you were a kid. Their heads swam and they had difficulty concentrating. Moving through the inner doors, they saw seven workers, all working on different stages of production of the rubber boats used by Abd-al-Hakim and Aaqaa, to transport the refugees. Mike knew his gun was now aimed at the two masterminds.

"I can't stand these fumes," Michael complained.

"Me neither," agreed Mike. "Everyone out," he shouted. The workers didn't need to be told twice and moved swiftly to the rear exit of the building. Everyone was suffering from the fumes. The workers had red eyes and a constant cough, despite their make-shift masks. It was proof, if any were needed, of the toxic conditions.

Mike was struggling and suddenly bent over, chocking for a second. Aaqaa ceased the moment and jumped on him. Abd-al-Hakim followed suit, which was a mistake. His clumsy attempt to help only tripped his partner up and all three were now on the floor. Mike managed to shift himself from the struggle. Aaqaa, realising he had lost the element of surprise, grabbed for the boat hook lying next to him and swung at Mike. Mike, was too quick and jumped to his feet, the hook narrowly missed his face. Before Aaqaa had another chance to strike, Mike brought his gun up and fired twice. Both bullets passed through Aaqaa, the second of which also hit Abd-al-Hakim's head. They both died instantly.

Mike emerged from the back of the shop and leaned against the wall. Michael approached him, but Mike waved him away. The workers stood around, visibly stunned. On realising their bosses were dead, some cheered, while others seemed indifferent. Michael went over to talk to them.

"They are a mixture of workers, really slaves of a sort. Some were promised passage, others money, which they rarely saw," Michael reported back to Mike.

"Ask them if there are a couple of finished boats we can take? And tell them that what's left is theirs. That should keep them happy."

Michael relayed Mike request to the workers.

"There's six finished, but their supervisor wants to talk to you. He says he speaks a little English."

"Okay," Mike said, "bring him over."

Michael beckoned to the man, who walked over slowly. He seemed worried that the next bullet might be for him, and not for no reason, Mike suspected.

The man spoke in broken English.

"You take boats, they're yours. But I help you and you take me, too."

Mike stared at him with cold blue eyes, and made him wait a few minutes before replying.

"Why do we need you?" he asked the scared little man.

"Because I will save your lives," the man fired back, smiling.

"And how are you going to do that?" Mike snapped at him. He grabbed the man and pulled him towards him.

"The boats will kill you," the supervisor clarified.

"We will take our chances," Mike said, pushing the man away.

"No," the man persisted. "I mean, they will definitely kill you."

"What's he babbling about?" Mike was becoming more than a little impatient. They had a long night ahead, and he had lots to arrange.

"Speak. If what you say makes sense, we will take you, otherwise, you can take a hike. Take it or leave it."

Mike stared at the little supervisor, who quickly decided that honesty was probably his best bet.

"Okay. Boats glue no good."

"What do you mean?"

"Glue for cupboards and toys, no good for boats. They fall apart when the water melts the glue."

Mike's face slowly showed realisation.

"How long has this been going on for?" he asked, grabbing the supervisor, who was now starting to regret his sales pitch.

"Since they started building them. The two you shot, they knew. They couldn't get new good glue." He put his hands up in a gesture of fatality. "I couldn't do anything, they would kill me."

Michael could see that Mike was not taking this news well, so he stepped between them.

Facing Mike, he said,

"Look he said he can save us. Let's find out what he means."

"Fine," Mike reluctantly agreed. He was starting to calm a little. This worm sent hundreds to their deaths, without a word; his story better be a good one.

"I have good news, sir," said the supervisor, looking a little hopeful. "The men you shot made lots of money, really lots, sirs."

Mike looked angry again.

"Do you think we want your bloody money, you little bastard." He began to raise his gun.

"No sir," the supervisor tried to protest. "I know what they did with it though."

Again, the gun came up.

Struggling with the words he needed, the supervisor continued, "They buy big boat. They not think I know, but Henry knows."

"Henry?" Mike looked enquiringly at Michael.

Michael shrugged. "Does it matter?"

"No, I suppose not. Right, Henry, where is this boat? I have been around this place a few times and I haven't seen any boats for weeks."

Henry, now looking more confident, pointed at the docks.

"I show you."

Mike nodded and pushed Henry forward.

"What about the others?" Michael asked.

"Let them take what they like, but warn them about the boats."

Michael passed on the message. Soon after, one man ran, screaming, into the building and begun kicking at the bodies.

Mike pulled him off and quietly offered, "They're dead now. They're gone."

Michael put his hand on Mike's shoulder.

"His whole family went with the last boat, Mike."

Mike let the man go and quietly led Henry away before the worker realised Henry's involvement and killed him.

The docks were a short walk away, down the front and to the left. As they walked, they could hear the waves and the neon light, still flickering. It was the last thing the flimsy boats saw as they left. No one spoke as they walked, especially Henry, who understood what the others were thinking. He, too, had a heavy heart, but he'd been too weak to do anything about it. Worse, he knew he would do the same again. It was who he had become. He soon let the feeling pass.

The docks were pitch black and there was no security on the gates. Possibly killed during the ISIS raid the previous day, Mike thought. He had known one of the guards, a good chap. Then, with sadness, he remembered the guard telling him that he had paid for his family's transport to Cyprus on those death boats; he had planned to follow them in few weeks, when he had earned enough for another passage.

They passed the gates and continued to where Henry had pointed. It was a reasonably sized dock. They walked for a few minutes before Henry gestured towards a concrete building. It was locked. Mike had to smash the large padlock with a very heavy chain link, almost a foot long and about ten pounds in weight, which took a few tries before the padlock finally yielded.

The heavy doors swung open to reveal two small dry docks

that were now filled with water. The gates for one of the docks was closed, but held a motor yacht. Mike guessed it to be about fifty feet long. Its name was written in Arabic (κορσέ οφ θε σεα). Henry looked very pleased with himself, throwing his arms around like a salesman presenting a house. Mike seemed less impressed, as did Michael. They were both thinking of the actual cost of this gleaming white gin palace.

Mike suggested he stay with the boat, while Michael went back to get the others. Discreetly, he told Michael he was sure they weren't the only ones who knew about the yacht. When news spread of the owners' deaths, others would soon think of taking it. Michael agreed and set off to the warehouse, which was not far away. Mike pushed Henry towards the boat and jumped onto the teak swim platform at the stern. The boat swayed slightly as it took on their weight, but being over 19,000 kg, the movement was hardly noticeable. It smelt new, the fibreglass was clean and polished, as was the stainless steel. It had two seats mounted forward at the back, which they walked around. Henry looked as if he was entering paradise; Mike had seen it all before. Henry was clearly more interested in the luxury it afforded. Mike quickly made his way to the bridge, which consisted of a double seat, and sat down. He started to look for a key, but one didn't easily materialise. Then Henry tapped him on the shoulder. Turning, Mike could see the little Arab's black-toothed grin as he swung a bunch of keys, to and fro, in Mike face.

"See, I am useful, sir," Henry said, very pleased with himself.

"So, where did you get these?" Mike enquired, looking carefully at the keys.

"They were just there on the table," Henry replied, now a lot less confident.

"No, they weren't. Henry, where did you get them?"

Henry shuffled around nervously before answering.

"They were at the warehouse. I grabbed them as we were

leaving. I knew we would need them," he lied.

"This is a half a million quid's worth of a rich man's toy. Henry, they don't come with roughly cut crap like these. They're all shiny, with gold key fobs, usually handed over by women you only see on the front pages of magazines. So, my guess is, you had plans of your own. Henry, these were given to you by another shady asshole like yourself, probably with equally bad teeth."

Mike stared at him, with a look that required a good, honest answer. Henry was reluctant, but couldn't think of anything that Mike may accept. In the end, he did something he despised, he told the truth.

"I hated those bastards you shot. They would have left me to be a slave to ISIS, or dead. They said they would take me. I saw them buy the boat, so they said I could go with them. But they lied, I could tell."

"I bet you could," Mike said.

"So, you thought you would go for a cruise yourself, is that it?"

Henry looked nervous.

"Ah, so not on your own, then," Mike answered for him.

"With whom, Henry?"

Henry didn't look good. All his plans were falling apart. He sat down and wiped his hands on his shirt.

"It was going to be me and the owner of the bar on the front, with his family. He's as bad as you, always pushing me around."

Mike almost felt sorry for him.

"When were you planning on going?" Mike asked.

"We don't have any time. He told me to wait for him to say."

Mike was inclined to believe him. He had met the barman on many days since his arrival. The barman wasn't one to talk much, and the word on the street was that he was not a person to mess with.

Mike nodded to Henry, as if to say okay, then turned his attention to the boat. The keys were rough, but they worked. The gauges came to life, and judging by them, the boat was fully fuelled. Next, he checked the radio, it also seemed to be working. Mike switched it off, he didn't want to alert anyone by mistake. He considered starting the engines but the noise would have given them away, so he switched off the ignition and moved of the seat. Down a few steps was the galley with imitation black marble, a microwave, a sink, and a stainless-steel oven. Straight ahead was the master bedroom, and to the right were two more bedrooms, one double and one with bunk beds. It was more than they needed, thought Mike, far more. He looked in the cupboards and found they were stacked with food and booze.

"And the old owners were planning a quick getaway!" he muttered to no one in particular.

He climbed back onto the upper deck, switched on the breakers, then returned to the galley to make a coffee.

"There's nothing to do now but wait," Mike told the quite miserable Henry.

Chapter Fourteen

Escape to Hell

Joan threw her arms around Michael as he came through the small warehouse doors. The others gathered around him.

"Where's Mike?" Ellie asked, concerned.

"He's fine," Michael said as he walked passed them all. He sat on the stairs to the office and told them the whole story, even the bit about Mike having to shoot the two traffickers. Based on their reactions, nobody seemed to judge Mike. Joan carried the babies and sat next to Michael. She had found a basket that was large enough to hold both babies, which she set down in front of her, all the while talking to them softly.

Ellie moved forward and took charge. She gave instructions for them to grab what they could and that they would make their way to the boat in ten minutes. After picking up a few bits that looked useful, they headed off.

The morning sun was rising as they stepped out, just enough to warm the air a little. They knew it would soon be scorching hot, as did the residents who were milling around, busy with their own lives and not really paying much attention to the group, other than the casual, curious glance at the new people. One individual, however, seemed more than a little interested. He walked purposefully in their direction. Less than six feet tall but wide, he had the appearance of someone who was very confident.

As he approached, Ellie could see his face had character, which was a polite way of saying he had scars and a broken nose, in two places at least. The man introduced himself as Abdul. He pointed to his bar and told them he ran it. Ellie vaguely recognised him, but she had only seen him a couple of times and certainly didn't know him.

"How can we help you, Abdul?" Ellie asked in the nicest way she could manage.

"Well, I don't know." Abdul was now blocking their way. "Call me curious, but where are you all heading, if you don't mind me asking?"

He spoke in good English.

Jack answered. "Actually, we do mind. Now, if we can't help you, goodbye."

Abdul took no offence, it seemed. Instead, he just laughed, a real belly laugh, which made them all nervous.

"Okay," said Jack, backing down a little, sensing the mood had changed.

"What?"

Abdul's mood changed again.

"I have been watching you and your murderous friends. I know exactly what happened last night. I know most of what goes on around here. Don't worry, though, they needed to die. You just saved me the job."

By now, the streets had mysteriously emptied. The group seemed destined to play out the standoff they were confronted with.

Michael spoke to Abdul in Arabic.

"What right have you to stop us. Get out of our way. You're out numbered and what is it that you want, anyway? This lady is with the UN, and this gentleman is English."

This may have carried some weight with most people in the town, but Abdul found it amusing and let out another belly laugh, waving his hand and whistling as he did.

From the top of the bar opposite, Abdul's wife and son appeared. The only thing that really caught the group's attention were the two Kalashnikov rifles, held in a relaxed manner by them both. More importantly, the guns were pointed at them.

"Now," Abdul began, "we stop playing foolish games, yes?"

"Yes," Ellie answered, quickly.

"I know about the boat. Or should we say yacht, or, more precisely, my yacht."

He waved to his wife, who disappeared. Their son stayed to cover the group for a short while, then they both came down. Abdul spoke again, this time, in a matter of fact manner. "Move this way," he said, pointing through the docks. All of them complied. The walk was short and they soon came to the broken door. Abdul's son went through first, followed by the group. Abdul followed, with his wife going through last, pulling the door shut behind her and wedging it with some wood.

Jack did not have a good feeling about this, and he wasn't alone. They walked to the yacht, where they met Mike, who had seen them coming. He had his nine millimetre drawn, holding it in both hands.

"So, what next?" began Abdul. A smile crossed his face, this time it was more like a cat sizing up a mouse.

"Well," replied Mike. "It's simple. You let them pass and we all go our separate ways."

This time Abdul was very serious.

"I like simple, too. So, drop your gun and go back to the town. Otherwise, my son cuts you in half, okay?"

"You know me, Abdul. You know what I do. Are you willing to bet I can't cut one of you down at least, before he does that?"

Abdul's son raised his rifle, but Abdul motioned for him to lower it. Abdul's smile was back, but this time he looked like a poker player. He took his time, letting the tension rise and watched everyone's reaction, trying to gauge how he could get the upper hand. Finally, he decided that Mike had a point; he loved his family too much.

"Here's the deal, my Army friend, we all want to get to

Greece, and you have the UN with you. How about we go together? You folk give your word that you will represent us, and after that, the boat is mine."

Abdul let the suggestion hang in the air. Mike looked across at Ellie, who was obviously unhappy. But she nodded. She knew it was the safest route, given the circumstances they'd found themselves in.

"Okay, Abdul. You have your deal. I can't promise the boat, though. The authorities will probably take it."

Abdul hesitated. He loved the boat, but his original intention had been to get his family out. He also had a lot of cash stashed away, so getting into Greece was all that mattered to him.

"Alright, but I'm captain." He stepped onto the boat, as if nothing untoward had gone on. He shook Mike's hand as he boarded.

The rest of the now large group boarded and made themselves comfortable, which on this craft was not hard at all. Abdul was unhappy to see Henry. It seems as though he didn't factor in Abdul's long term plans. Henry picked up on this and shrunk away, out of site. Abdul sent his wife back to town to pick up their belongings, including, and unknown to anyone else, a bag containing seven hundred thousand dollars, accumulated from his smuggling activities over the last twenty-five years.

Abdul seemed to know a lot about boats, much to Mike's relief. His own experience was limited to a small fishing launch he'd used as a child, as well as inflatable landing crafts from his days in the marines. But this yacht was a completely different prospect. While Abdul's son opened the hydraulic gate leading to the sea, Abdul expertly manoeuvred the thrusters and twin 428hp diesel engines out of the dry dock and into the basin, before gunning the engines, allowing them to cavitate in the dirty waters. He steadily directed them towards the open sea. Abdul only knew how to move forward. In his world, there was no reverse gear. He also had no time or patience for untrustworthy associates. So, as soon as they'd cleared the basin, he grabbed Henry by the back of his jacket. Henry protested. But to Mike's surprise, Abdul marched him to the back of the boat and, with one movement, threw him into the water. Without looking back, Abdul returned to the controls, opened the throttles, and took the craft up to a steady 18knots, by no means its top speed, but he was trying to conserve fuel, although the four hundred miles should have been in the range of the boat's tanks, with the reserves he had loaded. They had around 2000 litres of fuel, which would be enough for emergencies, he hoped.

He set the course on the Ray Marine plotter, then put it into auto pilot. Stepping down, he smoothly grabbed a bottle of Ouzo and smiled at Mike as he took a long pull from the bottle.

"I'd better get used to this stuff."

Mike couldn't help but like the guy. He was one of those rare breeds who hadn't let life grind them down. His was of the kind who got up fighting when anyone else would have been crying. Mike had no problem with losing Henry, he hadn't trusted him at all. The others were a little shocked though, but said nothing.

Chapter Fifteen

The Sentinel

Larnaca, a once thriving tourist location once dominated by tourists, t-shirts and sun lovers; now everyone was mixed together on the waterfront with tents and other malnourished, displaced people. Some had settled there for weeks, others were new arrivals. Everywhere, there was evidence of the human cost of war.

The sea, normally a place of wonder with its clarity and beauty, was now strewn with the remains of rubber boats and cheap life preservers, which were ironically named as their occupants, for the most part, did not have their lives preserved, not to mention their names, or who they were. Everything they had become was being reduced to news sound bites, at best, provoking a few gasps of horror from the world in between the latest dance competition results, which, ironically, would be the news that would inspire millions to pick up their phones.

Sula was a housewife and mother of two beautiful children, a boy and a girl. She used to work at a local restaurant and was very popular. Sometimes, if persuaded, she would dance for the customers, a traditional Cypriot dance called Hasapiko. It was always popular as patrons could join in. The slow, rhythmic up and down motion that gradually built up speed, could have taken its inspiration from the warm, blue waters around the island.

As she looked out towards the sea, scanning for new refugees, Sula's mind went back to those happier times. As a youngster, she had lived through the war with Turkey, never thinking she would see anything as terrible again. She was a tough woman, who had suffered badly herself in life and never hesitated in defying her husband, a local Policeman. She left her job to help with the growing human crisis at their door. He was concerned, as men needed to be, especially in Cyprus. The bills and everyday problems forced on them, from years of a bad government and corruption, made life hard. For many, it was difficult to take on another burden. Sula, however, saw it differently. In her mind, it proved there was always someone worse off than yourself and, accepting this, she thought, helped them as well as yourself.

Cyprus, was not an easy place for refugees. The asylum process, as laid out by the EU, was not followed here. Leaflets handed out to refugees were often in the wrong language. Applications made in good faith often led to prohibited refoulement and the deportation of legitimate refugees. Appeals, which were few and far between, were rejected, even by the supreme court, due to a mixture of poor legislation, procedure and lack of knowledge by judges. As with all countries, the responsibilities for doing the right thing ended where the law started, with the good people of that country, of which Sula was one.

The port at Larnaca was mainly a marina, surrounded by concrete arms. Its foremost arm is where Sula stood, watching. She was surrounded by a couple of local anglers who were catching small colourful fish, using a secret mixture including cheese paste, handed down generations. Sula chatted with them, putting the world to rights. Every now and then, she viewed through her binoculars, which were gifted by her grandfather. They were from the Second World War and had a mottled black leather covering, which had started peeling off at the edges, but they worked, somewhat. On a number of occasions, she'd spotted a refugee in the water, only to discover it was dirt inside the lenses. After a couple of false alarms, the local harbour master had promised to find her a better pair, but he had long since given up, and had asked her to leave the spotting to the professionals. Her dark eyes and burst of loud, forceful dialog, typical of the Mediterranean people in general, especially its women, was always too much for Mediterranean men. The saying, "Anything for a peaceful life", had surely originated here.

Stavros walked towards Sula, smiling. He couldn't help but admire her tenacity. He had also begun to learn a lot about the middle-aged women who held vigil along the harbour walls he patrolled each day. Sula had become a living statue, as predictable as marble itself. There was no doubt in his mind that she had saved many lives. The authorities, for sure, couldn't be everywhere. She had alerted them on quite a few occasions, to people struggling in the water, people who, without her efforts, would almost certainly have died, as, undoubtedly, thousands already had. It was an occurrence that had been witnessed by these poor women and men, whose job it had become to pull out the bodies from the sea, bloated, with eyes missing, most likely taken by the ever-opportunistic sea birds and sea life. It was a haunting, inescapable memory for those who had to retrieve them. A perfect job, Sula thought, for those in the power, the ones causing the atrocity.

Why, she thought, do we learn nothing from the past? When will we try something different? She looked up and smiled at Stavros. She had not known him well before the crisis, but had learned to like him a lot. He was a family man and had been the harbour master for twenty years. His skin was like leather and when he smiled, his face cracked into a dozen lines.

"Hi Sula," he said, his smile drooping a little. "Have you seen any new sightings?"

Sula shook her head. "None today, handsome." She flirted innocently with him. It was a game they played to kill time.

"Good, I think," he replied. Sula knew what he meant. "I

have a present for you," he said, reaching behind him. "It's an FM Radio. Technically, you should have a licence, but, well, I suppose we can let that go. It will work better than that phone you have. You may pick up the end of a signal, if it just came through. Otherwise, you just miss it. I have set it on channel sixteen, the emergency channel. You probably won't need to use any of the other channels."

Stavros went on to show the enthusiastic Sula how to operate it without killing the airway for everyone else. Sula listened patiently. She was not academic and had little education as her younger life had been frequently disrupted, but she was determined to learn the radio functions and its procedures. The wind picked up, hampering Stavros efforts, but after she successfully made a couple of test calls, he was convinced she knew enough to operate it on her own. He pulled his uniform around himself as protection against the wind.

"Okay, Sula, I'm going back. Stay in touch and I'll see what I can do about the binoculars."

Sula kissed him on the cheek and watched him walk away before turning her attention back to sea. It was going to be difficult now as the waves and white caps made it almost impossible to spot anything. The occasional orange life jacket would present itself and her heart would beat in her chest, but then the wind would throw it up into the air, as if to help put her mind at rest. Sula would be left wondering who the unfortunate owner was. Her wind-swept face always took on a more determined look, but, secretly in her mind, she could hear the voices of children out there, crying to be saved, along with their mother's cries as they drifted away from her, just out of reach. Sula was going nowhere until those cries were gone for good.

Chapter Sixteen

The Sea of Souls

Abdul and Mike sat opposite each other, both sipping brandy, courtesy of Abdul's bar. Mike asked Abdul to tell him more about himself, which he happily did. Abdul explained that he did not consider himself a Syrian. He was, as he explained, a desert Arab of the Beni Sakhr tribe, that was, he said a little sheepishly, until he had been disowned and kind of thrown out. He had many friends, but just as many enemies. The latter had started to outweigh the former, so he had moved to the coast, adopting a more western life in order to avoid contact with those who would, as he put it, drastically limit his manhood. He gestured towards Syria and his old bar, and told Mike that he had never drank before he had this. But temptation and proximity had proved too much. Abdul gestured upwards.

"May Allah forgive me."

To Mike, though, Abdul didn't look hopeful of redemption, nor did he seem too concerned about it as he took another sip from the crystal glass.

A shout from the deck alerted them. Both men jumped up and moved to the stern where Joan and Michael had been standing on deck. They'd been sharing a moment together whilst Ellie watched the babies. Now they were pointing out to sea.

What the men witnessed was surreal. There were literally hundreds of bodies passing by them. A crash came from the front of the yacht, and with it, the horrible realisation of what it was they'd hit.

Abdul rushed to the controls and abruptly switched off the

engines. The yacht slowed suddenly, throwing everyone aboard forward. Thankfully for them all, no one was injured. Ellie came up on deck carrying the children. She was not happy.

"What the hell, Abdul?" she shouted, as if he were a child. Abdul was caught off guard and looked just like a kid who had been told off. In response, he just pointed aft. Ellie immediately realised something was wrong. She carefully put down the children and walked to the stern. Mike and the others stood motionless, paralysed by the horror of the scene in front of them. The life jackets held the dead bodies in grotesque poses, heads lolling backwards, eyeless sockets looking up to the sky, as if seeking help. The bodies slowly bobbed up and down, transforming the Mediterranean into a wall 'less church of the praying damned'. Only, these were innocents. The sea had taken without malice or prejudice to age or colour, and unable to offer even a peaceful burial, which was its usual way.

Now, it seemed, even the sea resented the intrusion. No longer a beautiful dark blue, it was grey and dark, despite the strong sunlight. The group had been staring for too long.

They searched tirelessly, but no life emerged from the human slick. They all just wanted to leave, but no one wanted to suggest it. Jack was the first to speak.

"We can't take them, but can't leave them either?" he asked quietly.

Ellie answered the question no one wanted to.

"We have no choice. Their relatives will want to know what happened to them. If we sink the bodies, their families will be left guessing. All we can do is radio in the position to the Cyprus coast guard."

Michael followed up. "Shall we will say a prayer first, before we call it in? Does anyone disagree?" No one did. Everyone was just glad that a decision had been made.

Abdul went to the controls and switched to channel sixteen,

the worldwide frequency for emergencies.

"May Day Relay, May Day Relay?"

He repeated the message twice.

"This is the motor yacht Horse of the Seas, relaying a May Day Relay alert for bodies in the sea, at coordinate's 35°23'58.6"N 35°10'43.2"E, possibly four hundred souls. No survivor's visible, out."

He repeated the message in Arabic and French. The radio message came back in English, with a Greek accent.

"Horse of the Seas, this is the coast guard receiving you. Can you stay on the station and await our arrival? Horse of the Seas, over."

Abdul looked at the others. They nodded despite him looking concerned.

"If we stay, getting in is going to be difficult."

"If we don't, it could be worse," Ellie countered.

Abdul sighed, this was not his way, and this woman was starting to annoy him.

"Larnaca coast guard, this is Horse of the Seas. We are holding position with a two knot southerly drift. What is your ETA? Over."

"Horse of the Seas, Larnaca coast guard, we will be with you in forty minutes. Thank you for your help, over."

"Roger that, Larnaca coast guard. Horse of the Seas, over and out."

They sat in silence. Ellie and Joan fed the babies, who seemed no worse for their ordeal and were seemingly good sailors. The boat rocking gently and rhythmically; the water moving the boat from side to side seemed to soothe them

Abdul had moved them a hundred yards from the bodies to avoid contact. Mike kept himself busy cleaning his gun. Abdul watched him, as if trying to weigh him up.

Abdul had finally introduced his wife, Fatima, and son,

Abir, who were both in the Galley. He looked over to them and nodded. Abruptly, he turned to Mike. "Do you have children, soldier?"

"No," answered Mike, ignoring the inaccuracy. He was no longer a soldier.

"You're lucky, look at mine. He likes to cook. What kind of boy cooks, I ask you?"

"A chef," Mike replied, smiling.

"So you think that's funny? You and your western ways. I see your women," he said, glancing at Ellie. "Taking charge, wearing the trousers; it's not good. What kind of wife will want him?"

"One who can't cook." Mike was starting to enjoy winding Abdul up.

"You laugh, ha-ha, but men need to be men, and that's that." With that, Abdul ended the conversation.

Mike just smiled at Ellie, but she did not reciprocate. She didn't want to upset Abdul. He seemed to know his way around a boat, and he also didn't seem nearly as bad as she had first thought, which had come as a major relief. At first, she'd thought he was a monster, one who would kill them all at the first opportunity, with no remorse.

The sound of powerful engines approaching broke the silence. The coast guard's white and red boat approached them at an impressive speed. They did not try to board, though. Thanking Abdul over the radio, they set about their unenviable task. The fact they would need a bigger boat had entered a few of their minds, but no one was in the mood to joke.

Abdul started the engines and pulled away slowly, almost as if he were following a funeral procession, which wasn't far from the truth. They were several hundred yards away before he opened the throttle, taking the boat to cruising speed, leaving the usually happy, but now ominous, sound of sea gulls behind them, much to the relief of everyone on board.

Mike set watches to ensure they didn't miss any survivors. As the sea began to get rough, Michael was the first of them to get sick. He had never been good at sea, and his affliction had not been helped by their last encounter. Joan was surprised he had lasted this long. His retching and the look on his face was not to be studied for long on a rough sea by anyone who did not wish to be re-acquainted with their breakfast. Joan went to him. She had never suffered with sea sickness and, being a nurse, cleaning up after sick people was second nature to her. He was also her husband, she had to reminded herself, more than once.

Chapter Seventeen

επευφημίες και σας ευχαριστώ (Cheers and Thank You)

Sula's feet were killing her, so she pinched one of the fishermen's boxes and sat down. The weather was ridiculous. If it weren't for the fact she'd found someone in similar weather before, she would have been on her way home. It was only an hour until dark anyway. She had picked up the call from Abdul on her new radio. The disturbing news of the bodies gave her some hope, hope that someone may have survived. She had seen the coast guard's boat leave in the morning, knowing it would return laden with body bags. The fisherman next to her caught a black bream and was celebrating with his friends, which momentarily distracted her, then she spotted them.

The Horse of the Seas was riding the waves well. It came in to harbour at an angle, to avoid being swept against the dock wall. The captains of the gin palaces weren't particularly skilled, although, many jobs had materialised from people with more money than skill on the water.

Then she caught site of the name, or rather the drawing below it. It was a horse emerging from the spray of a wave. As time was getting on, she thought she would go and talk to the captain, to see if he had any new news.

Abdul swung the fifty-foot boat into the dock. Mike sat with his hands holding tightly onto his seat, but the yacht swung around and straightened up just as the gap between the wall came up. Abdul, he thought, was full of surprises, but he still didn't trust him one bit. Mike was not about to forget that Abdul had planned to steal the yacht from the traffickers. That, in itself, didn't put him off Abdul. He was probably just trying to protect his family, Mike reckoned. However, he was not about to let his guard down. Hopefully this was where they would part company, so it wouldn't matter either way.

Abdul's son jumped onto the dock and tied the boat. Abdul killed the engines and Michael jumped to shore, where he felt even dizzier. As anyone who's been to sea would know, it takes time for your body's balance system to realise you're on land. Land sickness they call it, not that Michael cared when Abdul pointed it out to him. All he knew was that he felt like crap.

Stavros and another man in uniform approached the boat. The other man introduced himself as a Customs officer. He requested documentation and the ship's log book. Abdul was now the one looking sick. All his earlier confidence seemed to drain out of him. He hated figures of authority. Under normal circumstances, he would have either bribed them, or run from them. On one occasion, he had used darker methods, as at the time it had proved necessary. But now, he was lost. Lowering his head, he mumbled something about losing their paperwork in a fire, which didn't go down well with the officer, who had heard it all before. Thankfully for Abdul, Ellie emerged from below the deck. Touching Mike's shoulder, she beckoned for him to follow her. Introducing herself, she handed the Customs officer the paperwork for Mike and herself, which seemed to relax him a little when she identified who she was. Ellie pointed to the dock and they left the boat to carry on talking on the dockside. At times, it seemed like Ellie was getting frustrated with the official, but she visibly held back and tried another tack instead.

Half an hour passed. Sula joined Stavros by the boat and started questioning Abdul, regarding the bodies he had found. She was disappointed to find that he knew little more than she knew already.

Noticing that the Customs officer was having difficulty with Ellie, Sula, pulling Stavros with her, went to see if they could help. Sula had also noticed the refugees on board. She was well aware of the difficulties they would face here in Cyprus.

Sula had been right. The Customs officer, Agda, which meant good hearted, was anything but. Six months ago, he was a different person. Now, however he had been worn down by constant lies and, occasionally, violence. This had come from people he had tried to help initially. Not only had this experience left him disillusioned, it had got him into trouble with his superiors. Over time, he had begun to harden his ways, and now his mannerisms and attitude were almost reduced to that of a traffic warden.

"No, you can't stay here." Agda could be heard saying.

"No, I don't know where you can go. And no, I can't help you. Try your embassy."

Was his a newly adopted vocabulary, one he rarely deviated from these days? Agda was starting to hate himself. He fondly recalled that he had once been a decent, young man. A man people had actually liked.

Agda saw Sula coming and resisted the urge to walk or run away.

"Stavros, you know my hands are tied," Agda pleaded with his friend.

"Don't look at me. You asked me to get you this job, so man up, my friend. Face the storm," Stavros returned, smiling. A storm was exactly what it turned out to be.

Sula let him have it, not for the first time, or even the twentieth time.

"Agda, have you seen the two babies in that boat. What do you want them to do? Go back on that sea? Your mother was here yesterday and we got on really well, so just you do the right thing!"

Poor Agda wondered how the proud job of protecting his country's borders had suddenly become about his mother. The only good thing was that this was the most genuine threat he'd had so far. In the past, he'd heard

"What would your girlfriend say if I told her you sent that old lady back to a war zone?" or "The priest was asking how you're handling things, what should I tell him?"

These, and many more, had become Agda and his colleague's diet of Sula's roasted tongue, served with a good serving of relish.

"Sula, you know better!"

"Don't Sula me," she said, grabbing his arm. "Come and see these kids."

Agda followed her, feeling more than a little stupid.

"There," Sula pointed. "People. Just like me and you." She was pleading with him. "We're making Greek history here, Agda. Don't you let it read something along the lines of the Greeks ignoring the suffering of an entire people on its doorstep, basically our neighbours."

Agda had almost always folded to the relentless attacks from Sula, mainly because he was a good man inside. However, he also knew it wasn't just up to him, his Sergeant would have the last say. Sula would have a more difficult job there, he thought. He also knew that if he kept making these type of decisions, which his Sergeant viewed as weak, he would lose his job. Agda was in a dilemma. He was sick of the arguments, but he was more sick of what he was becoming.

"Okay, Sula, you win. They can stay tonight, but none of them can leave the boat. You can take it up with the boss in the morning." Sula kissed him. There was still hope for him yet, she thought.

She turned to give the newcomers the good news. Abdul shook the young man's hand in gratitude, almost breaking it in the process, and handed him a bottle of single malt whisky before he left. Despite his initial protests against the gift, Agda took it. He didn't have any argument left in him anymore. Plus, he liked whisky.

Everyone said their goodbyes and arranged to meet in the morning to discuss things. Sula promised to call Bob at the UN for Ellie. Ellie wanted to let him know they were safe and, if possible, to pull some strings.

Ellie had taken to Sula immediately, she was her type of woman, and Ellie looked forward to meeting her in the morning.

Ellie ushered the others onto the yacht, so as not to concern Agda. Although Abdul complied, he was obviously put out. The meal being prepared for them was a Syrian fish dish called Sayadish. They cooking smells made them all look forward to it.

The dish was served on a large plate. Everyone sat around helping themselves, after which they all washed up and prayers were said. Sitting together around the food, on Abdul's prompt, they all started eating. Jack had never eaten this way, but soon found it a very sociable way to have a meal. It was served with uneven bread, which acted as a plate. Everyone complimented Fatima, who, for the first time, smiled.

The docks were partially lit by street lamps. Silver shadows littered the cobbles where the spray had fallen from the boats passing. It felt damp to anyone walking around, and a little colder than the streets of Larnaca. Sounds filtered up from the still busy restaurants and night life, massively diminished by the crisis, but still hanging on. It seemed unreal to the people on the boat, as did nearly everything that had happened that day. Mostly, they wanted to forget it, but few of them really thought that they could.

Sleep came easy as they were all exhausted. Abdul took the main cabin without discussion and no one felt up to an argument. Michael and Joan were given the other double, while Ellie and the babies had the bunks, with the babies on the bottom. Jack and Mike were content to take the couches, which lined the upper cabin. Given the luxury of the yacht, the couches were exceptionally comfortable. Abdul's son went up to the fly bridge with a blanket, which seemed to work for everyone, not that Abdul seemed to care.

The boat stayed silent. Romance did not shake the boat, much to everyone's relief, and the night passed without incident.

The next morning at eight, Mike and Jack were woken by the sound of knocking on the sliding rear doors, beautifully decorated with an etched marlin jumping out of the sea. Visible through the cut glass was the uniform of the Sergeant and two other Customs officers, which neither of them recognised.

Jack pointed below deck, and said, "Mike. You had better get Ellie, she is the only one with any authority here."

Mike nodded, rubbing his eyes. "A coffee might have been nice before this." He said, meaning every word.

"Even some breakfast," he muttered as he tumbled down the small steps. He slipped on the last one and let out less than diplomatic statements.

"Ellie," Mike whispered as he gentle tapped on the door. Jack wondered why he bothered after his outburst. Two things happened as a result: the babies started crying, and the Customs officers banged harder on the glass, shaking it.

"Okay, okay," shouted Jack. "We're coming." Saying that, he fell the two feet from the narrow bench he had been sleeping on, to the floor.

"Shit," Jack said, as he rubbed his hips, which he was sure would need replacing.

The door silently slid open to one side to reveal a true Greek, not the Adonis type of legend, but the forty-year-old, Customs officer type. One with a legend, that is, if you worked in the docks, or lived within hearing distance of them.

He was not tall, which was strike one, in Jack's book. Little guys, he thought, always gave more trouble than they had to, possibly to compensate for their lack of height. Also, it was obvious that no one ever commented on his fashion sense. His uniform needed throwing out and his shirt had either been mixed with child's clothing in the wash, or it had drastically shrunk. Likewise, his tie-tying skills seemed to have been lost years ago, that's if he ever learned them. His hat was a relic, no longer used by the coast guard. Due to his superiors restricting his duties to the docks, mainly with fishermen, his appearance had generally gone overlooked. He did, however, speak English on account of his wife, who was from Manchester.

This first thing Ellie heard when climbing up to meet him, was a Greek Manchester accent, which had to be heard to be appreciated.

"Hello, Mrs," I am Sergeant Spearos, of the Cyprus customs police. "I believe we need to talk."

Ellie greeted the Sergeant and offered him a seat and a drink, which Fatima left to prepare.

"I realise," she begun, "that our, and by that I mean all of us, presence here is unofficial. And you probably have a lot on your hands as it is." He nodded but didn't interrupt. "So, I was wondering if we could simplify the situation by placing all these people under my guardianship, so to speak, while we sort out the necessary paperwork and visas? I'm sure your Government and superiors would thank you for managing the workload. Anyway, that's my offer, I won't make it again. It's only giving me extra work," she said without blinking an eye.

The others looked on in amazement.

"What …" Michael began to say, but Mike held his shoulder and gave him a look, as if to say, "shut up".

"What's in it for you?" Spearos said, looking into Ellie's eyes, trying to spot what he'd missed.

"Nothing," replied Ellie. "I'm hoping for something not much different to what you're after. Perhaps a bit of positive news to tell my boss, or maybe some good publicity. Heaven knows the UN could use some."

Spearos nodded. That, he thought to himself, was true.

"What the hell," he conceded. "They're yours, but they don't leave the port without papers. Understand?" he cautioned, wagging his finger at Ellie, a gesture she privately hated. But, given the circumstances, she didn't reciprocate with a one-fingered response, which would have been her usual reaction.

The Sergeant finished his drink and, acting somewhat like a magnanimous king pardoning a servant for dropping a drink, he left. If he had turned around at that moment, he would have seen Ellie's delayed usual reaction.

Ellie suggested they all meet below deck. Just then, Sula arrived, smiling. She was just on time for the meeting.

"Good morning," she greeted in a warm Greek accent that seemed to welcome you in any language. She spoke in English as she realised that most of the boats occupants seem to understand it.

"Hello to you too, Sula," returned Ellie, greeting her with a hug. "We were just about to have a meeting; the Sergeant has let me be their guardian, while they get papers."

"Really?" Sula looked shocked.

"You must be pretty persuasive. The last time he said 'yes' to something that didn't come in a glass was when he was getting married." They both laughed. "But I don't want to intrude," Sula finished.

"Nonsense, without you we wouldn't be here. Can you spare the time?"

"Oh yes, my eyes need a rest anyway. Nice boat. Is it yours?"

"I wish. But if you ask Abdul, he will say it is, even though it's not."

Sula looked confused.

"It's complicated," Ellie clarified. "I'll explain inside."

The two passed the ornate doors and entered the lounge area. Everyone was sitting around looking a lot more relaxed.

"So, Ellie, what's next?" Jack asked.

"Well, let's start with introductions. This is Sula, and for those of you who didn't figure it out, she is the main reason we're still here."

A little clap went around the boat and Ellie joined in, leaving Sula a little embarrassed at the attention.

"It was nothing," she said, but they continued clapping.

Ellie broke the applaud.

"Okay, let's get started. This is where we are and it's nice to see you all happy, but hold off on being too optimistic. We have a long way to go yet. First question is, what do you want? We never had a chance to really discuss it. Second question is, where do you want to go from here? Let's go around clockwise and find out."

Michael was the first person on Ellie's side, if you left out Sula, which he only realised following a nudge in the ribs from Joan.

"We would like to get to England, if that's possible, with the babies. That's it, really. We have friends there who will be able to help us." Michael stopped and, after a pause, Mike spoke.

"Well, I will stay with Ellie until we get back to England. It's my job," he finished with a shrug. Ellie smiled at him.

Abdul shuffled around before he began speaking in the first person. "Abdul doesn't really care. He only wants to be close to home so he can go return when the war is over." His wife and son nodded in agreement.

"All reasonable requests, you would think, and if

governments were reasonable, I could tell you now that all that could happen. But chances are, they may not." Sula was instantly apologetic for mouthing her thoughts out loud.

"No, you're okay," reassured Ellie. The group mumbled their support and Sula smiled.

"Well," she began, looking like she was about to cry, "it's like this. I have become ashamed to be a Cypriot. My government has abandoned its morals, its humanity …" Unable to hold back her tears, she broke off. This speech had been a long time coming but Sula had not been ready for the flow of emotion. Joan changed places and sat with her, holding her close.

Comforted, Sula continued, "… It's not just here. Humanity is all over the world, but my country is killing its own people. Before that, we had the madness in Egypt, Iraq, Israel and now Jordan. Even countries like England won't help. Sorry, Ellie, but it's true, look at Rwanda."

Abdul looked confused.

"I'll explain later, Abdul," she assured him, not wanting to interrupt her flow of thought. "No country is excused … none."

Ellie's memory went to Rwanda. The Canadian UN troops had been hacked to death there, followed by the slaughter of millions, while the world watched and did nothing. After that, they either forgot, or didn't care.

The latter part of her sentence resonated with Abdul's thinking.

Mike waded in at that moment.

"You're right, Joan. No one here needs to be ashamed of their country's actions; they are all beyond redemption," Sula ended and looked around at the group.

Ellie put her hand up. "Sula, if you feel you can, can you let us know what the latest requirements are for getting visas? Long or short term."

Sula, wiped her eyes, feeling her strength return.

"The office you need is not the one on the front, where the refugees are queuing. They will just tell you to go to another office, but nothing is simple anymore. You can be turned down for many reasons, such as lack of papers."

Abdul interrupted. "I found ours last night," he said, waving some forms.

"What a surprise!" Mike said, smiling.

"Anyway," said Sula, looked pointedly at Abdul. "I am just saying, I wish I could guide you on where to go from here and that all will be fine, but I can't because chances are, it won't." She looked across at Ellie, for her to end the meeting.

"I will go into town with Mike, the rest of you stay here, and we will find out what we can. Does anyone need anything?"

No one answered; the boat seemed to say it all. Ellie and Mike picked up a few bits and headed off to town. The weather had calmed, and Sula walked with them. She left them when they reached the road to continue her vigil at the dock. Sula wished them well and pointed out a few locations where they could get help on the small tourist map she had brought for them. As they said their goodbyes, Sula agreed to join them for a meal that night. Waving, she made her way to look for more stranded refugees at sea.

Chapter Eighteen

Put the World to Rights

Ellie and Mike returned to the boat by mid-day, with no good news. They all sat around Ellie as she shared what they had found out.

"Apparently," Ellie began, quietly looking from one to another, "this is not going to be as straight forward as I thought. Cyprus, as Sula implied last night, are playing by the rules now. If I help you apply for refugee status here, it may not be granted. Instead, you may be given subsidiary protection, which sounds like it should be good thing, but isn't in reality. You would have limited or no rights to work, you won't be able to bring family to join you, and, more importantly, it would stop you applying for full refugee status elsewhere."

She let her words sink in. The group were silent. Joan spoke first.

"Surely they can see that we are refugees, anyone can see that," she said. She was almost pleading for her words to be accepted. Abdul and his family nodded while Michael held Joan close to him.

"There is little to be done, officially. Although, we do have a suggestion." Mike paused and looked up at the faces staring at him in anticipation. With a serious face, he continued, "It's not a guaranteed answer to your prayers, but it may be the only thing to do."

"What, Mike?" interrupted Michael. "At this point, anything is better than nothing."

"Okay, it's like this, we do nothing here officially. We make some calls and then we sail directly to the UK. Once we get there, we can apply for refugee status."

"Won't that get you into trouble?" Joan asked, looking genuinely concerned. "We may even get arrested." Her voice ended on a sharp note.

"We'll deal with that when it happens," Mike said firmly.

"I'm not so sure," said Abdul, "I know nothing about England, the UK or Britain, or for that matter, Great Britain."

"They're all same thing, almost," Ellie said smiling.

"Well, why can't they make up their minds," countered Abdul, looking around for support and not getting any. Eventually, his son nodded furiously, realising he was expected to. He even clapped to make up for his earlier silence. Abdul looked at him with a grudging smile.

"It's a really nice place," said Ellie. "The trick is going to be getting you in there. Fuel is going to be a problem. Does anyone have access to cash? This beast is going to take a few Euros to fill her up."

Silence descended again until Jack started to talk, but Abdul interrupted him, "Abdul has this. It's okay."

Ellie and Mike looked at each other and shrugged.

"Ask no questions, and be told no lies," Mike said.

"That's a good saying," said Abdul. "I like that." He started to laugh. "Now I go fishing in the dock, get fresh fish for tonight. You'll like it, you'll see. Abdul's wife great cook, Abdul great fisherman," he finished with a big grin.

"Well, I will get some wine," offered Mike. "Ellie and I are the only ones allowed beyond the dock, and I can't take another day of Abdul's hard liquor."

"What's wrong with my booze?" asked Abdul, clearly offended.

"Nothing, if having a permanent hangover is your thing," Mike returned, smiling at Abdul.

"Only happens if you stop drinking," quipped Abdul, as he got up and grabbed his fishing rod and some smelly paste. No one asked what it was, as long as it went outside with Abdul.

The afternoon went well. Ellie decided she had earned a rest. Besides, she told herself, when would she find herself on a luxury yacht in the Mediterranean again? So, she went to take a look at the fly bridge.

The afternoon rest period was all too short. The sun began to set, lighting up the sky with a mixture of colours, as it so often did after a storm. It had inspired feelings in everyone who had witnessed it, for generations: to paint, propose, enrich minds, encouraging souls to aim for better and, for some, an inspiration. Despite their recent experiences, the group were all taken in by the captivating sunset. Even Sula, who came to the dock every day, perhaps lured by the sun, found herself saying a prayer. They had no way of knowing that they all said the same prayer, which united them on that dock that night.

Prayers, Sula knew in her heart, were powerful. Possibly, she thought, the only real power on earth.

Abdul came back carrying his catch. Thankfully, thought Joan, his smelly bait did not return with him. Abdul had caught at least five good bream, which he proudly showed to anyone who seemed interested, before handing the bucket to his wife. He then poured himself a drink. Ellie and Joan just looked at each other.

The smell from the galley soon became intoxicating, producing an atmosphere of its own. Relaxed, smiles and jokes began to be swapped.

When Sula arrived, the evening was already well under way. The babies were awake and were being passed around to willing hands. Even Abdul took a turn. His face betraying the other side of the hard desert Arab persona he liked to project.

The food was served. Everyone made a big fuss of Fatima, Abdul looked on in confusion. Eating and sitting under the current circumstances, emboldened the group, who started to feel more confident with their surroundings.

Joan was first to point out the change.

"This is nice. A few days ago, we were all strangers, now look at us. I just wanted to say thank you to all of you for your help. It's a real pleasure to be dining with you all tonight."

"Thank you, Joan, from all of us."

"Why is it that people can be so easily crushed? Not just because of their circumstances, but by themselves even. If you know what I mean?" Joan asked curiously.

Ellie and Sula nodded, Abdul just shrugged.

"Abdul not let anyone make him feel bad. I make him feel bad first," he said, as if to himself. He passed the baby he was holding to Michael, who cradled it before answering.

"There's nothing wrong with protecting yourself. The point, surely, is that we shouldn't have to, and the world should …"

Mike cut him short. "What do you mean, Michael? Are you saying that everything should be nice, and that we should all love each other? Get real, this is the way it is." He sat back, obviously at odds with Michael's thinking.

"No, Mike," Ellie interjected, "I think you're wrong. Without ideals and goals towards achieving peace, our lives are surely worthless?"

"Yes, but you have to be realistic." Mike was not about to back down.

"Again, I disagree. Being realistic is just another way of saying you give up, or can't be bothered. It's just an excuse, in advance of failure."

"I agree," said Sula. She was warming to Ellie, but in her heart, she genuinely agreed with her.

"If only you knew how many times that excuse was used around here. The joke is, if you went back, say ten or twenty years, taking in a starving family would have been more than realistic. It would have been, without question, the thing to do. I know the population has increased, but back then, we would have seen it as a matter of principle, essential to maintain our decency, not an obligation. Now, it seems, it's not realistic to have any of those things. Well, I say sod realistic, I welcome the unrealistic."

"Wow." Ellie was impressed. The others clapped, even Abdul. Mike just moved his head to one side, which, if you knew him, meant he had given up.

Eager to move on, Mike continued,

"Let's just say I accept what you're saying. That's the way forward. So, how do we change things? The rich and powerful control this world. They also control the politicians; it's a very old story, which you all know very well."

Everyone nodded. Sula sat forward and began talking, the look on her face ensured everyone would listen and pay attention.

"I hear you Mike. As you say, it's not a new story. The other popular story goes something like this:

'What can one person do?' There are plenty more stories, but I won't bore you with platitudes. I have always believed in good and evil. The problem is that I mainly see evil. Perhaps that's the reason we despair at the thought of beating it. I am no genius, just a housewife, but some things seem simple to me. Why do we so easily accept that no 'one man' can stop evil, yet there are so many examples of 'one man' causing evil."

"That may be true, but …" Michael stopped and smiled. "I think the second opinion just peed on me." He looked down lovingly at the angelic face smiling up at him.

"I'd better change her," he said and went below deck.

"Where were we?" Ellie asked. "Oh yes, no 'one man'. I agree with Sula, one person can make a difference, but they need help, in the same way the evil man required support. That's possibly the problem, there aren't enough good people around."

"Exactly," Mike agreed. "The problem is dealing with the

other barriers, such as money, corruption and power-mad assholes trying to rule the world."

"So, do you just think we should give up, is that it?" Sula pushed Mike.

"Not quite. We just do what we do. We get on with life the best we can, doing good if you can."

Joan joined in, she was getting into the spirit of the evening.

"That's the best we can do on a Thursday night, with all our experience," she said, smiling.

"Alright. That settles it. We will solve the world's problems tonight," Ellie concluded, smiling back. Realising the conversation was getting lighter, the others joined in for fun. Ellie grabbed her bag and took out a pad and pen.

"What if we go around the room and propose a solution. Everyone gets to suggest, one solution, and then, when we have included our conditions, the ones we feel are most important, that becomes our constitution for the world. Agreed?"

"It beats playing charades," Joan quipped.

"Sounds like fun," said Michael, returning with the baby girl, Adara.

"Here, it's your turn," he said, and passed the baby to Mike.

It was unanimously agreed that Sula would go first as she had triggered this line of discussion.

"Remember, only one idea at a time. That way no one can take over," Ellie cautioned before handing over to Sula.

"Right, my first solution would be to always respect human rights."

Ellie wrote it down.

"Mike?" Ellie said.

"Oh, okay. Let's see. I was thinking about making corruption illegal, but I don't know how. It's already illegal, anyway!"

"That's fine," Ellie said as she wrote it down.

It was Abdul's turn next. Some faces cringed, but Ellie stared them down. "Abdul, you're up."

"Abdul wants to abolish politicians," he said, with an amazing confidence. The faces changed to admiration, and a little relief. Ellie wrote down: no politicians.

"Joan?" Ellie nodded at her.

"I want life to be sacred, no death sentences, no killing at the hands of human beings."

Ellie scribbled it down. "Fatima, your turn."

"No, I'm not playing."

"Everyone's playing, Fatima. Join in," Mike encouraged. "Your ideas are as good as any of ours."

She blushed and looked at Abdul.

"Alright, wife, say your mind."

"I want wise men and women to rule the world," she said shyly.

"You know, for my money, that's the best so far," Ellie praised her.

"What about you, Abir?" Mike said.

"You're old enough to carry a gun, what is your opinion?"

Abir also looked at Abdul, who nodded.

"I, Abir, want to vote. I want to say who governs me, like in America." Abdul's hand shot out and slapped Abir's head, making him fall forward.

"Hey," shouted Ellie. "None of that, everyone gets an opinion. Jack, your turn. You've been quite patient."

Jack looked seriously at the others. "I think something like our House of Lords, as a second house, is a proven good idea. If you take out the jobs for the boys, they have experts on everything, and they don't need to be wise, just qualified to advise."

"Thanks Jack. That leaves me ..." said Ellie. "I would definitely like to see an age limit for participants, say thirty-five. No one can gain enough experience before then, I don't think."

The others nodded in agreement.

"That seemed like a welcome opinion," Ellie concluded.

"So, what, if anything, are we going to do with this?" Michael nudged.

"I suggest we put it to a vote. Before we do, though, does anyone have any further suggestions?"

"I think," said Sula, thoughtfully, "there are two possible outcomes from this. We can have a good chat about putting the world to rights, like thousands of other people, and feel guilty for surviving while others die, or we can do something else."

"What we do?" Abdul asked. "It makes no difference, anyway. It's just talk. We talk all night, and we change nothing … nothing. Okay?"

"Very supportive," muttered Ellie. "But Abdul has a point. What are we saying, anyway?"

Michael picked up. "I think what we're saying is that people need better choices. I don't know a government, anywhere, that even comes close to that criteria, or meets those ideals."

"Or a country that is likely to spawn one," Abdul said. "They are all the same bloodless, corrupt self-seekers."

"You're not wrong about that, Abdul," agreed Mike.

"Okay, let's just say you're all correct. But the real problem is the bloody flags, and let's face it, people follow them, right or wrong!" Sula surmised.

"That's true, Sula, very true," Ellie affirmed. Everyone's mood was dampened, until the baby boy burped loudly, making everyone laugh.

"Well, that's telling us off for being negative!" Ellie said, wiping a tear away.

"So, let's say this was a real government, would people vote for it?"

"I would, I suppose," Mike volunteered.

"Me too," Abdul said. "And Abdul never votes."

Ellie looked around the room. "Do you all feel that way?"

They all nodded, some vigorously. "Then ask yourselves, would you vote for that government if it was made up of foreigners?"

It was a good question. They looked thoughtful.

"I suppose," began Michael, "it would depend on the existing government at the time, and the alternative options available. Look at my country now, I would vote for anyone not trying to kill me, let alone a dream team of wise men."

Ellie spoke again, very softly, "Alright. So, what are we saying is that it is possible?"

Mike moved forward on his seat. "I think that you, Ellie, should put it into a formal document and send it to the UN. You must know someone who might be interested in this type of thing?"

"Well," said Ellie, "if you want, I'll do it."

"Why not!" Joan said enthusiastically.

Sula's smile took over her face.

"Can you really do that, Ellie? Are you that important, and will they listen to you?"

Ellie was quick to respond.

"No, please don't get excited. Half an hour ago, this was just a party game. We've been through a lot, some of us more than others. This is one of those nice ideas that will require a lot more depth before anyone reads it, let alone act on it or present it, so relax, it's a bit of fun. I will try to do something, though."

"It is a great idea," Joan said. "Just imagine if all the great minds of the world all formed one government that was available to the world!"

"Okay," Mike said calmly. "Ellie has a point. Look, I'm a real cynic, but even I like the sound of this. The more we talk, the more bloody obvious it sounds, as these things always do … Until the cold light of morning, when the wine has worn off, and reality sets in."

"That may be true," Jack came to life, for the first time that evening. "In fact, we all know it is. But if this fantasy did work, it would make a difference. Think of all the people who don't vote. I heard on the radio today that Donald Trump is running for presidency. If he gets elected, it will prove anything can happen, the people are obviously desperate for something new. They're certainly fed up with the statuesque."

"Who?" queried Abdul.

"Yes," said Ellie. "Look at the UK. We voted ourselves out of Europe, which by the way, may not help us. But what it does prove is that people are turning in another direction ..." She let this hang in the air.

"Do it, then. Start a revolution," Mike said, pointing at her notepad. "Oh, and pass the wine."

That got a few more laughs from Sula. Deep inside, she felt something, but kept it to herself. She could have mentioned it there and then, especially since they all probably felt the same. It was the feeling you got when you found something special.

Even Abdul was excited. He stood up and proclaimed.

"We're revolutionaries now. Haay cool!" He ended with both his thumbs up. Mike laughed.

Chapter Nineteen

Viva Le Revolution

Ellie awoke with a headache and a brief recollection of the night before. She groaned to herself as she swung her legs from the bunk. Just in time, she realised she was on the top bunk, three feet from the floor. "Perfect," she said, still half asleep. The others were in a similar state, mumbling good mornings while queuing up for coffee. Fatima, the only one not suffering, was dutifully serving coffee with a look that held no sympathy whatsoever. "Fatima, you're a life saver," said Ellie. She, too, was met with a stony look and silence.

They gathered at the stern. Some sat in the seats, others stood looking over the harbour. It was a tranquil sight. The water was clear blue, small fish darted away from larger fish. Others, like mullet, could be seen in great numbers, sucking the algae from the dock walls. The scene brought everyone some peace, and even started to revive a few of them.

The peace was broken by Abdul and his fishing rod, and the accompanying smelly bait.

"Abdul, do you have to bring that stuff out here? We were just relaxing," Michael moaned.

"Very sorry," came Abdul's sarcastic response. "You got delicate tummy. Oh, I get nurse to rub it, Michael," he said laughing as he swung himself around to the starboard gangway, narrowly missing Michael with his bait bucket.

"Well, at least we'll eat!" interjected Ellie.

"If we can keep it down," Joan added, wishing she had abstained from the wine.

Sula was walking along the docks, heading towards them.

She was wearing a bright orange dress, which, thought Ellie, really suited her positive nature. She was smiling all over, much to the annoyance of the hungover group.

"Hi, fellow world changers," she greeted. "Who do we elect as the new leader of the Government Select?"

"Government what?" said Michael.

He sounded like he was in pain, which was probably genuine, thought Sula. She recognised the symptoms.

"You know, our proposal for making a better world."

"Oh that!" Michael moaned quietly.

Sula looked indignant.

"You of little faith. We are going to help millions, you'll see." With this, she jumped onto the boat. "Do I smell coffee?"

"In there." Michael pointed towards the galley.

Ellie was drifting off. The harbour, the boat, none of it seemed real. Somehow, reality was a thousand miles south, she thought, back in Aleppo. Did she really need bombs and bullets to feel alive? She shuddered. Something was missing though. The force that drove her had dulled, and she felt she had to get it back.

"I'm off to type this up. Do you have a computer on the boat?" she shouted over to Abdul.

"I think so," he replied. He hadn't put it there himself. After all, he'd stolen the boat, but he had seen one somewhere.

"Ask the wife," he shouted back, returning to his fishing. Ellie sighed. Now she remembered why she wasn't married. She headed back down to find Fatima.

Sula re-emerged, clutching a mug of coffee as if it were full of gold coins. Sitting down next to Joan, she raised the coffee to her lips like a holy sacrament.

"Where is Ellie off to with that much determination?"

"You must have inspired her, Sula. She's off to type up our revolutionary statement to the world," said Joan.

"Good," was all Sula said.

Chapter Twenty

England my England

Mia was sorting the laundry when the phone rang. She swore. Why does that bloody thing go off when I go outside … it better not be a bloody salesperson, she thought.

"Can I help you?" she answered in the nicest voice she could muster; still sounding irate.

"I hope so," replied the voice. Mia sat down.

"Dad!" she shouted as she sat down. "Where are you? Are you okay? When are you coming home? We didn't know if you were alive or dead."

"I'm fine, how are you?"

"Okay now, but we were all worried. Where are you?"

"Well, as it happens, I'm on a luxury yacht in Larnaca, Cyprus."

"Seriously, dad! You're swanning about the Mediterranean, while your family are stressed out worrying over you, you and you."

"Now, it's not that simple," interrupted Jack. "I have been bombed, shot at, inherited a family or two, or three, for that matter. Anyway, the yacht, is a new welcome addition to my life."

"Okay, dad. But what's this about new families? You have been behaving yourself, haven't you?"

"Nothing like that, you smutty-minded daughter, think clean thoughts. They are refugees, and they need help. Can you ask around and see what we can do for them. There is a husband and wife with two babies. They were rescued from Aleppo, and it's not been easy for them. We need to find them accommodation and work. She's a nurse, and he says he will do anything. Plus, they both speak English. See what you can do?"

"Alright, dad, I'll ask around. Is there anything you need?"

"No, I'm fine, thanks. I have to go now, but I will be home soon. Love you, sweetheart."

"Love you, dad."

Mia put the phone down to end the call, then set about calling the rest of the family. Suddenly, she realised she had forgotten to ask about her aunt, but took some comfort in knowing that her dad would have said something if there was bad news.

Chapter Twenty-One

Fallen Angel

Ellie sat down at the desk the captain would have used to navigate, before satellite navigation took over. Her plan was to work on the ideas they had all put together the night before. Her first thought, before she started typing, was that this was probably a big waste of her time, especially considering the other more urgent things she had to do. This thought led Ellie to another one: was she doing this to avoid facing what she should be doing; was she helping the others to avoid her job. The biggest question in her mind was, "what the hell am I doing, wasting my time doing this?" Ellie sat, as still as a statue, staring at the screen. A half-naked woman with a machine gun stared back at her. Presumably, she thought, the trafficker's choice of screen saver. This was confirmed as the blonde switched to a brunette with a rocket launcher.

Ellie violently pushed the keyboard away from her and ran into the galley, crying. Luckily, no one was there. Ellie's cry was joined by another, coming from the bunk bedroom. It was the little baby girl. Ellie wiped her tears and quickly opened the door to find the baby had slid to one side of the bunk and trapped her arm in the gap between the boards. Ellie gently removed her arm and checked it; it seemed fine and the baby stopped crying. "We have to find safer beds for you two. These are big people's beds," she whispered to the baby, who managed a smile back.

Ellie carried the baby girl to the stern to see if Joan could take her. As she walked through the cabin, she heard them telling Sula that she was typing up the ideas from last night.

She also heard Sula reply, "Good".

Ellie speeded up. She didn't want Sula to think she was going to finish the report, or whatever it was she was thinking.

"Sula," she called as she passed through the doors.

Sula turned. "Hi, Ellie."

Ellie slowed and walked towards her. Sula was just about to jump down to the dock, when she heard the baby scream. Ellie, caught off guard, lost her balance, tripped, then fell forward. Sula was closest to her and she reached out to catch the baby before Ellie fell to the deck.

Mike moved to help her, as did Joan. Suddenly, they all turned in utter confusion. Sula suddenly cried out for help. Her balance had been thrown off by the baby. She was going down fast, only not to the dock, but between the boat and the dock.

The noise her arms made as they broke was sickening. It could be heard across the dock. Joan was there first and grabbed the baby from Sula's useless arms before she fell further. As she went, her face and chin hit the hard fibreglass, knocking her unconscious. The rest of her limply fell the last few feet into the water.

Mike moved quickly and jumped to the dock, shouting for someone to call an ambulance. Sula's predicament was worse than he thought. She was being held up by a loose mooring rope, from a different craft that had moored near them during the night.

Mike could see no way to free her quickly. Her head lay between the boat and the dock. She was unconscious, but Mike called to her anyway, not expecting a response.

Mike stood up from where he had been crouching and looked up to see the horror and shock on the others' faces. Then everything moved in slow motion. Behind them, he could see the bow of the customs boat cutting through the water faster than most would in harbour; after all they were in charge.

Mike jumped into the water. Looking up through the clear water, he could clearly see Sula's legs held upwards towards the inside of the boat. Surfacing, he saw the huge motor launch moving quickly from the right. The swell hit Horse of the Seas. Its starboard side pushed against it with sickening predictability towards the dock, trapping Sula's head.

Mike had no chance to reach her. He swung his hands at her legs, but only felt empty water. That's when he saw blood and bone exploding in the water around him, like leftovers from a meal thrown overboard.

What was left of Sula's head filtered through the crystal-clear waters, while a hundred eager colourful little fish, darted in and out, forming a terrible decoration to the macabre scene.

He surfaced and swam away as quickly as he could. Finding a ladder, he climbed out and sat on the dock, witnessing the distress of the others as, one by one, they realised Sula's fate. Ellie was hysterical, the only time he had seen her like that. Jack was trying to comfort her. Everyone else was crying. Abdul, as hard as he looked, sat bent over with his hands over his head as the sirens from the ambulance made its way past the harbour walls. It soon came through the security gates and its flashing lights stopped. The sound of the siren winding down added to the unreal atmosphere the group were experiencing.

The medics were quick to realise it was now a recovery job, not a rescue. They radioed the message to the coast guard. Mike hoped Stavros would not get the call.

The police arrived in their own vehicles and efficiently sealed off the area before the recovery process began. They lifted her remains from the water; the very same waters she had worked so hard to prevent others drowning in. It did not take them long, a grim testament to the amount of practice they'd had recently.

Mike saw a local policeman arrive, held up by two other

officers. He was distraught beyond consolation. Mike guessed it was Sula's husband, so he walked towards him. The other officers waved him away. Finally, when he had seen enough, his two colleagues helped him to their car and drove away.

The day went by with police interviews and questions. Stavros did turn up, visibly shaken over the news. He, too, didn't want to talk.

"Sula had been a much loved person," Ellie observed as they sat drinking coffee in the lounge area. Everyone agreed. "If only I ..."

Mike cut her off mid-sentence. "It was no one's fault, Ellie. What's next, will we blame the baby? This was an accident, they happen. We just have to live with it."

Jack spoke next. "She seemed the type of person who wouldn't have wanted us to look for blame."

"You're right," Joan said. "We should honour her memory. She lived for others. Does anyone have any ideas as to what we could do to remember her by, something real?"

"Let's think it over and talk tomorrow," Mike suggested.

It was a welcome suggestion as no one was really in the mood to talk. Grateful, they wandered off to do their own thing.

Chapter Twenty-Two

Legacy

Ellie awoke from a deep dream. Slowly, yesterday's events filtered into her mind, like a bad dream. Only this time, she knew this was reality. Her body slumped back onto the bed. As she lay there, she thought of the best way to handle the tragedy, as was typical of the next day when there was more clarity.

She had only known Sula a short while, but she felt she was a kindred spirit. Ellie recalled her passion for other people and how she'd been the only one amongst them to really stand behind the statements they'd all come up with. Sula's suggestion had been simple: that the new Government be obliged to respect human rights.

A thought occurred to her then: had the people of the world reached a point where they were ready to vote away from the status quo? A quote from one of her favourite historical people came to her. It was one she used to live by. Time had dulled her memory, but she smiled as Henry Ford's words came back to her:

"Whether you think you can, or you think you can't, you're probably right."

Ellie knew that if she had said 'we can' to Sula, she may have been alive today. But she also knew that bad things happened, no matter what you did. What was left to do now? To honour Sula seemed obvious, she thought, as she continued writing up the report, hoping to send it to the UN soon. At least they would think she'd been doing something for the last few weeks, but mostly, this was going to be for Sula. She swore to herself that she would do a good job.

Ellie thought that she would finish the document in a couple of hours, but that deadline came and went. The more she wrote, the more intrigued she became. Things were starting to make more sense to her, and she found it harder to write things down without thinking some of it was a bit obvious. The only thing holding her back was the inarguable fact that, despite thousands of years of government and democracy, the plainly obvious points they had all come up with were conspicuous through their non-existence, even in the constitutions of the most developed countries.

The other point that, not surprisingly, became apparent was that you could argue on most of the principles: "What if this happened?" type of questions. Thinking deeply about this, Ellie decided this was probably the main reason to keep all the points raised. The devil was in the compromise, she thought. Well, our ideas are not flexible she thought. Ellie realised that that too was a recipe for failure. It was a conundrum. It was obvious to her now that everything they had come up with was a principle. They could be followed, wherever possible. The checks and balances were up to the individuals who had been chosen to lead the new form of government. Remembering Jack's wish, that a second house be appointed, she recognised that they were doing the best they could; maybe the best mankind could do. Evil hides in the cracks, where it can ambush good intentions, she thought to herself.

So, Ellie started another section, looking to clarify those thoughts further, to assist the reader. She went on to the advice section, which was like a template for the user:

If you have chosen well, the individuals will be from all parts of the community. The selection of a person, say from amongst men and women who had worked at a lathe for forty years, would depend on the person's characteristics. If there was a person stood by a machine, a person whom anyone could chat over a problem with, knowing they would receive a wise answer, for the young or old; or, a person who was simply known for listening without any return expectations, one who kept confidences; this person would also be a wise choice.

Perhaps they weren't academic, or didn't have a glittering career behind them, but their strength lay in their ability of knowing right from wrong. Another characteristic to look for would be someone's ability to help you see the difference for yourself. Also teachers, ones who were loved by their pupils right up to the point they left school; the very same teachers who were disliked by those just joining in their first year. These were the men and women who would never dream of becoming politicians. And the few who did try, were worn down by a corrupt inept system, geared to destroying good, even when it resided in the best of people.

Ellie, by now, was thoroughly getting into the project, even enjoying it. It was turning out to be a cathartic exercise for her. The task of writing up their points had seemed unbearable this morning, but it had actually helped. In hindsight, she was surprised at her own earlier rejection of the idea. Had she thought the whole thing was a waste of time? What, she wondered, had changed for her? The answer was now obvious, working on it had resulted in the creation of a living, breathing thing. More importantly, it had started to make sense. Her thoughts were interrupted by Mike placing his hand on her shoulder.

"Are you okay?" he asked.

"Yes, I'm fine, considering."

"What are you writing, if it's not too personal a question?"

"No, not at all. Actually, you own part of it. It's the notes from the game we played the other night, the one Sula was quite serious about it. I felt I owed her …"

"You don't, you know, but if it helps …" said Mike, trying to sound understanding.

"No, Mike. It's more than that. That's how I was feeling when I dashed out to see Sula. I had decided not to bother with it, and was going to tell her so."

"So, what changed your mind? You didn't kill her, you know! You're not responsible."

"Yes, I know, it's more that. Since I started writing this, the more important it seems. Don't ask me why, it just makes sense."

"Come on, Ellie. It's nice that you're doing this, but ..."

Ellie interrupted. "Don't do that, I'm serious, very serious. People are fed up, even in Western countries. Think of the good that could be done by wiser people in poorer countries, where every time a new leader takes over, he or she treats it like a lottery win. There are more examples than we have time to count, and those are just the ones we know about. What about those who got away with it?

"If the UN passed a resolution to have Government Select on the ballot, people could have another alternative, but the people would still need to vote for it. It would still be their choice. Isn't that adding to democracy?"

Mike sat down, and pondered a response. "What about countries like Russia and China, let alone North Korea?" he came up with.

"You're right, Mike, they will veto it, but if they don't have to participate, they may let it through. Especially if the European countries agree to participate first. This is always going to be about 'suck it and see.'"

"Would they even consider it, Ellie?" Mike asked, genuinely interested.

"That may be a sticking point. I would have to persuade some pretty influential people to back it, and they have a lot of other things on their mind right now. But we're just sending this as a potential project, something to throw into the mix of ideas."

Mike stood up to leave. "No harm, no foul. Give it a try, you raise some good points. Let's see if anyone else will agree, or even listen!"

Mike left Ellie to her work and walked aft. Abdul had opened a whisky bottle, so Mike sat down to help him with it.

"Not good business this. Always good people. I think Allah is lonely for nice company. Sula was nice company," Abdul said, draining his glass and taking the bottle from Mike, who had poured himself one.

"She was, Abdul, she was."

The pair sat in silence with their thoughts, slowly finishing the bottle while the radio played soulful tunes in the background.

Outside, the others gathered. Joan and Michael held the babies and Jack was trying to talk to Abdul's son, teaching him some English, with a little success.

"I'm going to call my daughter again. Sorry, buddy, but you can't come with me," Jack said, patting the youngster on the back before jumping off the boat onto the dock.

Ellie hadn't typed half of what she needed to. She realised this was more than a day's work, so she packed up for the day and saved her work on a USB stick she had brought from England. She had kept it on her through everything. A friend had bought it for her and it was both waterproof and shockproof. The stick held all her data and private letters.

Ellie walked back through the boat and, on learning where Jack was headed, ran after him. He hadn't gone far. She gave him a hug when she reached him.

"What was that for?" he asked, surprised.

"No reason. Actually, it was more for me. I am having a difficult time keeping my eye on reality, I just spent the last few hours typing up the outcome of our game, and I don't know if I'm doing it because I believe in it, or if it's out of grief and guilt."

"Well," Jack began, stopping for a moment. "I have been thinking about that to. Sula had a point, and we have to believe that our actions mean something. I know that's not exactly what she said, but, I think, that is what she meant."

Ellie started to walk again, to help her think.

"Okay, accepting all that, it's still a hell of a long shot. Every time I think about the problems, getting a proposal like that, if that's what it is, through to someone who will look at it, let alone accept it, is going to be tough."

"Don't think that far ahead, Ellie. If you do, you will grind to a halt, just take the next step in the process, you may surprise yourself. At the very least, you can always say you tried, which is more than most people can say. After all, you joined the UN to make a difference. Who better to write and propose this than those around that table last night."

Ellie gave her brother another hug and they walked off to make some calls, Jack to his daughter, and Ellie to Bob and her other contacts in the UN.

Chapter Twenty-Three

The Voyage into the Unknown

Night fell on Cyprus. To the occupants of the yacht, nightfall seemed to be slower than usual, almost like a silent last post for the lady who kept vigil on the dock. Even the wind stopped blowing, the water turned black, appearing like the ceramic of a luxurious watch. It was peaceful and everyone was quiet, consumed with their own thoughts as the sun gently disappeared.

Ellie and Jack broke the silence as their feet moved along the boat, sending a small wave over the harbour.

Ellie sat amongst the group and Jack found a seat behind them.

"What I found out today is neither good nor bad. One thing's for sure, though, we were right not to process any paperwork for you here. We need to do that in the UK, which means we need to sail around the Med to the Straights of Gibraltar, then into the Atlantic and around to England. It's about two thousand eight hundred miles, give or take. With the fuel consumption alone, it will cost over two and a half thousand euros, minimum. Abdul, you seem to be the money man, is that even possible?" Abdul nodded.

"Wow! Okay," Ellie exclaimed. "The next problem is, according to the internet site I used, it will take us about eight to ten days, or longer, to reach there, weather permitting. So, here's the bad news, there are no guarantees that, when we get there, you will be able to stay, or even gain entry."

The atmosphere and faces in the room dropped. Ellie quickly continued.

"I have, however, called in a few favours and spread a fair amount of bullshit regarding you assisting me in a study I am doing on behalf of the UN, on solutions to conflicts."

Ellie let that sink in. "It wouldn't normally be within my remit, or even close to it, but a good friend of mine, who has been following our progress, has backdated his request for me to compile a report covering the local population and their ideas. It's a survey to demonstrate that the UN are doing their best to try and find solutions, and get ahead of problems. Anyway, this would explain why you need special status. So, with a bit of luck, someone will swallow that crap and stamp some visas. In the meantime, I have to finish a report that looks worthy of my bullshit."

"Well done," Abdul said, clapping and thanking Ellie.

"You're welcome, I think," Ellie replied, with misgivings written all over her face.

"So, we have a lot to do. We need to plan a course as we won't reach England on one tank or even two. We will need places to fill up and replenish our food supplies," Mike added.

Joan stood up.

"We also need things for the babies. Abdul, we will need some cash," she said, looking at him. Abdul looked if he was going to refuse, but one raised eyebrow from Ellie dissuaded him.

"Abdul is happy to help, no problem," he said without any enthusiasm.

Ellie suggested they start arrangements in the morning. As they stood up to leave, a shout from the dock made them all stop. It was Stavros, the Customs officer, asking if he could board. Mike immediately agreed. Abdul looked a little put out as no one seemed to have grasped that he was captain, and it was starting to get to him. Stavros stepped inside and removed his hat.

"Thank you," he began. "It's been a very sad day for us all.

Sula seemed to like you and we wondered if you would like to come to the funeral?"

Ellie looked at the others, and then turned to Stavros. "We will be leaving soon. When is the funeral is taking place?"

"Tomorrow morning, at her husband's request. He doesn't want the process drawn out, for the sake of their children. So, here is the address. You may all attend. I have arranged special permission. I'd better be going, and I will let her husband know you sent your best."

"Thank you," said Ellie.

Stavros left and they all went about the business of tiding the boat up for departure. Fatima went to cook, despite offers from Joan and Ellie; even Mike offered.

That night passed slow. No one slept well, and the next day dragged on too. They were all apprehensive about the trip, especially what lay for them in England. The things they needed for the baby were bought with Abdul's money. They also picked up sea bands for sickness and travel pills.

The funeral was attended by a lot of people from the island. Sula had been very popular, the group slipped away as soon as it was over, after passing their condolences to Sula's family. They had a lot of preparations to do before they could depart.

The boat was moved to the other side of the dock to allow refuelling. Finally, all was ready for them to leave.

In the meantime, Ellie had been working hard on her report. By now, it resembled the American Constitution in size and, in some small ways, content. Finally, after re-reading it twice, she felt happy to send it off.

Sitting, looking at the finished document, Ellie felt a little proud. Not only for herself, but for everyone who had contributed to the idea. She asked herself whether she dare to hope that the powers that be might take it seriously. Then stopped and reminded herself that, if nothing else, if it persuaded the UK to give visas to the group, it would have been worth the effort. So, connecting with the harbour network, compliments of Stavros, she sent the file to her London office for the attention of her boss, Bob.

Chapter Twenty-Four

Pass the Parcel

Bob was sitting at his desk in London where he spent most of his time working as a director for the World Food Programme (WFP). Prior to this posting, he used to work for, and head up, UNITAR, or the United Nations Institute for Training and Research.

To anyone who was curious enough to look into the workings of the UN, they would have soon realised what a poor description this was. It was anything, but organised, with over 130,000 field workers, in over 120 different countries. There were 193 different countries listed as member states, with the number growing.

Despite its lack of organisation, its resources were huge: 167 helicopters, 7 ships, 59 aeroplanes, 14,000 vehicles, 350 medical clinics, and goodness knows how many buildings. On top of this, it is split into at least 108 different departments on a worldwide basis, dealing with everything from women's rights to rape and, of course, food.

So, when Bob opened the email from Ellie, he had no idea what to do with it. However, as he read it, he was taken aback by its simplicity and honesty.

Bob soon realised that he was also becoming a believer, but, he reminded himself, it would make little difference to the outcome. He would have his work cut out, even if he used it as an excuse to persuade the immigration department in the UK to give Ellie visas. Getting anyone to take it seriously as a proposition was a different matter altogether.

He had noticed that Ellie had sent copies to Alexander

Spacy, Jane Trelawney. Alex headed up UNITAR and Jane the UNHCR, the United Nations High Commission for Refugees.

Ellie had carried out this bold move for no other reason but the fact that the three ladies had had a few too many drinks at a UN get-together for a charity, which, much to her shame, she couldn't remember the name of. The ladies had a good chat that night, revealing a lot more about each other than they would normally have done had they been sober. Each phoned the other the next morning, swearing an oath of secrecy to each other, not that they had revealed anything too terrible, but embarrassment was definitely on the cards. Ellie hoped it would be enough leverage to get her report read.

Bob, on the other hand, looked at the email recipients list and couldn't for the life of him work out why she had chosen these people to send copies to. Each copy of the report, he noted, was headed with the UN mandate, which read:

"To save succeeding generations from the scourge of war, to reaffirm faith in fundamental human rights, to establish conditions under which justice and respect for the obligations arising from treaties and other sources of international law can be maintained, and to promote social progress and better standards of life in larger freedom."

Ellie had known it would have minimal impact. As anyone who had been around the UN knew, it was not known so much for the action it took, it was more about the words and speeches made. However, the words they had used were good ones, albeit a little naïve, but that was the point. She'd smiled as she pasted it in. Unfortunately, she thought, as she pressed the send button, their report had little, or no, hope of triggering anything. Ellie was more than aware that more important issues were being ignored by member states, whose votes were used to veto peaceful propositions, which were aimed at saving lives. She also knew that the organisation was full of people with good intentions, and they were usually the ones suffering from depression, from when things went another way, as she was told by an old member of staff on joining. Cynics would find food here; evil would find a place to work. The good came here to starve and die. At the time, Ellie had thought she was just old, but the longer she stayed, the more those words rang true. Anyway, thought Ellie, the job is done.

Bob saved the file to his desktop and sat back to consider who the best people would be to share it with, apart from immigration. Anyway, he thought, he only intended to give them an outline of the project that "he had commissioned". But right now, he was stuck, so he did what he always did when he had a dilemma, he decided to ask his old mentor, Al Stevens. Al was semi-retired now, but he still held an advisory position with the UN on a number of matters. He had joined in 1975 and held a number of posts during his service. He'd also been the one responsible for Bob's recruitment in the late eighties. Bob had been a manager for a clothing store before he left to find something more challenging. Luckily, he bumped into Al at a charity ball, and the rest was history. That's that sorted, Bob thought, and went to have a late dinner. His secretary was out so he left her a message:

"Check the document; email it to Al at UN HQ."

His secretary, Eunis, knew Al as well. They had met on many occasions when he had visited Bob. Al always had a nice thing to say to her and always asked after her husband, Barry, who had an affliction concerning his voice, where he could only whisper. Bob, knowing how she liked to joke about it, always had a new one for her, something about a quiet life, or something similar.

The next morning was beautiful. Sunny but cool. England at its best. One of those days when the English didn't envy anyone, not the Spanish or Greeks, nobody. On these days, the

English were content, probably because they knew it wouldn't last. But, for that one day, everyone lived happily in denial.

Eunis parked her car in the staff car park and made her way through the double doors. Security knew her well, but she still had to go through the usual scan and security check routine before being let in. Her office was on the ninth floor and she shared the lift with three other people she had never seen before. Not an unusual occurrence in the UN building. No one spoke, not because they were anti-social, as most people were in lifts, but because they had the added excuse of never knowing what language they would need to use.

Eunis reached her office and went through her usual routine: she took off her coat, then switched the coffee machine on before sitting down to check her emails. There were a few spam emails, which she simply deleted, and one or two that needed Bob's and her attention. Although she had noticed the sticky note from Bob, she had stuck to her routine. With her essentials over, she read it. It pointed to the memory stick that had been left on her desk, so she loaded it up. She knew Ellie and was intrigued to see her name on the document. The whole office floor had been anxiously waiting news of her, and everyone was massively relieved to know she had turned up in Greece. She wouldn't have been the first to die in the field, many had in the past; UN work came with a high risk.

Eunis read the report and realised it was far more than just a report. She stopped several times to collect her thoughts as a great deal of what she was reading seemed idealistic, which didn't seem like the Ellie she knew. Ellie had always been very grounded in her opinions. She wondered what had brought on this revolutionary thinking in Ellie.

As she read on, she started to understand a little of what the group were trying to say. More to the point, she had witnessed England vote against a fairly popular Prime minster, with

Brexit, and there were plenty of other examples around the world. She wondered if the world's population, as a whole, had reached a turning point with the quintessential politicians of the last hundred years or more. Maybe, she speculated, this idea has a chance. She smiled.

"And pigs may fly," she said out loud.

It took her all afternoon to proof-read the document. It would have taken longer had it not been for Ellie's excellent grammar. Satisfied with the content, she loaded it up to an email. Eunis had been so engrossed in the report, she had not bothered with her coffee and was starting to feel a headache coming on. Realising she was dehydrated, she grabbed a glass of water and took two aspirins before looking at Bob's poorly written note. Doctors, she thought, were better. She pushed the send button on the email and shut off the screen.

"I deserve a break," she mumbled to herself.

Downstairs, on the first floor, there was a canteen, a pretty good one by most work standards, probably because they never knew who might be visiting. Even heads of state had popped in for a coffee. Eunis grabbed a prawn sandwich and an orange juice and sat down on an empty table, where, luckily, someone had left a newspaper. She opened it to look at the headlines. One of them read, "Dance Diva shows all". Sighing out loud, she turned to the next page with hope. "Internet email scandal, Hillary Clinton accused again". She suddenly froze in motion, looking at the news piece. Something stirred inside her, something she was familiar with. She had felt it before, the same feeling one got when they knew they'd made a big mistake, but unsure of where or when. Then it came to her. Eunis dropped her sandwich and stood up. As quickly as she could, without making a scene, she made her way to the lift. As expected, now that she was in a hurry, the lift seemed to take an age. Finally, she was on the ninth floor and almost diving behind her desk. She turned the screen on and checked her emails again. What she saw next, made her feel sick. She had not sent the email with Ellie's report attached to Al at the UN. Instead, she had emailed it to everyone at the UN, or, at least, that was the distribution list she had accidentally chosen. She had, she realised unconsciously read 'Al' as 'all'.

Wars, she thought, had been started by less. However, a crucial part of her job was to ensure the accuracy of recipients of emails. It was paramount. Eunis wondered how she could have made such a basic mistake. Then it sunk in: it didn't matter, she was solely responsible and she knew she had to let Bob know. So she rang his mobile.

"Hi, Bob."

"Hi, Eunis."

"Little problem, I'm afraid."

"How little?"

"I'm not sure. That report you asked me to proof-read and send off ..."

"Yes?"

"How bad would it be if it had a wider audience?"

"How wide are we talking?"

"I sent it to everyone in the UN who is on the mailing list."

Silence.

"Bob, are you there?"

More silence.

"Bob, speak to me."

"Oh crap."

"Bob, your scaring me."

"I'm on my way in."

He hung up.

Chapter Twenty-Five

Deep Blue Sea

Farewells said, and few tears later, the Horse of the Seas left Larnaca harbour. The weather was fair and the crew were all standing on deck, waving to Stavros. Ellie couldn't help thinking she could see Sula, still standing there, the sentinel on the dock. How many lives would now be lost because she was no longer there to look out for them? she thought, then she turned away and went below deck. The emotions were too much for her to bear. She wasn't alone in her thinking.

Abdul stayed at the helm just looking out to sea instead of setting the yacht to auto pilot, checking his gauges every now and then. He had been through a great deal in his life: he had seen his parents die of diseases and his friends blown up, but throughout, he had endured, which had made him resilient. The people he was used to living around were hard survivors like himself. If they hadn't been, he would have witnessed their deaths. This was the lesson life had taught him and it had kept him alive. At this moment, he was in a dilemma. The people he now found himself with were also tough, but somehow, they had remained human. Something he feared he had not done. It was not that he had committed any horrific deed, but he was not proud of what he had done to survive and protect his family. Although, he knew, he would do it all again if they were in danger. He also knew that he would protect his new-found friends; something inside him told him they were worth it, that they would do the same for him. He looked out to sea, a little calmer now that he had made a decision.

Their first fuel stop was planned for Heraklion, in Crete.

Stavros had called ahead for them, so that they would not be hassled unduly. It seemed like all was firmly in place, so everyone settled down for the journey. Despite their planned fuel stops, they carried two drums of additional fuel and everyone was banned from smoking on the stern. It would take them over a day's sailing to cover the 450 nautical miles to Crete. Although they journeyed in luxury, it was still tiring for them. Abdul suggested they set up watches to try to avoid collisions with discarded flotsam, and containers frequently lost from ships carrying containers. Although the newer containers were designed to sink, there were still enough older models floating around. At fifteen knots, they would tear the bottom out of the yacht, despite its thick hull. After Abdul explained this, they all kept a good eye out on their watch. No one wanted to end up in the water, not after what they'd seen in the waters on their way to Cyprus.

The day was exhilarating. The sea bands on their wrists seemed to be doing their job; no one was sick. They enjoyed the yacht as it did what it did best, which was to cut through the water like a knife. Abdul kept the speed down, despite protests from his son, who tried to grab the controls at the earliest opportunity just to tease his dad. Abdul was not laughing, but inside he was quietly enjoying the banter with his son.

Before nightfall, everyone went on deck to watch the sunset. Abdul even stopped the engines so they could drift in peace. The experience was intoxicating. The silent boat barely moved on the still water. The warm evening with the cool breeze only added to the experience. Abdul threw a line over the side and soon caught their dinner. One fish, a Dorado, took him five minutes to reel in, with Abdul chasing it around the boat before Mike, who had found a fishing gaff clipped to the roof, pulled it on board. It was a spectacular green and yellow in colour. Abdul explained that this was a great fish to eat, but at over fifteen kilos, Fatima had her work cut out.

They ate in silence. Everyone was tired and deep in their own thoughts. They were discovering that the sea made you drowsier than usual. Mike commented on the food and it was agreed all around that they were being spoilt by Fatima. She tried not to look too pleased with the attention, but it showed anyway. After dinner, one by one they said goodnight. Some were sleeping on the benches they were sitting on during dinner, so they all retired for the night swiftly.

Those who slept, dreamt. Those who didn't, day dreamed. Everyone on the boat had a hope or dream of their own. Ellie's woke her up. She could still remember her dream: she was standing in front of a big crowd and they were shouting something, but she couldn't remember what. The others were there, too, but they seemed out of place. She remembered feeling overwhelmed, even a little scared. Unable to go back to sleep, she stood up, deciding to have a quiet walk before trying to get back to sleep. The walk helped her settle and the rhythmic sound of the twin engines, helped her drop off; this time into a dreamless sleep, or least not one she would remember.

In the morning, they emerged from their beds or bunks and made their way to the galley, where Fatima dutifully passed out coffee. It was so thick you could stand a spoon in it; a typical Arab blend and very strong. Abdul announced that they would see land in about an hour, which brought on a round of applause.

The Heraklion stop turned out to be hostile and boring. It was not at all what they'd been looking forward to, despite Stavros's call. They were treated roughly and told they could not leave the boat. This angered Ellie and Mike, but they decided not to make a fuss in case the rest of the group and the boat were impounded. Ellie told Mike that she was finally starting to realise how refugees felt. They refuelled and left for Marsala before the day was out. The miserable atmosphere was somewhat heightened by the pleasure of being back at sea, where they were free to move around without permission, despite the limited space they had.

The television on the boat had not always worked well, but for some reason it worked fine in the middle of the Mediterranean. Everyone, except Fatima, gathered to watch the news. CNN, understandably, concentrated on the upcoming presidency of Donald Trump. Debate after debate followed on all the accusations against him: of being a racist to a woman hater, which sparked some lively debates amongst the group themselves. Although none of them were planning to go to the USA, the general feeling was that Tump could potentially spark a worldwide move against refugees. One that, in general, could affect them personally. As usual, though, the debate took on a wider perspective of the world. Joan was particularly vocal on the subject.

"Personally, I am fed up with the so-called superpowers playing power games in the name of war, then complaining when the consequences turn up at their borders."

"I agree," said Abdul. "It's not just war. When they get their way, they screw us in business, then act like saints when they give some of what they stole back as charity. Then they expecting us to be grateful."

Everyone looked at Abdul, that was the most eloquent speech he had made since they had known him. A few gave him a little clap. "Thank you, Abdul. You're not the big stupid lug we thought, eh?"

"I'm sure no one thought that, Abdul," Ellie said. "You do raise a good point though, the world economy is literally set up on win and lose, and on surpluses and deficits. And where does Africa and Asia fit in this equation? It's not as winners, which is insane. When you put deficit next to a country's name, its people starve."

"That true, Ellie," Mike acknowledged. "But the problem is much bigger than that. Each country develops at its own pace. Surely you can't be suggesting that Africa could have all the luxuries of America?"

"No, Mike, but one shouldn't be a parasite on the back of the other, especially just to maintain useless luxuries, half of which we throw away. There must be a better system, a better way to run things. The biggest problem seems to be population. There's simply too many of us."

"You're right there," Joan joined in, "but China tried its best to sort out the problem, with its one child rule, but that didn't work out very well, especially when you take into account the nation's preference for boys over girls."

Jack shuffled in his seat and decided to contribute to the discussion. "It all comes down to what we were talking about the other day, about when wise people rule the world instead of greedy ones. The world would truly be a better place. However, I really don't see this happening anytime soon, so we muddle through. You, Ellie, joined the United Nations, and you did that to make a difference. It's only a small difference, but it is a difference. The real trick is to have thousands more like you, if not millions. I hate to say it but, it would take an enormous effort for the people in the Western world to understand that, if they don't do something, their final choices will be to either take in all the refugees of the world, or do the unthinkable and kill millions of them. You know, it just occurred to me that that's just what we're doing. We're killing millions of people. We're actually helping and encouraging them to kill each other. Wouldn't it be a revelation, a real story, a genuine horror story, if we discovered that this was the plan all along, perpetrated by one or more of the superpowers. Or maybe they have already worked this out, and, although they're not working together, because their aim is the same, they might as well be as far as the so-called third world is concerned."

The group looked shocked but were in agreement.

"It's hard to knock that logic." Mike spoke for them all. "So, what's the answer, Jack?"

"If you're looking for an Oracle, Mike, you've come to the wrong place. I am simply a truck driver. The only thing that makes me special is the way I was brought up. My father deserves all the credit for that. He would have said that it was all a matter of decency. Of course, the real trick would be to get the world to be decent. On that subject, my father would've said, 'it all comes to education', and it does. So, if we can get the world educated and brought up as my father brought me up, then we could be onto something. However, you still have the problem of population control, which, if I'm not mistaken, is a bit of a sticky subject. I did a bit of research before I left England. You know what I found out? All the countries with the lowest number of literate people, were also the countries currently at war."

Silence met Jack's revelation. Then Ellie decided to speak up. "As we are just chatting here, it doesn't really matter, but in most religions, there is some form of Armageddon, an end to all things, and if there isn't, there should be. So, if you believe in something greater than yourself, then you may feel our efforts to change the world is a futile exercise. Unless, of course, you feel that God would judge you on your efforts, in which case it becomes very important indeed."

Joan spoke up. "I believe it is important that we try, even if it seems impossible, or maybe because of just that. If we don't challenge ourselves, what would we gain? What God would reward us if we took the easy option? More to the point, what satisfaction would there be in it for us?"

"You make a good point. I can't say that I have been particularly religious throughout my life, but I have prayed. What man doesn't when he is being shot at. Although, I'm not sure if that counts? Let's say that I follow the option of keeping God happy, just in case," said Mike.

No one was paying attention to the television, which had been left on. A typical occurrence amongst people of this generation, where one somehow picked up on the most appropriate time to pay attention to the TV screen. Call it sixth sense, but all eyes turned to the television. The United Nations was the news topic. Apparently, a leaked document had come to the attention of the press, and had been interpreted as a proposed resolution before the UN.

The UN denied this, pointing out that this document was taken from an internal email, one not meant for public release. At best, it had been marked as discussion point. There were no plans, now or in the future, to put these before the United Nations as a proposal or resolution for any practical purposes.

None of this would've been particularly interesting if it weren't for the fact that, at the end of the news piece, the female reporter mentioned Government Select.

"It can't be," Ellie murmured nervously.

"What did you do, Ellie?" Mike asked.

"Nothing really, I just sent it to Bob and two others. Certainly not to the whole of the UN. I'm sure he wouldn't have sent it out widely to everyone, so it has to be some sort of mistake."

"Well, we got the publicity," noted Abdul. "That's what you wanted, wasn't it?"

"Not like this!" said Ellie, looking decidedly worried. "Then again, I suppose we really didn't expect it to go anywhere really, so perhaps it will get noticed at least." A smile formed across her face.

"Let's try another channel," suggested Mike.

Michael, who had been playing with the babies had avoided participating in the discussion. He switched to the BBC News channel. There, streaming across the bottom of the page, was their story. Although they weren't mentioned by name, the destructive phrase "Gone Viral" was damaging enough.

"What the hell, Ellie. You could have wiped it before you sent it."

"Abdul, you twit, I emailed it, and it's not that type of virus."

"Oh, what then?"

"It means the word is spreading very fast indeed. Like a virus, but in a good way."

"Is there any money in it for us?" Abdul asked hopefully.

"I would normally say no, but who knows nowadays. That's not why I sent it, though, and I don't believe that's the reason you said those things the other night." Ellie looked around the cabin.

"No," Joan affirmed quickly.

"But Abdul is like us, we have nothing and I don't blame him for asking, do you?"

"No, I suppose not. Sorry, Abdul," Ellie said sincerely.

"Let's listen. I want to hear the whole story. It's bound to come up."

Chapter Twenty-Six

King Canute

Bob awoke with the feeling that something had gone wrong. He crawled out of bed, showered and put on his best suit. The drive to the UN offices would have been uneventful had it not been for the radio. Every time the news came on, it mentioned Government Select, the new revolution. The people's government they were calling it. By the time he reached the office, he had fully accepted his fate. There was no way this going to die down. If he didn't know Ellie better, he would have sworn that he had been set up, but he knew her too well and she was as straight as a dice. Besides, he thought to himself, the idea was a good one. Just then, a thought occurred to him. If he made it look like it had intentionally been shared widely, that it had been his idea to publicly push it into the open for debate, he could play both sides. Now he felt better, he parked the car and headed into the building.

Eunis was always the first one in, and she too was dreading the day. Although, the whole affair added a little excitement to her life. She had never been so directly associated with a breaking story before.

As Bob walked in, Eunis started to talk, but Bob cut her off.

"Don't worry, Eunis. You did just fine."

"I …"

"Not another word, Eunis. You did just what I asked you to do, you understand?"

"Yes …" she played along. Although she was confused, Bob was happy so she felt it was best to leave it at that.

"Do you want a coffee, Bob?" she asked.

"Definitely. Thank you, Eunis." Bob smiled as he walked into his office.

He hadn't sat down for more than a minute before the phone rang.

"It's John Summerville for you."

"Okay, put him through. John, how are you keeping?"

"Fine and you?" came the gruff voice. "Now, what's all this Government Select stuff? I hear it came from your office?"

"Well, yes. It did. I commissioned one of my staff to conduct a study, a kind of reach out to the people sort of thing. You know, public relations. If we ever needed it, it's now."

"We need it, although I'm not convinced this is a good thing, Bob. It's a big distraction from our core work."

"It doesn't seem to have any negative press," Bob said hopefully.

"No, that's true. But isn't it all a bit idealistic … pie in the sky type of nonsense?"

"A little," conceded Bob. "It shows were being proactive, though."

"Yes, but I mean, nobody's going to take it seriously, are they?"

Bob knew his boss was digging to see if Government Select held water, or, in his case, a potential knighthood. It was common knowledge that he had his eye on a gong.

"Well, I would imagine some of the African states may take an interest. Imagine what would happen if it came up trumps!"

"Please don't say Trump. I have had nightmares since that man bought his way into the White House. God knows what he'll do after his inauguration, have Putin for lunch and serve Chinese takeaway probably. The man's a menace."

"But he did ride in on a wave of popularity; it does seem to be the way to the public's heart these days."

"True, very true," John said, mulling over Bob's remarks.

"Okay, just let's play it by ear and see how it goes. Who knows! Goodbye, Bob, keep up the good work."

"Goodbye, John."

Bob sat back in his new swivel chair and sighed. He wasn't a deep thinker and his mind wandered to when he had fallen backwards on his old chair, several times.

Eunis, who had been eavesdropping on Bob's side of the conversation, as good secretaries do, just smiled. She could spot the UN quickstep anywhere. They did it so much, she thought, that it ought to be on *Strictly Come Dancing*. The guest politicians would be great at it. This time she laughed to herself.

Chapter Twenty-Seven

Fishy

The sea stayed calm as the group looked forward to a better reception in Masala, Sicily. The travel guide they'd found on board the yacht, along with some other travel brochures, suggested the chocolate drink in Masala was to die for. They all hoped they got the chance to try it.

The favourite pastime seemed to take place at the front of the boat, not Titanic-style, just sunbathing on the platform. Michael and Joan were rarely there, though. They stayed below deck, looking after the children. Both felt guilty enjoying the yacht in the way the others did, as they remembered the friends and family they'd left behind in Aleppo. From the news, it seemed like Aleppo had entered a new version of hell, the new and improved version of hell for the twenty-first century. That's how Abdul had described it, and it seemed to fit.

Ellie, for no reason she could fathom, found herself writing up notes from the discussion they'd had the day before. She stopped typing for a moment to ponder over why this group always seemed to come up with such profound ideas. It was not that they were particularly original or gifted, but they seemed to bring together other people's ideas in a way that worked. Sort of like a wheel and engine from two different minds, which were destined to come together at some point.

Ellie watched Abdul, who was working on the Ray Marine navigation system. In truth, he had only started studying it a few weeks earlier, just before they'd embarked on their journey. His knowledge was purely theory-based only. Luckily for the group, he was a lot more gifted than anyone suspected, and, for that matter, a lot less devious. He was just a man trying to survive and look after his family. Given his experiences over the years, even the best of us would have followed a similar path, thought Ellie. Anyway, he seemed to be getting the hang of the machine, her thoughts continued.

Jack was sunbathing with Abdul's son, doing his best to teach him English. The young man already had a grasp of the basics and was really impressing Jack as he pushed forward quicker than Jack could teach.

Movement caught Mike's eye. Turning to the side of boat, he saw a huge fin. Mike froze before tapping on the bridge window, frantically signing for Abdul to stop the boat, which he duly did. Abdul and Michael joined Mike as he pointed to what could have passed as a scene from the National Geographic channel. A massive shark circled the boat.

"What kind of shark is that? Do you know?" enquired Michael.

"Yes," said Abdul. "But I can't believe it."

"What is it, father?" his son asked.

"It's an extremely rare Mediterranean Great White shark."

"No way!" exclaimed Mike. "You mean bloody Jaws."

"That's the one," said Joan as she joined them.

"What's Jaws?" Abdul said.

"It's a film," Mike said.

"Oh, well this is fish, not film." Abdul stated the obvious. "Anyway, it won't bother us. It's just after fish hanging around the boat. Can we go now?"

Mike looked incredulously at Abdul. "Yes, I suppose we can."

They took photos of the rare shark and moved on. Abdul was right, it soon lost interest in the them and stopped circling when the food ran out.

Chapter Twenty-Eight
Paparazzi

Jo Sparks hung around. He literally just hung around waiting for things to happen. It was his job. Of course, the secret was knowing where and when to hang around, and, especially, who to hang around.

His real name was Kevin Prosser, but he'd changed it. Partly to give himself a different image, and, ironically, to give himself a level of anonymity from his real life.

He could make a lot of money with the right photos. The right photos were either rare shots of celebrities, or embarrassing shots of anyone in the public eye. These photos would bring in the best returns. Magazine sales didn't depend on interesting content. What was deemed as entertaining, or, at least, what was enjoyable at a base level, was what the public desired from its glossy magazines that covered the fake lives of successful people.

The only serious part of the whole business for Jo, was the money he made. As for the misery they caused for the celebrities they stalked, well, Jo's conscience survived on a regular dose of the age-old cliché: "they wanted the fame, therefore, everything that came with it, including him, were just par for the course". Money blindness was an age-old disease, common amongst pimps, politicians and businessmen the world over and, so far, there was no cure. Why, he thought, should he be different?

This morning he had been hanging around the UN building on an assignment. This was how he referred to his daily activities, probably to feel more like an MI5 agent and less like an unshaven button-pusher, whose true talent lay in leaving his morals at home when leaving for work.

He had already snapped a couple of dozen shots of Bob and his boss coming and going from the building. Just as he was starting to think he was wasting his time, both returned to the building. Jo was just about to call it a day when he saw Bob opening the doors to leave again. He raised his camera and zoomed in, with the sound of a gentle whirr as he watched through the lens, he witnessed a car pull up. Two men jumped out and his finger was instantly on the button. The camera shutter sliced the air and light into segments of time as efficiently as a Michelin Chef chopping an onion. The scene he captured would be on the front of every paper in the morning, and he would be paying off the mortgage for years with the takings from the images he was capturing at that moment. Then it was over. The car sped off. All that was left were security guards running out with radios in hand.

Bob lay on the floor, dead. He had taken two shots to the head and one to the heart. Jo kept taking photos, switching to HD video as the ambulance and police turned up. Soon, there were too many vehicles surrounding the area for him to get a clean shot, so he packed up. A short while later, he uploaded the pictures and sent them to his agent. The message subject read, "Nuclear material".

Chapter Twenty-Nine

Stealth

Ellie was enjoying her time with Joan and the babies when she received the news. They'd been watching television intermittently when the programme was interrupted by a news flash. Ellie sat frozen in front of TV, tears rolling down her checks. "Why? For God's sake, why?" It had to be related to her report, she thought to herself.

Mike came in to see what the fuss was about. Joan simply pointed at the TV. Mike was shocked into silence, this couldn't be happening.

"This is ridiculous," Mike finally commented, then slumped down. He hadn't known Bob well, but he had seemed like an okay guy to him.

When the others found out, the question each had was, "Why?"

"What was in that report, Ellie?" Mike asked.

"Nothing bad enough to get Bob killed, if that's what you're asking."

"No, of course not but, well, there had to be something."

"Take a look for yourself, there is a copy on the computer."

Mike went to check the computer, while the others comforted Ellie. Well, all except Abdul, who had followed Mike.

Ellie was right, Mike thought, there wasn't anything in the report that would trigger a murder, especially as it was still only under discussion. It would have been different if some country had Government Select on the ballot paper. Even then, he thought, it would probably have had the opposite effect. They would have gone after the accomplice, not Bob. He was just the messenger. The irony hit him then: Bob would not have been the first messenger to be blamed, or, for that matter, killed.

Abdul sat down beside Mike.

"What do you think, Abdul?" Mike asked, genuinely interested in the Arab's opinion. He was starting to admire the man ever since he threw Henry overboard.

"I think this is very strange. Abdul thinks this is silly thing to kill over. Something else was going on here. That's what I think, I think we better keep heads down."

With this, Abdul walked off, leaving Mike none the wiser and more than a little worried.

The Port of Marsala turned out to be the complete opposite of Greece. As it happened, the Italians, especially the Sicilians, had great respect for wealth, and a million and a half dollars' worth of boat screamed wealth to them. Whether it was actual respect, or just the hope of some of the wealth rubbing off, they would never know, but they had the freedom to wander, at least for a couple of days.

The group decided to walk around town together. They packed a few bottles of water and said goodbye to Ellie, who had volunteered to look after the babies. She pointed out that she was in no mood to enjoy herself, anyway.

Ellie played with the children after the others left. The children were at an age where it was enough to have a few meaningful chats about life and how it sucks, all said in a happy, talking to baby, voice. One that was familiar amongst parents who were not in the mood to talk about fluffy bunnies.

The afternoon was very hot so Ellie put the children in their new baskets for a nap below deck. While there, she heard and felt someone moving around on the boat. She felt their presence more than she heard it. Whoever it was, they had a very gentle touch. For some reason unknown to her, the hairs on the back of her neck stood up and she suddenly felt very vulnerable. Ellie thought about shouting up, but something told her not to. Her rational side told her it was probably one of the others who had forgotten something or simply had enough of the heat. Despite this thought, she moved quietly from the cabin and into Abdul's. There she rummaged around until she found what she was looking for. Under the bed, wrapped in a sheet, was one of the Kalashnikov rifles Abdul had brought on board. She held it and studied it; she had no clue how to use one of these, although, looking at it, the mechanism seemed fairly simple. There was a lever to pull back, which she did, thanks to a few films she had watched. Below the lever, there was a smaller lever with three settings. She guessed that it was probably safe in the position it was in, so she pushed it down one.

Now, with her heart beating loud enough to wake the babies and shaking arms, she made her way out of the cabin. Carrying a AK47 was no mean feat for a lady who was better suited to comforting babies, and the doors were very narrow. Once out, she could see up into the lounge area, or at least some of it. The stairs and the angle obstructed her view. Ellie almost lay on the steps as she gradually made her way up. Just then, an unfamiliar voice came from the lounge. Whoever it was spoke in English, with an unmistakable Italian accent.

"Why you sneak around, Ellie? Come and join me. We need to talk," the voice commanded in a voice that could have played the snake in a Disney cartoon.

"Who are you?" Ellie called out as forcefully as she could muster. "And what are you doing on our boat without permission?"

"This is your boat, Ellie? Really, your boat?"

"Yes, our boat," Ellie answered, at little less sure of herself now.

"We both know that's a little lie, Ellie. Don't we? Please, let's not play games, Ellie."

"What do you want?" Ellie said as calmly as she could. She knew was on very lose ground and was starting to get nervous.

"I don't care about the stupid boat, Ellie. I want the man called Mike, who is with you, and the dirty Arab and his family. I think his name is Abdul. Then you can keep the boat, and you and your friends can go wherever you want."

"Why do you want Mike and Abdul?"

"You don't want to ask so many questions, Ellie. Think of the babies. You see, I know all about you and your little crew. Now, for the last time, come here and we'll wait together. Don't make me come down there."

Ellie thought hard. What possible connection could Mike have to Abdul and his family? Then realisation swept over her and she felt a chill run through her, despite the heat.

"You know the people traffickers? Is that what this is about?" Ellie asked.

The sound of a slight clap came from above. You could, Ellie thought, hear the sarcasm in the clap.

"Well done, Ellie, well done. But you're not completely right though. It's not personal to me. I have never met them, but, at this point, it really doesn't matter. Your friend Mike upset a lot of people, people who relied on those traffickers for a very good income, and still do. You see, Mike only paused the process. It is back up and running again. Only, those running it are the family members of those Mike killed. They want him, and anyone else connected to the deaths of their family members, dead, as anyone would. So, as good friends do, my employers wanted to help them find justice and a little peace. You understand, don't you? Mike's boss had to die, and now I will kill Mike. Done, everyone's happy."

"Where does Abdul fit into this?"

"Well, that's another story. He was going to die, anyway. He had planned to steal the boat, only he's not a very good thief. So, he dies too, along with his family, for good measure."

Ellie doubted Abdul wasn't a good thief, but she had most of what she wanted to know. On hearing the reason behind Bob's death, her nerves had gone. Now she was just angry.

"Why would you leave the rest of us alive as witnesses?"

Silence.

"You got me there, Ellie."

Ellie heard movement and looked up to see the head of a middle-aged man. He had a pot-marked face, over tanned, with jet black hair. Seeing the AK47 pointed at him, he raised his gun, but Ellie was prepared and pulled the trigger. The resulting noise deafened her, which would have been bad enough, but the body she had shot four times fell down the stairs on top of her, knocking her out.

When the others returned, it was Fatima who discovered Ellie and called for help. Mike dragged the body off Ellie. He placed the rifle and the pistol on the galley top, then carried Ellie up the stairs. He laid her down on the bench seat. She seemed to be breathing and unhurt, so Mike asked Joan to get some water. He soaked a towel and gently stroked her head.

Abdul sat opposite, looking sadly at Ellie. "This is what I feared."

"What?" said Mike. "What do you know?"

"Nothing you don't, Mike. You killed the traffickers, and this is their revenge."

"How do two assholes like that reach out to me like this?" Mike asked.

"Two assholes who pass fresh hookers to the Russian mafia, that's who."

"How is that possible? They're dead."

"Family not dead," Abdul stated. "They carry on family business."

"Why didn't you say something?" Mike looked up from Ellie.

"Abdul hoped they not know who did it. Abdul hoped they get bored and move on."

"Really, Abdul! Seriously?"

"Yeah, pretty stupid, eh?"

"Yeah, pretty bloody stupid."

"You know, they're after us all now, Mike. Those Russians, they nasty bastards."

"No kidding. He doesn't look Russian, though." Mike pointed to the corpse.

"No, he probably Italian. Do it for the money. No one going miss him."

Ellie started to stir. Regaining consciousness, she looked distressed before throwing her arms around Mike and crying.

"What's going on? What have I done?"

"You did what you had to," Mike said, in a serious tone.

"The babies!" Ellie tried to get up.

"They're fine," Joan reassured her.

Ellie sat up with Mike's help and Jack came over and held her hand. He, too, looked shocked. Michael and Joan went to attend to the babies, who had slept through the whole drama.

Abdul opened a bottle of brandy and drank from the bottle, and sighed. "We got to get the hell out of here, right now."

Mike nodded, but Ellie paced her hand on his shoulder. "Mike, we have to call the police. He attacked us."

"You shot him with a Kalashnikov, Ellie. You didn't hit him with a rolling pin. Besides, you did a good job; four out ten bullets hit him, the other six are going to cause a problem if it rains. It's a miracle no one heard anything."

Ellie went quiet. She decided to leave this to them. She felt as fragile as tissue paper and was in no state to make decisions.

Abdul wrapped the body in a sheet and placed him in a corner in the engine room, then prepared the boat for departure. They called the coast guard and the harbour master, as if nothing was wrong, to say they were filling up with fuel. Mike felt they wouldn't question them too much as they'd already been told they weren't staying. They all had questions and everyone wanted to talk, but Mike persuaded them to wait until they were at sea.

The motor yacht blipped its engines, before pulling itself from its dock. The momentum took it back towards the craft behind it, then, just at the right moment, Abdul gently engaged the engines. The yacht moved forward. Abdul increased the power slightly on the port engine to steer the boat straight, then, levelling with the starboard, he repeated this manoeuvre to guide them out to the fuel barge, where his son tied up.

Abdul jumped onto the barge and approached the man next to the pump. Behind him, Mike also jumped onto the barge. The man approached them, speaking in Italian, "Mi. Potet aiutaie? (Can I help you?)"

Abdul pointed at the pumps, making a gesture to fill up. The man reached for the pumps as Abdul unscrewed the petrol cap, which was set flush below the rail. As he tried to lift the pump, it clattered and a padlock stopped it moving.

"'Scusa (my fault)," The man said, before heading towards a small cabin built up on the barge. It was no more than a box, but it was designed to keep the rain off. Mike followed him and, as he came level with the hut, saw a hand protruding from the bottom of the door. The man, realising what Mike had seen, turned, pistol in hand. Mike was quick; he grabbed the top of the pistol with his left hand and deftly turned it, bringing his right hand up take over the trigger, then stepped back. The man was quick to throw up his hands.

Abdul patted Mike on the back. "You're a handy man to have around, Mike."

The man was escorted back to the cabin on the barge and seated. Meanwhile, Abdul knocked off the padlock and filled the boat up.

"This complicates things," Mike said to Ellie, who was replacing shock with anger.

"It's likely he knows something. You or Abdul can get him to talk, right?"

"Maybe, but that's not the point. If we take him with us, we will have half the Italian navy looking for us. He has to stay here to account for the dead pump attendant."

"Won't he just point them at us?" Jack asked.

"He can't do that without implicating himself even more. Can you, my little Italian hitman?" Mike said, squeezing the hitman's cheeks. "If he does, his employer is going to get very mad. He wants us dead, not arrested. So, as soon as Abdul's finished, we'll tie him to his victim and leave. I know it's not a perfect plan, but it's the best I can do. We just have to hope the police are more used to this kind of thing than we are, and just be glad they have someone to blame."

"Okay," Ellie said, much to Mike's surprise.

"Really?" He looked at Ellie

"Really!" she confirmed. "I'm sick of being in the middle of all this. The government is like an obstacle, when they should be helping, instead. We're only trying to do the right thing. Following the rules has got us nowhere, and I don't intend to spend a day behind bars while the Italian police work out how to read and write."

"Good for you," Mike said, smiling.

Abdul joined them after refuelling; he had heard the end of conversation.

"From here to England, we have to keep our heads down."

"What then?" asked Ellie.

Neither of the men answered

Chapter Thirty

Media

The agency Jo Sparks used was called Pre Prints Ltd. It was run by Ian Pink, a well-known character in the industry. Ian received the email from Jo Sparks. It had the word "nuclear" in the subject line, so he opened it without thought. Although Jo possessed a great deal of enthusiasm, Ian thought to himself, Jo wasn't generally prone to exaggeration, like many of the other photographers were. Nevertheless, Ian had become immune to the fantastical subject headings Jo used, presumably there to grab his attention.

This email turned out to be different. Ian didn't recognise the poor victim of the shooting immediately, although he did recognise the building. He turned the volume up on the news, which he kept on permanently in his office. On the TV screen, the scene matched the photos on his computer. The same event was playing out on TV, only the news only showed shots of ambulances leaving and police wandering around behind tape.

He hit speed dial on his desk phone for the Mirror while simultaneously barking instructions to call the other papers. Then he remembered he also had a video file. He wiped the saliva forming round his mouth before shouting new orders to his team.

Bob's name had not been released by the police yet. They needed to inform Bob's family first.

Chief Inspector George King was one of the first on the scene. He had been on the force for twenty-five years and had no ambitions to go further as he had reached as close to the brass as he wanted to go. George didn't have a political bone in his body, his blood was pure blue, old fashioned policeman. During his career, if he hadn't solved so many crimes, he would have been asked to retire somewhere quiet years ago. But, at a time where you only had a chance of getting caught if you were a terrorist or a driver, George was the exception. He stuck to cases and was, to an extent, a judge on the street. That's exactly what the force needed. Crooks respected him from afar, and youngsters soon learned to do the same. He was a tall man, six foot three, with chiselled features that were quite literally from knife attacks. Somehow, he'd remained approachable, and even liked by some. If the authorities had known that he was also, personally, responsible for recruiting fifty yard officers and retaining more than most could count, he may possibly have gained some respect from those in authority above him. The brass, though, were more concerned that he may float past them. When they realised he wasn't interested in a promotion, they gave him a hard time by pushing him to look trendy, which, to be fair to them, was the only way forward in the system they found themselves in.

George, for the most part, was unconcerned. He had long ago decided that he was on borrowed time. However, with this came a sense of freedom, which had a knock-on effect of making him very difficult to manage. Which Chief Constable would want his burglary conviction rate to drop to near nothing?

One of the benefits of being George was that he had a tendency to get all the high profile interesting cases. The brass wanted them solved and solved quickly. The assassination of a UN senior manager, codenamed "Royal Jelly", was definitely in the hands of George. The codename itself was similar to the ones used for George's previous cases, partly due to his name, but also the wobbly nature of the investigations.

George started to get a feel for the case, but one thing didn't fit. A young constable had informed him about Bob's connection to a viral internet and YouTube sensation. George recalled the news piece, but hadn't really listened to it as it had come on late and he was falling asleep in front of the TV. The young bobby brought him up to speed, but the connection didn't make sense, not that murders or other crimes had to nowadays. It was typical to hear of youngsters blowing themselves up after a couple of sessions on a religious website. George shuddered.

"Is anyone going to get the coffee?" he asked, looking directly at a woman police officer, without blinking an eye. She smiled and left to get them. He was, despite his total PC blindness, popular with anyone who spent time around him. The woman police officer had been chosen because she was closest, and she knew it. George would have fought tooth and nail to get a good WPC as he called them. Anyone who worked with him knew that sex and race meant nothing, and neither did etiquette. If you were good, that was good enough for George.

The other inspector he worked closely with was James Hatten, a clever young copper who had managed to endear himself to George over the three years he'd worked with him. He approached George and stood next to him.

"We found the shooter's car, it was set on fire in a side road, but no leads so far."

"I don't think there are going to be many, unless December twenty-fifth comes early this year," George answered sarcastically.

"It goes without saying and appears to be a professional hit, but why?"

"I'm not sure yet. I don't buy this media Government Select crap. Why would anyone kill the poor bloke for that? From what I heard, he didn't even write it. There's no more to this than meets the eye. I'll give my left nut if I'm wrong."

James's mobile rang. He smiled at George.

"How do you like your turkey? With all the trimmings? Because Christmas is closer than you think."

George, rubbed his hands together and pleaded like a child, "Please, daddy, don't make me wait until the morning."

"Okay, you can open one present now," James laughed.

Ian Pink was happy. The kind of happy that comes from increasing zeros on your account, or, in this case, his and Jo's. The various news sources had picked up the video file, and the papers were fighting amongst themselves for the shoots on offer. It was a good day, thought Ian. Ian's secretary interrupted his thoughts when George King and James walked in. Ian recognised them both.

"Can I help you gents?"

"You know you can, Ian," George said, smiling.

Chapter Thirty-One

Plain Sailing

The Horse of the Seas was living up to her name as she galloped over the waves. Abdul was throwing caution to the wind, literally opening the throttles of the twin Volvo Penta's, lifting her sleek white body as she danced over the waves. Occasionally, she leapt like a new born antelope, glad to be born, and splashed down majestically before continuing with her dance.

Inside, it was a little different. The slamming down on the waves was making a few of them feel a little green about the gills. No one complained, though, they just wanted to get as far away from the dead bodies as possible. They had left one body at the refuelling cabin, the other they'd unceremoniously dumped overboard in a very deep part of the Mediterranean, with a weight attached to his feet. If anyone felt bad about it, it wasn't mentioned.

For four hours, Abdul kept up the pace. Then he gradually pulled back on the throttles to bring the pace down to a more comfortable fifteen knots, roughly about half of what they had been doing.

"I think I know why they call it plain sailing now. We spent half the time flying," Mike joked.

Ellie smiled for the first time in a while. "What are we going to do, Mike? These people could follow us for ever, or until they kill us."

"I truthfully don't know. Any enemy I ever fought, generally had the decency to stay ahead of me. At the least, they went home when I did. But, this is different. We'll figure it out, though. So, first things first. Let's try the satellite and see if we can pick up some news."

The TV was already turned on, but it had been useless while they were bouncing around. Now that the boat was steady, they scanned the channels before settling on the BBC and CNN. At one point, they picked up a carefully edited version of the shooting. Ellie still couldn't believe what she was seeing. It seemed unreal. Hell, she thought, she had killed someone. It still felt like a bad dream and it jolted her a little when she remembered the events. Jack knew what she was going through and put his arm round his sister.

"Well, no news is good news, I suppose. My guess is that the police have worked out who the bodies belong to and they're not putting much of a priority on finding the perpetrators," Mike said.

Ellie took a little comfort from his words, but she knew what had happened. It was something she would live with for the rest of her life, no matter the outcome of the legal side of things.

The one constant on board were the babies. They were a reminder of the fact that there were more important things to worry about. Joan did most of the caring, but Michael helped as much as he could. Both had had totally accepted the babies as their own. Joan took very naturally to motherhood, that much was obvious to everyone. It was also obvious that Michael would make a good father, too.

Mike, on the other hand, had little to do while they were cruising between ports, so he helped clean up. He tried to do as much exercise as he could, and always took his shirt off when doing so. This was mainly due to his limited wardrobe, but it added some pleasure and admiration from the women on board.

Ellie also watched Joan and Michael. She was reminded of a boyfriend she'd had when she was younger. His name was Marcos and he had beautiful, long blond hair, which his father wanted him to cut. There had been a time when his father had tried to cut it, while Marcos was asleep. If he hadn't woken up screaming and made a quick escape by running out of the room, he would have been all set to join the marines.

Marcos, in general, though, was quite a manly man, one who loved playing rugby and other sports. But he had a more gentle side to him.

As Ellie sat watching, she allowed her mind to go back to her days with Marcos. Why hadn't she married Marcos? she wondered. After all, he had asked her, and her father. For some reason, one better known to the east wind, she had turned him down. It had broken his heart; she'd been surprised at how hard her rejection hit him. She almost caved in but, even back then, she was stubborn.

"You know what!" Ellie exclaimed loudly, making them all jump.

"What?" Mike responded, jumping in the air. Ellie laughed.

"Okay, sorry! That was a little over enthusiastic, I just wanted to say, to hell with the Russian mafia or any other bloody mafia. Seriously, we have had super powers trying to kill us. I'm not going to rush around naked, crying my eyes out over threats."

Ellie hesitated.

"That's a shame," Abdul said with a huge grin on his face.

"You can shut up, too!" Ellie snapped.

Now everyone was laughing. The laughter extended for hours, into the night, with everyone using the excuse to let off steam. Later that night, lying in her top bunk, feeling the gentle rhythm of the boat, Ellie swore to herself that no one was going to hurt these new friends she had made. They had become very special to her.

Dawn broke with a light shower of rain. It was welcomed in the hot summer weather they were experiencing, and it transformed the relatively calm sea into a million tiny explosions. Somehow, despite being quite loud, the explosions were relaxing to listen to, as soothing as one's mother telling a story. The effect on the group was remarkable; they all seemed calmer, despite what they had been through.

Palma was their next stop, although they didn't linger there for long. The port was large and easy to manoeuvre in and out from. It was tempting to stay and look around if they had had permission to do so. Instead, they announced their intention to refuel and leave. Although, they were given a three-hour grace, during which, once again, they weren't allowed to leave the dock. The yacht was obviously making a difference. So far, wherever they went, they seemed to receive a better welcome, certainly better than the normal band of refugees turning up unannounced.

However, when the captain, Abdul, made himself known, customs was always a little taken back. They probably assumed Mike or Ellie held that role. Or that's how it seemed to the group. Paranoia on the yacht was as rife as racism.

As they left, Abdul hugged the shore. They passed the beautiful Gothic Style Cathedral on the front, possibly one of the most beautiful buildings in the world. Their next stop, announced Abdul, would be Gibraltar.

Ellie looked forward to being back on British soil. While docked at Palma, she'd had the time to call into her office. They told her they would arrange for someone to meet her in Gibraltar. They were due to dock there in just over a day's time.

She had spoken to Eunis, Bob's secretary, who was distraught by the incident and was happy to hear Ellie's voice. Ellie had also spoken to John Summerville. She had felt the need to confide in him, after all, he was her boss now that Bob was gone. Ellie reported the whole story to him, leaving out the part where she shot a man, glossing over it with the attempt on their life at the fuel pump. Although, Ellie got the feeling John had been informed of the incident, anyway. He had promised to share the information about the trafficking ring with the other agencies. Ellie knew what he meant: trafficking humans was rightfully high on everyone's shit list of things to eliminate.

Each journey between ports was different. On this trip, everyone slept like logs, far longer than the usual eight hours. Ellie and Joan entertained the babies and Michael started writing a few letters to some friends in England. He hoped they could send them by special delivery from Gibraltar, so that the letters reached his friends before their arrival in England. Despite Ellie's reassurances, he was very concerned about their status and the reception they were to expect on reaching the UK. He was also worried about the babies; neither he nor Joan could bear the thought of being parted from them now.

The boat purred on. It might as well have been the *Mary Celeste* for all the life visible through her dimly lit cabin windows. Under the circumstances, nobody noticed the little blip on the radar, one that seemed to have stayed at approximately the same distance on the edge of the screen. It never sped up or down, matching all their manoeuvres, like-for-like.

Chapter Thirty-Two

Payback

To many, John Summerville may have seemed to be a career opportunist, one who didn't give a crap about anyone but himself and his career advancement. This was a fairly accurate description of John. However, underneath all of this, there laid a patriot and a man of action. His time at Oxford had helped him with the belief that he and his schoolmates were destined to lead the country, or at least a large part of it. Unlike his classmates, though, it didn't just end there. John was also a man of principle.

Those who were described as terrorists, the mafia or just plain evil, did not want to cross John Summerville. His hatred for these parasites lay deep. He sat thumbing through the list of telephone numbers he had for some of the most powerful people in the UK and picked one, the Defence Secretary, or Leon, as he was known to John. He knew Leon would have the same level of commitment regarding people traffickers. The only difference between them was that John belonged to a generally peaceful organisation, namely the UN. Leon, however, had a good bit of control over the SAS. "Just the man I need to talk to," John said to himself as he dialled the number. As expected, John had to get past the civil servants and personal assistants before Leon came on the line.

"Leon, hi. How are you keeping?"

"Fine, John. You?"

"Good, thanks. Look, I know you're busy so I'll get straight to the point. I know you have been looking, or at least MI6 have been looking, for people traffickers. As it so happens, through my contacts in the field, we have become aware of a pretty vile group. They seem to have links to the Russian mafia, or so my source informs me, probably through Istanbul. I thought the information might be of use to you."

"Well, yes. Obviously. But Istanbul and the Russian mafia are not exactly new news, John. Besides, I'm not about to get the PM's to push for a strike on Turkish soil."

"Yes, I thought you'd say that, but this info is about a group in Syria. I also have it on good authority that they just had my deputy killed outside our offices."

"I heard about that. I'm very sorry. Did you know him well?"

"Quite well. He was a good man and certainly didn't deserve to be shot."

"Wasn't he responsible for the Government Select report leak from the UN?"

"Not him. It was a lady who worked under him, and a group that are currently on a boat on their way here. Which reminds me, I need a small favour with regards to that …"

"Well, it's funny that you contacted me. The PM is in a bit of a flap over that report of yours, especially with the media having started their wild speculation that this proposed Government Select of wise persons should be placed on the ballot everywhere. What with the Brexit vote and Trump, well … you can see where this is heading."

"Wow! Yes, I hadn't thought about that," he lied. "I had no idea it was being taken that seriously, but now that you mention it, I can see the PM getting her expensive knickers in a twist over it. What can I do?"

"Tell me more about these people on the boat. Do they need to be picked up, and is the boat seaworthy?"

"Oh, yes. You could say that. Look, I'll send over a full report. When you have had the chance to read it, give me a call. Our first priority, though, is these traffickers. We can't let criminals kill off

UN personnel at will, especially on a London street."

"No, you're right, John. Send over the details and leave the rest to me. We must get together at the club one night. Is next Tuesday good for you?"

"Sounds perfect, goodbye."

The old-boy network is still functioning, thought John as he put the phone down. This time at least, he mused, it was for an unselfish purpose.

Four hours later, Leon was opening a highly confidential email from John. As he read the details, he could feel his blood pressure rising. Opening one of the small drawers, he pulled out a small silver pill box, one that originated from the Victorian era. It had been well used and kept, with a few dents from rough handling. The pill box held blood pressure pills, and Valium. He swallowed both down with his coffee, and then buzzed his assistant.

"Get the PM on the line and advice those who need to know … I need a Cobra meeting convened urgently."

Six hours later, in the Mediterranean, the Red Sea, a super yacht built by German shipbuilders, Linesell, cruised along. Linesell were possibly the best builders of the incredible marine palaces available today. The Red Sea was by no means their largest yacht. However, at 150 meters, she was impressive by any standards. Her Russian crew and owner were trailing another yacht, which, although impressive itself, would have been dwarfed by the Red Sea.

They were cruising in luxury that few people could ever imagine. The rooms were filled with ladies of the night, and some men of the same occupation. None of them would have looked out of place on the cover of a Vogue magazine. The other occupants were surrounded by body guards and guests in the largest state room. The owner was Sakharov Nikolay (Kola) Semeyonovich, who was simply known as Kola to his friends.

To the agencies trying to bring him down, he was Coca Kola, an obvious double play on his occupation as a drug dealer, not as a fizzy drinks salesman. He was a medium sized man who, until you caught his eyes, would probably have passed by you without notice. But when his silver-grey eyes met yours, it was an experience you would not forget. When he talked, which was seldom, he whispered, especially when issuing instructions to his employees. The effect of his whispering took place on an almost physic level, akin to telepathy. Those who served him closely soon learned to read his requirements from his nods and looks. This was sufficient to instruct them on when to act. Those who complied with this requirement, survived, with riches. Those who didn't, disappeared.

Kola was playing this game in person, which was unusual for him. Normally, he wouldn't have been within a hundred miles of an assassination. Somehow, the combination of a sea pursuit in his favourite toy, combined with the added debauchery it provided, proved to be an irresistible opportunity. His motives were also partly driven by his desire to amuse his new guests, two of whom were technically his competition. However, the trip was also a good will gesture, to help free up some of the inevitable tensions between rivals.

He also hoped to overwhelm the newcomers into the business. History had taught him that, in the case of deceased drug lords, their deaths were often attributed, but rarely proven, to have been committed by either a disgruntled employee with ambition, or the opposition. Kola had planned this trip in an attempt to reduce the chance of both eventualities. Although, he was under no illusions. He knew this was not a long-term fix. Being drunk and out of their minds, though, was a good, traditional means of learning their weaknesses. As a bonus, he got to play the role of master of all he surveyed, which was his favourite pastime.

Cobra assembled in private. The name was a simple derivation from the room the meeting was usually held in: Cabinet Office Briefing Room A. The nature of the business carried out there was anything but simple. Today's meeting had a few legal implications, which the home secretary was busy pointing out to his colleagues: firing missiles at Syria was allowed, but would become questionable in Parliament; firing at Russian registered ships was a whole different kettle of fish. The argument went on for some time. Finally, the points that won the argument were that a UN official had been assassinated. And, thanks, in no small part, to some very good HD footage, voluntarily handed in to police in a gesture of good will, they were able to trace the assassins and extract a confession from them. Paid assassins and loyalty rarely went together, so a deal had soon been struck.

Then, with the help of the Royal Navy, MI6 had located the yacht in the Mediterranean. They were also asked to trace the whereabouts of the 'The Horse of the Seas'. It soon became apparent that the 'Red Sea' was closing in fast on the smaller boat. As the pieces of the jigsaw puzzle came together, it was clear to the government that they had to act, and fast.

Chapter Thirty-Three

There's Always a Bigger Fish

After a good nap, Abdul busied himself with checking their course and position. They were making good time, he thought, given they were halfway to their destination. His mind wondered about all the fuel he was paying for, then, to add to his worries he wondered about what would happen next. Once he was done paying the way for these people to reach safety, there was a strong chance that they would probably take the boat off him. He shuddered. This boat was his first real chance to get ahead in life. The cash he was carrying would help, but what if they took the cash, too? He shuddered again. A bleep coming from the consul diverted his attention. It was the anti-collision alarm he had set to prevent them bumping into something. Although, the only object on the radar was behind them, moving fast in their direction.

Abdul woke Mike.

"What is it?" Mike stood up rubbing his eyes.

"Maybe nothing, but check this out." Abdul pointed to the radar. He had already switched off the alarm.

"What am I looking at?" Mike asked.

"That!" Abdul pointed to the blip on the screen.

"Okay," Mike mumbled, looking no wiser.

"It's a large craft and it's heading straight at us at speed."

"Okay, I get that. Can we see it?"

"Maybe." Abdul reached for the binoculars.

He and Mike climbed the stairs to the fly bridge. Abdul made his way to the rear seats and sat, resting on the rail. To Mike, he took an age. It was like watching someone trying to thread a needle when you wanted to do it for them.

"Abdul, what do you see?" Mike was getting frustrated.

"Oh, yes. I see a beautiful yacht. Kind of makes this one look like a dinghy, I think."

"Let me see," Mike insisted.

Mike took a few seconds to get in focus before he saw the Red Sea through the binoculars. He could clearly see her name.

"Have you ever heard of a yacht called the Red Sea, Abdul?"

"No, never heard of it."

"Okay, can you get an internet signal here?"

Abdul shook his head. "Sorry, buddy."

By now, Ellie had joined them. They brought her up to speed with what was happening. At the mention of the Red Sea, fear lined her face.

"What's up, Ellie?"

"What's up is that we are being hunted by the Russian mafia. To add to that, a boat named the Red Sea is closing on us."

"Shit, you're right. Why didn't I think of that!" Mike exclaimed.

"Can we go faster, Abdul?"

"Not fast enough, Mike."

Mike dragged Abdul below decks and looked seriously at him. "What arms do we have on board, and no lies?"

Abdul had no intention of lying. "We've got three Kalashnikovs and a fair bit of ammo."

"Do you have anything heavier?"

"Never need anything heavier. You got anything, Mike."

"Yeah," Mike muttered, "but it won't be much good at sea on this boat, there's too much movement.'

"What you got?" Abdul was intrigued.

"A fifty cal."

"Oh, sweet."

"Yes, but it will be like trying to shoot a duck from a roller coaster."

"I suppose, but fun, eh," Abdul said, smiling.

Mike couldn't believe Abdul at times, but he laughed anyway.

The two went off to gather their arms and were soon carrying the guns back to the fly bridge. They looked aft for the ship, but didn't need binoculars this time. The Red Sea was clearly visible, but it wasn't until Abdul picked up the binoculars to take a closer look that the magnitude of their situation became very clear.

Mike saw the binoculars slip from Abdul's hands. Taking them from him, Mike focused on the front of the Red Sea. He couldn't believe his eyes.

The whole front deck of the luxury super yacht was festooned with people in swimwear, holding everything from rifles, to machine guns and, more ominously, rocket propelled grenades. Mike was fairly sure he saw a hand-held Sam missile launcher. He passed the binoculars around.

Mike estimated they had about four minutes before they came into range, depending very much on what armament was being held on the deck of the Red Sea. That, it occurred to him, could throw his estimate way off.

He turned to the others and shouted for them to put their life jackets on and to get the raft ready. Although, both seemed a little absurd, given the circumstances. At least it would keep everyone busy, he reckoned. He raised his fifty cal to determine its effectiveness. It was likely that it wouldn't be very useful. The cross hairs jumped around as if he was on a bouncy castle.

Abdul and his family looked as composed as one could be. They busied themselves loading magazines and setting up barriers, using tables made of the finest teak.

Mike didn't bother with cover. He lay overlooking the stairs, set his bi-pod up and adjusted his sights. He guessed the monster yacht would stop some way off. As crazy as it seemed, this felt like a day out shooting bottles. The bikini clad women looked, for all the part, like they'd been take right off an American arms convention poster. If, however, they were going to enjoy the shooting, they could not get too close, or they would have to hang off the rails. He doubted whether their mafia boss would be pleased with a group of drunken hookers shooting down at the lower decks.

Mike took aim. A few seconds later, he spotted his target, who wasn't armed and was calmly moving around and patting his guests on the back and pointing, in the way a good gamekeeper would when pointing out a stag or some potential birds to his wealthy client.

Mike followed his movements closely, every second or so getting a glimpse of the red-shirted gamekeeper, as he had named him in his head.

The waves were not consistent, but the super yacht was close enough for Mike's powerful telescopic sights to hone in on its target.

Boom! A spray of water shot up, drenching the fly bridge and temporarily distracting Mike.

"Bastards are starting with the big stuff …" Mike shouted. Before he could finish his sentence, Abdul and his family let rip with the Kalashnikovs.

The super yacht was just in range, and the return fire caught the Russian's by surprise. On his deck, the gamekeeper could be seen yelling orders to his crew. Abdul and his family opened fire again. This time they allowed for the drop the bullets suffered at long range.

Suddenly, an audible whoosh flew past the small yacht. The Red Sea shattered into a thousand pieces of glass and fire. Secondary explosions ripped her apart. Within seconds, she was starting to sink. This luxurious craft had not been designed as a war ship and its hull split into pieces of thick, but ultimately useless, fibreglass. Those on board were either vaporised, or in small enough pieces for the fishes of the Mediterranean Sea to feast on.

The sea where the yacht once stood was now a bubbling patch of debris and oil. No one had survived.

On board the Horse of the Seas, the group came together. Abdul helped Mike up from his prone position and, at the same time, cleared the stairs for Ellie and the others, who hadn't even had time to don their life vests. Joan and Mike were the last to join them, holding the babies, who were gently crying.

"Wow!" Abdul uttered. "Those Russians make great machine guns."

"I hate to burst your bubble, Abdul, but I don't think that was you, despite your fantastic efforts, by the way."

Abdul's family looked at each other, smiling with pride. Who are these people? thought Mike.

"Who then?" Mike asked the question that was at the forefront of everyone's mind. He glanced over to Ellie. They had both seen similar outcomes before, although neither had been present during a live strike.

"That," Ellie clarified, "was a drone strike. For once, I am glad they spent my tax payments wisely."

Further away, in Latakia, another two explosions were heard. One in a small shop in the high street, the second on an expensive Spanish-style villa on the sea front. Both had devastating effects on the inhabitants.

When the crew of the Horse of the Seas had ensured there was no one left alive to rescue, they all moved down to the lounge area. They sat and looked at each other in disbelief. Abdul acted and moved to the bridge to start up the engines. He set course for Gibraltar and put the yacht on auto pilot, resetting the radar alarm before sitting by his wife and son. Much to everyone's surprise, he hugged them and began to cry.

The thought of losing them had overwhelmed him. He had

to let it out. Mike was not as surprised. He'd seen the biggest of men fall helplessly apart in battle, for far less traumatic reasons. Many a times he had told the men that there was no shame in it. In any case, no one judged Abdul. If anything, Abdul had grown to a new perspective in their eyes.

They all welcomed an early night as they were due to dock in Gibraltar in the early hours.

Chapter Thirty-Four

Home Coming

The Gibraltar harbour was well lit but, unusually, they were met by the harbour master.

They all made their way to the deck and watched as a massive rock passed them on the right. It wasn't anything like the pictures one saw of it. Down at sea level and lit up, it was like the kraken of the Norwegian legend, rising up from the sea. No wonder Spain wanted it, Mike thought, and no wonder we won't give it to them.

They were led to a prime docking point and, as they tied up, they were met by a man and a woman, neither of whom were familiar to Ellie or Mike. They introduced themselves as Liz and Peter and explained that they had been sent from the British Government. They were there to escort all of them to their hotel.

As it happened, though, instead of a conventional hotel, there were taken to a cruise ship, not dissimilar to the ill-fated Red Sea. The Sunborn Gibraltar was a 189-room floating hotel, with spa and casino, where they all had allocated rooms, courtesy of the UK government. The look on everyone's face was one of amazement. The last twenty-four hours had been surreal for them, to say the least.

They were given itinerary's, which included a map of the ship. Based on the itinerary, they were all due to meet at a conference room later for breakfast, which was only five hours away, so they took the opportunity to get a little more sleep, agreeing to meet up at breakfast.

The food was, as you would expect on a luxury cruiser,

everything you could want, and a lot more than you could possibly eat. Although, Jack and Abdul gave it a good try.

Joan and Michael were last to show up again, having had to tend to the babies. They ate in silence, and when it was time for the meeting, they left the restaurant and made their way to the conference room, through the maze of corridors.

The room was four times larger than was needed, but they sat down and helped themselves to the lemon flavoured mineral water that had been provided.

Facing them was a screen. Mike commented that if they tried to sell him time share, he was off.

Soon they were joined by Peter and Liz, who set up their laptops and handed out some folders. It was starting to feel like an insurance seminar to those who had been unfortunate enough to have experienced one. Abdul was quite enjoying it all; he had never seen anything like it. His wife and son, on the other hand, were starting to look a little overwhelmed. Mike simply hated the clean-cut office surroundings. Even the beautiful view through the windows didn't help his increasing bad mood.

Ellie felt at home, as did Michael and Joan. This setting was typical of the university they'd attended, only far more classy. The wave-like patterns on the floor and the wood effect walls were stylish without being over the top.

Liz spoke first. "Hello everyone, and welcome home to Ellie, Mike and Jack. Welcome also to our visitors. Before we continue, can we begin with introductions please, starting clockwise. Please state your names, and perhaps tell us a little about yourself."

Oh crap! It is an insurance seminar, thought Mike.

Liz spoke first. She was the type one would immediately think was a social worker, and not in a good way, either. As it so happens, she had once been a social worker back in the days.

"You first, dear," Liz said to Joan.

"I'm Joan," Joan began, slightly nervous. "I am a nurse and this is Adnan and Adara."

"Michael, my name is Michael," Michael stated, equally nervous. "I am a nurse, too."

When it was his turn, Jack stood up. "Jack, and I am a driver for an aid charity."

"Mike, I work for the UN.," Mike sounded as though he was firing off a few rounds.

"Ellie, and I work for the UN."

"Abdul. I'm a captain, of the Horse of the Seas, and this is my family. My wife, Fatima, and my son, Abir."

"Well, thank you all. I am Liz and I am a consulate worker. Peter is also from the government. Now, the reason you are getting the VIP treatment, if you weren't already aware, is because you have become 'very important people,'" she quoted, using her fingers to make a point. "Let me hand you over to Peter, he will explain in more detail."

Peter was a tall military-looking chap with short hair, dressed in a nice but basic suit with a tie that looked like his mother had picked it out.

"Please," Peter began, "open the folders in front of you."

They followed his instructions, like kids at the start of an exam, before ruffling through the contents. The plain black folders consisted mainly of newspaper clippings and a few transcripts from meetings.

Mike looked down and then across to Ellie with a big smile. "You set this up, didn't you?"

The look on Ellie's face answered his question.

"Really! How in the hell? I knew things had leaked, and that our press have a tendency to exaggerate, but this can't be right." He looked at Ellie in complete shock.

The others were also looking at front page headlines, which read:

"Government Select Experts, the people's choice"

"Wise is Wonderful"

And in The Sun, "Government SEX on the ballot. See page three"

The Mail read, "The Mail had it right, years ago"

"The Mirror hailed the new socialist revolution"

"What is going? Ellie was incredulous.

"Well, your report, manifesto, whatever you want to call it has taken off, in a big way. All predictions pools are saying that it will run endlessly. Every time there's an election, someone will call out for Government Select to be on the ballot."

"And what is wrong with that, exactly?" Joan said before she could stop herself.

"What's wrong ..." Liz took the lead, "... is that it doesn't work that way."

Jack stood up, looking upset. "You know what? I am sick of hearing that stupid saying. What does it mean, anyway? You ask the person on the phone why their company can't deliver when you need them to, and the answer is always, 'It doesn't work that way', I could go on for hours with other examples. Just because something's new, it doesn't mean it won't work. If you applied this to every new idea, progress would stop entirely."

Jack sat down; he was tying himself into knots. However, he got a clap from the others.

Peter held up his hands to quieten the room, which didn't make him popular.

"The point is that we have a democracy and the rules don't allow for foreigners or groups to be individually elected. We, and many other countries, have been in touch to discuss this in depth. We feel this kind of proposal could undermine years of legislation and tradition."

"And corruption," Mike added.

Ellie responded. "What do you expect from us, Liz?"

“We want you to help us defuse the whole thing, give statements saying it was just a game, and that it was not meant to be taken seriously. You know, a couple of appearances on TV, just laugh the whole thing down and out.”

“What if we like the idea of Government Select taking off? What if we decide to ride this wave of popularity?” Ellie returned, smiling.

Liz played along and smiled back, albeit a crooked one. “Then your friends will not be getting any help from our government, or any other for that matter. I’m sure you know what I mean.”

Everyone in the room recognised the threat, especially as it was delivered by an expert ex-social worker, one who had a degree in saving her own backside, no matter what the consequences.

Abdul made to speak, but Ellie, guessing what he might say, laid her hand over his and squeezed it. Abdul reluctantly sat down. Before Ellie spoke, she looked around, trying to catch the group’s attention.

“Can we have some time to discuss this?” she asked Liz, giving her the best smile she could.

“Let’s reconvene here tomorrow,” Liz agreed reluctantly.

Everyone got up and headed out the room. Ellie still held on to Abdul’s hand.

Chapter Thirty-Five

Pirates

The group met back at the boat. The meeting with Liz and Peter had shaken them, surprisingly. The report Ellie had compiled had not been anything serious, not until Sula's death at least, when it had seemed like an appropriate memorial to her. More than this, though, the reception the report had seen, as shown on the news, had been quite pleasing to them. None of them had anticipated the backlash it was now attracting from the UK government.

Sat in the lounge, Jack spoke first. He'd had enough time to ponder over the discussion and to say he was angry was an understatement. He stood up and struggled for words. Ellie put a hand on his shoulder to help calm him.

"Who do they bloody think they are? Where do they think we are? This is Britain. I don't know about the rest of you, but I'm not putting a foot on any stage and knocking what was a pretty good idea, albeit naïve perhaps. I couldn't give a hoot in hell if they think it threatens some politician's dreams of power, or whatever he or she wants. They can piss off."

A small clap of support followed his outburst. Abdul was beginning to think he better understood where the British got their reputation for being such a tough nation. Talk like that in Syria, he thought, even amongst friends, meant you disappeared the next day.

"Jack has a very good point," Ellie said, hugging her brother with pride written all over her face.

Mike stood up.

"If those bastards think they're going to bribe me, well they don't know me," he said and abruptly sat down again.

Joan spoke next, a great deal quieter than the others. "I agree with you all, but where does that leave the rest of us? I can't ask you to go against your principles, but I have to admit, those people scare me."

Michael just put his arm around her. She was clearly speaking on behalf of them both. Abdul moved over to the liquor cabinet and poured himself a brandy.

"Maybe I should drop you lot off in England, then keep going with Joan and Michael. We could take our chances in Germany. I heard, while I was back at the bar, that they have an open-door policy."

The room was silent for a moment. No one wanted to admit it, but that seemed like a good idea. After a while, Ellie spoke.

"I don't think that's going to be necessary. Although Abdul, Joan, and Michael, it is entirely up to you." Ellie paused and nodded at Abdul's wife and son. "You must do what you feel is best for yourselves. However, I don't think you should give up on Britain just yet. The press are having a field day with this, so I strongly believe that those two are bluffing. If we tell them we will think it over on the way back, they won't be able to do a thing about it. In the meantime, I will make some calls. The rest of you may want to consider doing the same. Let's play them at their own game. Let's find out how powerful this whole thing is. Purely judging from the papers we have seen, in addition to the over-reaction we just witnessed, my guess is they will back down."

Michael stirred in his seat. "Am I the only one who thinks this is a dream. Just the other night, this was simply a means of passing the time. Now, it's an international incident and people are dying. I can't get my mind around how this has happened?"

"Stranger things have happened, Michael," Ellie said. "A little brown chap was thrown off a train in South Africa. He was so riled up, he threw the British Empire out of India, and he held no power in the political office. People will follow the truth, especially when they get tired of the lies, and maybe that's what this is. You can't con everyone for ever. It's possible that those few, well-chosen words were the simple message people realised they needed in a sea of bullshit."

Another supportive clap went around, with Michael clapping the loudest.

"So, what do you want to do?" Abdul said, pointing at the boats wheel.

Ellie thought for a moment, then, in unison, she and Mike decided: "Let's get the hell out of here."

The boat was refuelled and well underway before the two civil servants realised they were gone. The group had become quite adept at packing up quickly. The sea was glass calm and, despite the threats they had endured, everyone seemed upbeat and positive. Ellie was amazed at the level of strength one could get if those around you stuck together, especially if they showed they genuinely cared. Somehow, she knew, the friendships made on this boat, would last a lifetime.

Mike couldn't stop smiling as he announced, "Argg, we are Pirates of the Caribbean now."

"The what?" Abdul looked baffled.

Everyone laughed, a combination of amusement at Mike's broadcast and Abdul's confused face.

Back in Britain, neither Liz or Peter were laughing. In fact, they were faced with a mixture of emotions, ones they were not particularly used to. Initially, they spent two hours running around the docks to determine whether the yacht had been moved. They followed this up with a call to the harbour master, who mentioned he had seen a boat leaving, but wasn't sure of its name, although, nothing had seemed suspicious, so he hadn't challenged it. Peter decided on their next steps and informed

Liz. To say she looked stunned was an understatement. Liz was someone who expected to be obeyed. She let off a tyrannical speech, which only made Peter look around to see who she was shouting at. When he realised he was the only audience, he simply walked off, much to Liz's frustration and increased fury. She ran after him and grabbed his jacket.

"This is important, Peter. Do not walk away while I'm talking to you. They can't get away with this," she fumed.

Peter smiled down at the short, red-faced woman.

"Did you not get that we we're not being serious, you silly woman. I would have done the same bloody thing, only I might have planted one on my nose on the way out. That chap, Jack, he looked as if he just might have this morning. Go and pack, we are going home. Oh, and by the way, home may not be the same for long, not as we know it anyway. So its best we get back soon, especially if we want to see the old corrupt England, the one we love so much. Liz stood, frozen to the spot, as Peter calmly removed her hand from his jacket and walked off.

The Horse of the Seas headed towards Porto in Portugal. From there, she was headed for Santander and across the Bay of Biscay to Breast. A shorter than usual journey would have had them in Jersey, prior to their final destination, Southampton.

Their stopover in Porto went smoothly. Despite their anticipation of trouble, no one was there to meet them. In fact, they may well have been tourists, of which there were many, coming and going from the port. They decided to stay and rest for a couple of days, taking the opportunity to visit restaurants and see the sights, which they did together. It wasn't until they got back to the boat that they realised that they'd chosen to stay together, despite their personalities. As individuals, in the truest sense, each usually preferred their own company. This fact sunk in deep with Mike. He had always been a bit of a loner and, as he sat with a whisky in his hand, he pondered his change of heart.

Not only, he mused, had he accepted the group's suggestion to stay together, a large part of him truly wanted to. He felt good around them. It wasn't solely because he wanted to protect them, which was the first explanation that came to him. "No," he told himself, "I can't hide behind that excuse." Something had changed in him. Perhaps he was getting older. This thought put an end to his ponderings. He decided he'd had enough of mopping around, so he put on the TV. He flipped the remote to the news channel and, sure enough, they were still making the new stories. Although, the emphasis had switched to them as individuals, rather than the content of the report, which was now being referred to as the proposition.

"Come and see this," Mike shouted out to the others.

They gathered around as Mike switched from CNN to the BBC and then over to Al Jazeera, which, surprisingly, had the best coverage. The world was speculating as to when and where the authors of the proposition would appear. The best guess they had was on the money, England. Most people thought Plymouth was a much more realistic option. In reality, though, they'd chosen to dock in Southampton. Ellie still had a home there, a short distance away from the port, and only twenty minutes from the airport. The drive to London was only a couple of hours away, too.

After the news reports, they settled down to watch one of the programmes, the *One Talk Show*, with a studio audience. It felt strange and somewhat absurd to be hearing their ideas, ones that had been voiced casually over a few drinks with friends, being discussed very seriously by strangers, even one or two celebrities.

The talk show audience who were against the proposition, who were openly attacking it, seemed to have less vigour than those who were defended the group's ideas. The opposition lacked the passion the pro group demonstrated. The supporters didn't want to change a word of Ellie's report. They were almost at the point where they seemed obsessed. Or maybe, Ellie suggested, they just didn't feel they were justified in changing someone else's work.

Eventually, the TV was switched off. It was clear to everyone that the report had outgrown itself, certainly its original intention, if it had one to begin with.

Ellie had called her office the day before. They were none too happy to hear about the civil servants and their thinly-veiled threats. Ellie's colleagues had implied that a complaint would be put to the UK government. They were glad Ellie had called as they had wanted to discuss something else, which she now shared with the group.

"I have something to tell you all. I spoke to my boss yesterday. They were more than a little angry with the welcome we had in Gibraltar. In response, they will, apparently, be raising a complaint with the Foreign Ministry today. Although, that's not the big news. The UN have been getting some very negative press over the last few years. Their public relations people, and yes they do exist, concluded that the main reason behind this negativity was the public's perception of the UN across the globe. The UN is, and was, perceived as being toothless and ineffective. If you think about it, it's not surprising really. When you look at the attempted genocides and massacres, which have gone on under their watch, the numbers are growing to the point where they're losing count? So, in reality, it is no longer a case of perception, but an accepted truth. The ones in authority seem to have given up on excuses. Instead, admitting to it being a fact. One thing that's come out of this soul-searching amongst the UN bosses is that they do like our report, or proposition, whichever you want to call it. Apparently, they feel it could be the key they have been looking for, one that will unlock the potential; the potential democracy promised the world, but never delivered on."

"They really said that?" Mike said, laughing.

"Seriously, Mike, that's what they said, and they meant it. They will meet us in Southampton and grant us diplomatic status under the UN. All of us. We are due to meet with them to discuss the best way forward."

"Sounds good to Abdul. Me and my family safe. I get to keep my boat and everyone happy."

"I didn't mention the boat," Ellie quickly corrected Abdul.

"I keep boat, you'll see!" Abdul said with a huge grin spread over his face.

"Well, I'll drink to that," stated Jack. "Surely we deserve a bit of a celebration. After all, we just survived the Russian's bombs, killed off some of the Russian mafia and, my favourite by far, we stuck a finger up at the UK government. We may never do anything so cool for as long as we live."

"Good point," said Mike, who was already drinking from a bottle.

"Well, I'm going to put the babies to bed and I will join you after. Michael, what do you say?" Joan hesitated slightly.

"Well, I don't usually drink, but pass me a glass."

Joan smiled and quickly disappeared below deck to put the children down.

Ellie grabbed a bottle and looked at Jack.

"Well, if you can't beat them, join them," she said, enjoying the light mood that engulfed them.

Abdul moved away and opened what was obviously a hidden compartment. It was under the cushions. From there, he brought out two bottles of Louis Tre brandy.

"Wow, Abdul!" Mike was impressed. "You have been holding back, haven't you? Do you have any idea what that golden ambrosia costs?"

"What? Well, I wasn't there when it was bought."

Chapter Thirty-Six

The Empire Strikes Back

The phone in John Summerville's office rang. Immediately, his secretary was on the line to him.

"It's Leon Castle for you, John."

"Thanks, please put him through … Leon, how are you? I was just about to call you."

"I thought you might. Do you know an Ellie Summers and her brother?"

"Yes, you know I do, Leon. Let me ask you, do you know a couple of civil servants with a penchant for bribery and threats?"

"Well, they're not mine, but yes, I suppose they did threaten the group."

"From that, I infer this was an act of bribery. Agreed?"

"Come on, John. You must know that this so-called proposition needs to be nipped in the bud. It's horrendous."

"The question is, horrendous for whom? Right?"

"Well, for all of us, I would think, John. Come on … a committee of wise men? It sounds biblical."

"Agreed, but we still swear by the bible, don't we? It's still a best seller!"

"Oh, very good, John. But let's be honest, who is going to take this seriously?"

"Well, the PM for one, it seems, Leon. She definitely seems to be wetting herself over this one. By the way, does that damage leather?"

"Alright, enough is enough, John. What do you want to make this go away?"

"On this one, I can't help you, or the foreign secretary. The

UN is dancing to a new tune, one you may not like. Its chorus is the proposition and Government Select."

"Now you have to be kidding. I know the UN's brains trust were a little short on electrons, but this …"

"They're thinking of changing the flag to incorporate a round table surrounded by owls … Sorry, Leon. That one was a joke!"

"Great. I'll let the PM know. She'll wish she'd let the Russian mob have them. Goodbye, my friend. See you on the other side."

The PM's office held four people, the Defence Minister, Leon, a tall blond man with a look of self-importance on his face, and Sir Charles Wandsworth, who never asked for a career in politics. It had been forced upon him by his mother, and now enforced by his wife. The PM made up the fourth person in attendance. She sat quietly, looking through papers. The men waited for her to speak. To them, it seemed like she was taking an age. It was, in fact, seven minutes. None of the men were used to being kept waiting, least of all in this manner. Sir Charles started to speak. A raised hand, which stayed elevated, caught him in mid-word. He refrained from finishing off the word until the PM brought her hand down. As if nothing had happened, she gave the men a sweet smile.

"Gentlemen, thank you for taking the time to see me. After all, you must all be very busy right now. I received a call from the UN Secretary General, and he had a lot to say. I imagine you don't need me to fill you in on the details. Would I be fairly accurate if I were to say that your efforts to quietly deal with this matter match that of an elephant trainer, one who was trying out ice dancing as a new idea?"

"Well, Ma'am," started Leon. "This does, on the face of it, seem to have got a little ahead of us."

"A little is resting the tip of its helmet on the beautifully crafted Chippendale seat to my left, Leon. Sir Charles, I hope the queen's sword didn't make you feel too inadequate, because, quite frankly, I need answers or balls on this table."

Without thinking, a very red Sir Charles sat up a little, lowered his hand and adjusted himself, then coughed.

"Still there, I hope? For Marge's sake at least. And how is the wife? Good, did you say?" teased the PM.

"It's in hand, Ma'am. We will deal with this," he affirmed and looked over to Leon, who nodded in agreement. "We have some lines of action that will work. Hopefully this will eliminate the problem, Ma'am."

"Why, then, do I feel worse? Do I really need to know the details?"

"No, Ma'am, you don't," Leon interjected swiftly.

"Then I bid you farewell, gentlemen. I have a little problem with junior doctors who apparently suffer from insomnia. I need to deal with that."

Leon and Sir Charles looked at each other, but didn't move quickly enough.

"Gentlemen, I understand your avid appreciation of punishment, but they don't pay me enough to moonlight as a dominatrix for two sweaty toffs. Call me if this Government Select takes over, now out."

Leon was still too slow.

"Leon, dear, I was joking. Anyway, you have my number." She winked.

Leon was too shocked to move.

"Get out," she shouted.

Leon moved.

The group enjoyed their time in Porto, the food was magnificent, the weather had been warm and the people were friendly. They were all reluctant to leave, but knew they must, for no other reason other than politics and political promises, which often had a shelf life. They needed to return to the UK, to take the UN up on their promise.

Once again, they tidied up the yacht and departed to Santander. The weather had picked up, the journey was going to be choppy. In anticipation of its subsequent effects, everyone dosed up on Dramamine for the sickness, put their sea bands on around their wrists and prepared for the worse.

As it turned out, it wasn't as bad as they had thought. Once away from the coast, with the southerly wind behind them, they made good time. When passing around the Costa de Motre, they were sheltered by the land, so Abdul reduced their speed and carefully took them along the coast to enjoy the scenery. The scene was breath-taking and had the instant effect of relaxation, until black smoke billowed from the exhaust and one of the engines spluttered to a stop.

Abdul stopped the other engine and lowered the anchor. Luckily, he thought, they weren't in deep water. He opened the hatch to the engine room and went below. Despite looking for more than an hour, neither he nor Mike could find the problem. Going with caution, they decided to limp in on one engine and get it looked at in Santander.

Abdul looked crestfallen. None of them truly realised how fond of the boat he had become. One by one, they went up to sit by him at the wheel, trying to distract him from his worries, but no one really helped, he was beyond consoling.

The wind stayed from the south, and they sheltered behind the land for this leg of their journey. Fatima made some of Abdul's favourite soup and homemade bread. Mike was taken aback. He told them that no woman had ever made him bread, which got a glance of disbelief from Abdul and his family.

"Really, Mike?"

"Yes," Mike said. "Women in the west rarely make bread, unfortunately."

For the first time that day, Abdul laughed. In fact, he laughed on and off all night long, simply from repeating, "Western women don't make bread, ha!"

Ellie started to look quite embarrassed and tried to avoid Abdul. But he ended up asking her the inevitable, "Surely you make bread, Ellie?"

"Well," she started. "I'm sure I could. It just never came up."

"Fatima will teach you. Then you will get a husband. No bread, no husband." He said this with such authority, Ellie found herself agreeing. She looked at Fatima and thanked her. Fatima just looked at her as if she was defective or broken, Ellie couldn't decide which. Maybe, she speculated, there may be something in what Abdul had said. She shrugged, it couldn't hurt to try. Besides, her 'Lady in red silk' perfume hadn't worked.

They approached Santander harbour slowly, having informed the harbour master of their engine problems. The master, in return, had been good enough to call an engineer, who later turned out to be his nephew. They docked and went for a drink while Abdul and the engineer looked over the problem.

The dock was heaving with travellers and foot and car passengers for the ferry, which connected with Plymouth. The bars along the front were all packed.

As they had the babies with them, they looked for a café down a back street. Finding one where a few locals were drinking coffee and playing dominos, they grabbed some seats and squeezed around the only free table outside. A waitress approached and offered some tapas to go with the drinks. Mike explained that this was a mixture of small, prepared food, which the Spanish ate in bars and coffee shops. Often, the two merged into one, where coffee and liquor were served in both. As it turned out, it was the tastiest meal they'd had in a while, and they were genuinely sorry Abdul wasn't there to enjoy it. His family, as always, had also stayed by his side and were missing the feast. They all decided to take some back for them.

The day drew on. Although some wine and beer had joined the coffee, Joan insisted they return to the yacht. As an unwritten rule, the group preferred to stick together, so they paid the bill and left. By this time, their waitress, who happened to be the bar owner, seemed more like a friend. They were sorry to have to leave.

They passed the shops and crossed the busy road on their way to the harbour, where they were met by a happy Abdul. He quickly explained that an object had jammed the water intake and overheated the engine. It had been a simple fix for the engineer to sort out. Then the harbour master came up to ask them to move the boat. Apparently, they had been shown to a larger mooring, where a slightly larger boat with a similar name had been moored. It was the same make, only a metre longer, with the name 'Sea Horse'.

Abdul protested before the move, having already filled out the necessary forms, even though he had explained they were leaving the next morning. The harbour master was adamant but pleasant, and insisted they move. Mike pointed out that the Spanish had been very nice in general, and that Abdul should just comply. He also whispered in Abdul's ear, reminding him of their need to keep their heads down until they arrived in England. Abdul agreed, patted Mike on the back, and waved his agreement to the harbour master, who waved back in acknowledgement.

The ropes were released and they moved a hundred meters further towards the sea side of the dock.

That evening, they ate the last of the tapas, telling Abdul's family what they had missed. Abdul sarcastically thanked them on behalf of himself and his family. "Wishing they all get sea sickness," he joked and pointed at the babies. "And you two as well." He received smiles in return.

The morning brought the party-goers decent hangovers,

much to Abdul's delight. All the usual bacon sandwich jokes came out. Only because Abdul was a liberal Muslim, it was changed to a mackerel sandwich. It was just as effective, though. Abdul had woken early and refuelled the boat with the help of his son. He was still a little worried about the engines and was impatient to hear them at top speed again. The occupants were either on the deck or at the stern as the boat left harbour. Marine engines have an evocative sound as they churn the water, sputtering it out of the cooling outlets, releasing steam to the atmosphere. The smell of diesel was an acquired taste, which most on board had started to associate with freedom or even home. It was for this reason that they all joined together on deck, as well as to take in the sights.

Those who have ever experienced an explosion knew that the experience, unlike most others in life, was not easier the next time. This one was no exception to the bomb-hardened crew.

A shock wave moved effectively across the water, pushing the Horse of the Seas along at twice its pace. The rear etched, patio door screens shattered, throwing glass in Abdul's direction. He had enough on his hands with trying to keep the yacht under control so it didn't hit the other boats bouncing around him.

Pieces of glass fibre and metal rained down around them. A sickening reminder of the previous day. Thankfully, the main shock travelled at ninety degrees to them; also, they were at least sixty yards from the blast. Everyone was calling out names, but, luckily, they were all unharmed. Michael and Joan had left the babies below, sleeping, and were relieved to find them awake and unharmed. Abdul took the boat to an empty mooring and surveyed the damage.

Smoke and sirens filled the air, even a helicopter chopped at the air above them for a while. The group sat with coffee in their laps, shaking and tired from their ordeal.

A paramedic asked to come on board and started checking everyone for possible injuries. He also concluded they'd been lucky. His words reverberated in Mike's mind so he asked the medic which mooring the accident had occurred at, assuming a gas leak or something. A chill spread through him and the others who were listening. The explosion took place at the very mooring they were moved from. No one on board the Horse of the Seas was thinking 'gas explosion' anymore.

Once they were alone on the yacht, they discussed what to do.

Ellie, who seemed more affected than the others, spoke in a shaky voice. "I was almost certain we had moved away from this kind of thing, that we were in the clear. I wish I had never written that stupid report and emailed it. Look at the trouble it has caused."

"You couldn't have known, Ellie." Jack walked over to hold her. She was crying and very shaken from the recent event.

"Who though?" Jack asked.

"The Russians," said Abdul. "They're mean people to take on."

"No." Ellie wiped away her tears. "This is something else, I'm sure."

"I'm going to walk over and see if I can find out anything," Mike said as he started walking over the broken glass to where the door had been.

The whole area was taped off, but Mike recognised the mechanic who had repaired their boat. Having forgotten his name, Mike tapped him on the shoulder.

"Hi, remember me?"

The mechanic nodded.

"Hello, señor. You and your friends are very lucky that you moved, I think."

"You can say that again! Was anyone hurt?"

"No, they were lucky as well. No one was hurt around the

boat, either. Bit of a miracle." The mechanic looking skywards and crossed himself on his dirty overalls.

"Anyone know what caused it?"

"No, probably leaky gas pipe. That's usually what happens."

"Yes, I guess you're right. Anyway, nice seeing you again. Oh, you wouldn't know someone who could fix the glass sliding doors on our boat, would you?"

"Yeah, I can do it," answered the mechanic. "But it will cost you. That glass not cheap, and I don't do that fancy engraving stuff either. Would tomorrow work for you?"

"Yes. Are you sure you can get the glass that quick?" Mike enquired cautiously.

"No problem, señor, see you in the morning."

Mike went back to their boat and cheered Abdul up with news about the glass. Abdul had been quite pissed off about the glass and was delighted when Mike told him he had arranged for it to be fixed. Mike hoped he would be as happy when he received the bill.

Chapter Thirty-Seven

PM with Attitude

Leon Castle and Charles Wandsworth waited outside the PM's office. Neither of them wanted to be there. So far, they had managed to avoid talking to each other, but Charles could hold back no more.

"Leon, I shouldn't be here with you. This is down to you and you know it."

"I hope you joking, I really do. I am going to assume that you have forgotten the other day at the club: our little chat, over a very good beef wellington? I am fairly sure the phrase "just do it" was slipped in by you at the end of the conversation."

"And I was fairly sure you would bring that up. However, I am also sure that I didn't tell you to send some alcoholic, ex-SAS madman to Spain to blow up half the Santander Harbour."

"That's not very fair and, as a matter of fact, he didn't do it."

"So, who did?"

"This isn't going to sound good, but if you think it through, you will realise that his idea held some merit at the time."

"So, who the bloody hell did it?"

"Promise you won't laugh!"

"Considering where I'm sitting, I can make that promise."

"Okay, it was Manwell."

"From Fawlty Towers and I am from bloody Barcelona, Manwell?"

"No, of course not. He came highly recommended and served in the army. Anyway, our man decided it would look less suspicious to have another chap place the bomb. Our man did all the intelligence work, though. It was just one of those things you can't allow for."

"Obviously, and stop calling this dick head 'our man'. He's all your man."

"Well, I will send you a full report. We need to work together here and convince this woman, which is not going to be easy."

"No kidding, especially after your last performance. What do you suggest? Chocolates?"

"Do you think that would help, and do we have time?"

Charles looked at Leon as if he was seeing him for the first time. The door opened and the PM's advisors walked out, doing a great job of avoiding either of the two men waiting outside.

Charles and Leon got up and started towards the door, but, before they could get there, the PM stepped out.

"Hello, gentlemen. Now, you know how much I respect the both of you." She raised her hand to stop them from responding.

"So, I will tell you that what I should do now is march you both into my office, sit you down, offer you both a drink, and then give you a speech about how valuable you are to me, and the country, which is why it hurts me to let you both go. But, as I said, I respect you far too much to lie to you like that, so just consider yourselves fired and get out my sight immediately. Who do you think we are, the bloody mafia? These are UK citizens, all of them for sure now, thanks to you two morons. I thought you meant a smear campaign, not semtex, you wankers. You're very lucky no one was killed. Now get out of here."

Both men left without another word.

Chapter Thirty-Eight

Faith

After being questioned by the Guardia Civil, the group left Santander. The forecast was not good but the vote to leave was unanimous. None of them wanted to stay, they were too concerned for their lives after the bombing.

Ellie was trying to reach England and John Summerville. She finally she got through after several attempts.

"John, is that you?"

"No, just putting you through now," came the polite response.

"Ellie."

"John, thank God. Have you seen the news? We're fairly certain that was meant for us."

"I guessed as much. I also think someone cocked up. Two ministers lost their cabinet posts yesterday and I think it was connected to the bombing. But, no one's talking, so we may never know the truth. Listen to this, though, the British government are offering your friends political asylum, and eventual citizenship. We received the call today. I wondered whether it was because we embarrassed them into it, by making them our offer, or whether it's a means of deflecting from the heat of the bombing. In any case, the newspapers are reporting a possible accident, not a bombing. I think we would be wise to go along with that story. So, ask your people not to rock the boat. Okay?"

"Fine," said Ellie. Then she screamed as a large wave threw the boat sideways.

"Are you there, Ellie? Is everything okay?" John shouted

down the line a couple of times before a battered but uninjured Ellie grabbed the phone.

"I'm fine … but, about that rocking the boat …"

Ellie said her goodbyes to John and went to inform the others of John's news. This time, nobody suggested a party, despite being overjoyed with the news, mostly because their attention had turned to the weather.

Jack and Mike voiced their outrage at the bombing, but could see the point in accepting a version of the truth that claimed it was an accident, at least for the sake of the others.

Everyone was surprised that a government like the UK would have anything to do with those types of practices, and it was somewhat satisfying that the ministers concerned were fired.

As they sailed, the waves started to pick up. Abdul had to admit that he hadn't gotten around to working out the computer thing on the console that spat out weather reports. However, that didn't stop him furiously pushing buttons as the waves got larger.

Over the last week, he'd learned a lot about the art of taking the waves. To avoid being capsized, it was best to stay in a position that was head on to them, leaving only a small angle to the waves. This seemed to smooth out the transition by sliding over the side of the waves, instead of crashing over them, or worse, into them. The trick was to avoid a big one that was coming down on you. This, however, forced him to make constant course changes in order to stay abreast.

Abdul ordered everyone to put on their life jackets and stay in the lounge. He didn't say it, but he didn't want anyone trapped below deck if they went down fast. He also ran through how to launch the life crafts with Mike and Jack, pointing out that he didn't expect they'd be using them. He didn't hide his anxiety well though; Mike and Jack hung on to his every word.

The waves had gone from scarily big, to terrifyingly huge.

They climbed one side of each wave and then rode down the other side, like a rollercoaster. The anticipation during those seconds, while they waited for the inevitable crash at the bottom, gave their imaginations just long enough to think up horrifying endings to that inevitable crescendo of screaming metal and fibreglass.

Time and time again, this went on. Their journey should have taken around five hours; they were now past the seventh hour.

Mike made his way to the wheelhouse to see what the plotter showed, only to find it flickering on and off as the waves shook the boat. Not wanting to disturb Abdul's concentration with stupid questions, he returned to his seat. Joan and Michael were eager to understand how much longer this would go on for as the babies hadn't been changed, for fear of an accident. They were understandably upset. Mike tried to keep them calm by telling them that he thought they were close, which wasn't much of a lie as he had seen land showing on the plotter in between the flickers.

Michael and Ellie were violently sick, despite the pills and bands. Even Abdul looked like he was only just holding it back. The relentless ride was playing on Fatima's emotions and, on one particularly monstrous wave, she screamed out hysterically. Abdul looked around for the first time in hours and shouted something to her. It was unintelligible to the group, even to Joan and Michael, but must have been abundantly clear to Fatima because she recovered her composure immediately.

Finally, the waves backed down. They had just passed a drop off in the ocean as they approached the harbour. The waves were now their allies as they surfed in on them, like a Californian beach bum. They could have switched the engines off and they'd still be speeding to the harbour.

They called the harbour master, who was very surprised to

hear from anyone coming out of the storm, which apparently measured eleven on the Beaufort scale. They found their berth and just wanted to just sleep, but Mike and Michael decided to keep watch, just in case, especially after what happened in Santander. Mike took the first watch, but nothing more than mullet jumping disturbed the night air. He was tired but enjoying the calm so much, he let Michael sleep. Mike carried his watch through to the morning, only stopping to sleep when Ellie, who was an early riser, told him to use her bunk. Mike didn't argue. It was still warm from her occupancy, with a slightly perfumed odour of a woman. He was asleep in seconds. Thankfully, dreaming was a private affair. The children slept below him.

Later in the morning, everyone but Mike was up. The topic of conversation was on the validity of Ellie's claim regarding their possible UK citizenship. Ellie was so caught up in the discussion, she joked that she hoped hers was still safe. Nobody laughed so she cunningly pretended she'd said something else. Jack had gone to get a paper. When he returned, he threw it to Michael.

"It's confirmed. They sure didn't waste any time. It's on the front page. Apparently, we're heroes for bringing down the people traffickers. Not that we don't deserve it, but what bullshit. They could have killed us back there." Then Ellie remembered what John Summerville had said about rocking the boat.

"Then again," she added quickly, "we do deserve it, come to think of it. Why not make the most of your celebrity status. I'm told it never lasts."

The other news was less gratifying. Reports that the Syrian government forces had finally captured what was left of Aleppo, subdued everyone. Hundreds of thousands had been displaced. Joan wept as Jack read out the news, even Michael couldn't console her. Joan had grown up there and had no idea who had survived, only that thousands hadn't.

The paper showed pictures of small children, who were freezing to death with the onset of winter temperatures. Although Joan couldn't identify any of them as family, she absolutely identified with their plight.

"The world has really gone crazy, hasn't it?" Joan managed between sobs.

"They know and sit in rooms watching this, but not in the way we do. They know they can put an end to all of this. They must see that big brown-eyed girl or boy sitting in the snow, shivering. What goes through their minds then? Surely, demons must rule their minds. Someone please explain, if any of you can, how politicians or UN directors can sit around in a large room or hall, pushing pieces of paper between them like this is some game, despite their serious but bland faces. I would have more respect for them if they threw chairs at each other in frustration. Then, there is the person who gets up and goes to work, makes a bomb, with the full support of his country, then tells his family that 'it's just a job'. Well, that metal object he has just bolted together, will tear a child apart, or just another person. It's time they walked away. My God in heaven, why can't all the war initiators just walk away?" Joan was clearly going deep into her emotions, so they left her alone.

Eventually, she got up and went below deck. Nobody said a word, but they all agreed with her.

"The world has been like this for a long time," Mike said once Joan was out of earshot.

"I have been party to this. I know I always thought I was fighting for the right side, but perhaps the only right side is the one that refuses to fight. Joan is right; from now on, I will never pick up another gun. If I have to die for this principle, I will. My mind can't justify my actions any more. Ellie, I will formally hand in my resignation as my position requires a willingness to kill, and that's just not me anymore. I can't believe God has kept me alive just to break all his commandments. I'm sure he has better plans for me. Look at what we have been through. I cannot believe we all survived for nothing. This proposition makes sense. From now on, I will work to promote it, if it needs me. To be fair, though, it seems to be doing fine on its own."

"Are you sure, Mike?" Ellie asked cautiously. "You have been through a lot. Why don't you sleep on it? I respect what you've said, I even applaud it. I just want you to be sure, that's all."

"I will sleep on it, but nothing will have changed in the morning. My mind is made up." The look on Mike's face was convincing enough for Ellie.

"I admire you for what you have said, Mike. It's not easy to go down another path." Jack patted Mike on the shoulder. "I also feel the proposition we have put together is worthy of the publicity it's getting. If you think it through, it's possible that it is the way it is, due to the fact that no one has been there to push it. It stands alone. Maybe we should consider leaving it that way. There's a chance we may damage it. I know that sounds crazy, but please, all of you, think it over. If it could do some good, if the press interview us and we all throw our opinions on top of it, it could lose the message it seems to be portraying. Can we talk about this tonight?"

"We ought to," Ellie said. "You make a good point. Although, we all need to agree on it. No one person owns this idea."

Chapter Thirty-Nine

The Movement

The event had been put together hastily. Permission had been sought and granted, in writing, from the council. However, both organisers had not anticipated the response they were getting. A make shift platform had been erected and a PA system set up, along with a few road markers and banners, but that was about it.

The police had informed them that traffic coming into Southampton had been estimated, by their patrols, as being almost on par with the boat show, or the balloon festival; some of Hampshire's largest event. The event organisers were also made aware that the police had not been informed of such high participation numbers, and that they simply did not have the man power to cope if things went south, as the chief put it.

Anna and Joss, students from Southampton University, had been following the progress of the proposition closely. In-line with their avid interest, they decided to call a rally to determine the true reaction to the report. After all, they were studying politics, and this would give them something to write about. Furthermore, they both liked the simplicity of the proposition. It had a pure feel to it, which embodied the feelings and values most people they had surveyed conveyed. At least, that was what they wanted to prove, one way or another. Anna was a good-looking girl, but her beauty was concealed by her unkempt hair and a Peruvian hat. Her toned body was also hidden beneath old Oxfam skirts and a retro denim jacket. Joss was the opposite. He was skinny and awkward, but tried hard to dress well. He wore jeans, a smart blue shirt and a polo neck jumper, not modern, but it suited him. He differed from most people, he knew of Anna's beauty, despite her camouflage.

Their plans to increase attendance via social media had back-fired somewhat. It had been too effective and they were beginning to panic. People in authority, people who had a lot more experience than themselves, were also starting to worry. Even the police had been caught out. The chief constable was explaining their options, which, they all agreed, were shrinking by the hour. Finally, it was decided that it was too late to cancel. Instead, the organisers were told to increase their efforts to provide some barriers. When the magnitude of their actions dawned on them, and once they realised who the organisers were, the thought of leaving the barrier setup to the kids was scrapped. The police took over and made some calls. In no time, effective barriers were starting to be erected. This was thanks to an emergency plan the police had put in place, in the event the rally invite went viral. The chief was reluctant to become more involved in this event than was needed, but it seemed there was no choice.

In less than two hours, the barriers were up, leave was cancelled and extra police were drafted in. People began to arrive and so did the portable toilets. Opportunistic burger vans, anxious to take advantage of a free pitch, and even the Red Cross, had put together a small team in lieu of the mass publicity expected. The Southampton Common started to resemble an ant's nest.

The numbers grew and, much to Anna and Joss's relief, the weather was holding, although it was cold. Anna and Joss thought it best to get started, despite the fact people were still arriving. It was already half an hour past the published start time. They'd already agreed that Anna was the best speaker, so she grabbed the microphone and walked onto the stage and introduced herself.

"Hello, I am Anna Corin, and my partner, who's just off stage, is Joss Winder. We are students at Southampton University and, quite frankly, we weren't expecting more than twenty people. Instead, you're here in the hundreds, possibly thousands, and you're still coming. Wow."

The crowd shouted and screamed, but in a good way. They were encouraging Anna, and she took confidence from their support.

"Thank you. We are all here to talk about a phenomenon sweeping the world. Some of you may just know it as the proposition or Government Select." More screams emanated from the audience.

"We like it, too." More screams belted from the crowd.

"What is this, a Cold Play concert?"

The crowd laughed.

"Okay. Many of you will have your print outs. Who wants to come up and share their thoughts? I am thinking a limit of two minutes each, until we fall asleep."

More laughs and a mass of hands shot up.

"This could turn real nasty if you don't behave. So, can we show that we can be as sensible as the proposition today. No pushing fighting or pissing off the law, what do you say?"

The crowd roared their agreement.

"I'll take that as yes. Let's see if it works. Slowly, make your way to the front, do not push past anyone, or someone will get hurt. Listeners should be as cool as those speaking up here. Am I right?"

A giant 'yes' came from the crowd, which was growing by the minute. The police kept themselves positioned at the edges, just watching. From what they could see things were going well so far. A man came up on stage and spoke to Anna before he was handed the mic.

"I'm Daniel, and I'm over here from Zimbabwe, as a student.

This proposition would change the face of my country, and the only perceived obstacle is getting it on the ballot, but it is cool man, it's cool. I hope it makes it through the usual hurdles because we need this, now."

He handed the mic back to Anna, she, in turn, handed it to another voluntary speaker. Each one provided a different perspective. It was soon clear that the proposition meant different things to different people. However, a common theme was seen to emerge, despite the diversity of the speakers' perceptions. No one really cared whether the new government was made up of their fellow countrymen. Most of the crowd were in agreement. As one lady said, the flags has been used to cover up evil for too long. She went on to say that flags were the key dividers of nations in this new one world we now lived in. They were the currency of the greedy and the power hungry; they were the excuses for genocide; the rallying call for the stupid, and the cannon fodder. It was time to see the world looking back from the moon, not from across a sea, or a mountain or a desert.

She never offered her name and walked slowly off the stage and disappeared into the crowd, which, thought Anna was just perfect.

The event went on for hours. Finally, the police called it a day. Surprisingly, everyone left like mist leaving a valley. Not one arrest was made, and no parking tickets were issued as everyone with the power to do so, was at the park. Anyway, no one remembered a day like this. No doubt the press would pick it up and blow it up into the next Woodstock minus the music.

Due to the monumental turn out, demographic questions hadn't been asked of the crowd. To compensate for this, questions were asked online to establish who was there. Even allowing for false claims, the mixture was amazing, not only with ages, but ethnicity, too. The following day, the newspaper proclaimed: *One small step for mankind; giant leaps off a cliff for the world's politicians.* Another news source published the proposition on its inside pages. It didn't publish it all but covered the main part of the document.

The Headlines read:

Here It Is Folks

This is the proposition, leaked to this paper exclusively today

The Constitution of Government Select

Section One

All legislative Powers herein granted shall be vested in an Independent congress, which shall consist of a formulated group of uniquely gifted individuals. Chosen by the people of the world to serve and protect, without prejudice, forsaking all family or interests or loyalties they may previously had or held, with the absolute knowledge that their actions have been sanctioned by world decree, and that their service will be applauded into perpetuity, by order of this world decree, without exception. There will also be a second house, similarly chosen, that will be known as The House of Ethics.

Section Two

The congress will be elected by the people of the country it is to represent, by a margin of no less than fifty percent of the turnout on that election. The House of Ethics shall be considered part of the congress, until the congress is sworn in, from then it will be separate, but part of the Government as a whole. No campaign will be run in any manner whatsoever, only a notification in the form of a leaflet will be distributed to the populace, regarding the services Government Select offer and a link to online information. This will be reported in the media in the same way. However, no prospective member will campaign, or suffer being removed from the Government Select proposition.

Replacements to either House will be made by the World Body.

Section Three

No Person shall be a Representative, who shall not have attained to the age of thirty-five when the congress is formed. They will be eligible, with no other consideration of sex, colour, religion, or sexual orientation or affliction whatsoever. Neither will criminal convictions prevent eligibility, if justice has been served before the appointment.

Section Four

The congress will have selected a speaker before the election, as will The House of Ethics; no person's vote will have preference over another. Each vote on matters of state must be by a majority. The legislation will then be passed to The House of Ethics for final approval. If approval is not forthcoming, the bill will be handed back for amendment, only once. Should there still be a difference of opinion, after a final vote between the houses, the congress's bill will pass.

Elections will be held every five years. Every qualifying applicant for the ballot must be added. Any discrepancies will lead to the dissolution of Government Select.

Section Five

The Government will not have the right to apply legislation to sanction the death of any individual within its country.

The Government will not have the right to declare war. All decisions of this nature will be referred to the Emergency Council for a decision, and in doing so, dissolving Government Select.

Section Six

No official in either the Congress or The House of Ethics shall receive remuneration, or gifts of any type, while in office, or after, into perpetuity on penalty of law; other than that agreed by the world body.

Section Seven

A medical body will be set up within the World Body in order to monitor the health of both Houses. They will have absolute power to remove a member from either House.

Section Eight

The purpose of the Houses will be to represent all the people of their elected country, without bias to sex, colour, religion, sexual orientation or affliction.

The purpose of the Houses will be to bring prosperity to the country they govern as a whole, without knowingly or unethically hurting another or damaging the environment.

The purpose of the Houses will be to promote world peace.

The duty of the Houses will be to uphold human rights, to the exclusion of its own safety.

Section Nine

It should be noted, and made clear to the voters, of Section Seven's objectives, so that it is clear that a member of Government Select has to be medically and mentally fit for the duty at hand. Also, that no further restrictions on change will be burdened on the congress to help forward these goals, and not to hamper its progress.

Chapter Forty

The Meeting

Evening fell upon them. Abdul had bought some meat for his wife to prepare, despite sincere offers from Joan and Ellie to cook. Even Mike offered, but Ellie turned him down. Apparently, he had cooked for her before. The nights were getting colder, so Abdul switched on the heating.

Adnan and Adara, the two babies, were nestled between Michael and Joan. They were generally quiet babies, but tonight, they were silent.

They ate the aromatic meat Fatima had prepared, with couscous. The air filled with the aromas of the herbs and spices used, making the cabin seem exotic.

Ellie spoke first.

"Further to this morning's update in the paper, which we could have dismissed as a passing interest, the news today, for those of you who missed it, is about a rally that was held. I quote '*reported a gathering in Southampton's main park. Estimated attendance was over ten thousand people, from all over the country. It is believed that thousands more would have attended had it not been for the roads being jammed by others trying to attend.*' They all came to hear and talk about our report. What originally started as a toss-up between charades or putting the world to rights, has now turned into a worldwide event.

"What we decide now may well have consequences for a lot of people. I say that to remind ourselves to take this seriously. We will be back in the UK in two or three days' time, where we will be questioned, and we will be expected to have answers. That is the purpose of our gathering tonight. One last thing, we are also here for Sula and for the other lives lost, lives that may have continued to live under dire circumstances, but none the less, lost. This is no longer an evening's entertainment, this is as important as it gets."

"Speaking for myself, I'm scared out of my skin." Jack waved his hand. "You ask if I have an opinion. No, I don't. If I had known my opinion was to be taken this seriously, I wouldn't have had one back then. Who am I to tell the world how to live? For that matter, who are we?"

Ellie looked over at Jack.

"Jack, I understand why you might be feeling like that, but your idea of a second house could be the difference between this working or falling flat on its face. Every government needs checks and balances."

"But that's not my idea, really. The UK have used it for years."

"That's not the point, Jack. Nothing anyone said back then is particularly new, but that's what makes it feasible. The ideas on their own have been tried, or at least most of them have, but collectively, they have never been tried."

"Alright, I see your point, as long as no one asks me to get up and explain myself."

"That's why we're here. Does anyone feel they want or need to defend what we did?"

Nobody spoke for a while, so Mike addressed the group.

"That's the answer then. We pledge, here and now, not to answer specific questions relating to the proposition. Is that okay with everyone?"

They all agreed and focused on the details for the next couple of hours. They went through "what if" and "if someone asks" scenarios and agreed on acceptable responses, which mainly consisted of bland replies. Then Jack suggested that they put together a written response, one they could default to when asked difficult questions. It was a good idea and Ellie was chosen to draft it.

At the end of their discussion, most of them decided to go to bed. Abdul stayed with Mike and Jack, and they had a few more drinks. The three men chatted about their time together and the odds of them meeting. They talked well into the night about the strangeness of their situation and where they were now. Looking around the cabin, with its luxurious wood settings and fittings, in direct contrast to their adventure, Mike postulated that they could have just as easily been left to die in a ditch in Syria, or end up as slaves of ISIS. Abdul had come from humble beginnings and every day was a wonder to him. Jack asked him how he seemed to cope with whatever came along, seemingly without effort, always taking things in his stride. Abdul looked around before answering, as if to make sure it was just the three of them within earshot, then told them a story from his past. A story about his father, who, he told them, was a religious man, one who always followed the Koran's teachings. He had raised ten children, five boys and five girls; Abdul was the youngest. His father had worked as a mason for thirty years. He'd been proud of his work and always carried it out to the highest standard. One day, after finishing a large job for a local business man, the businessman complained about the standard of the work, hoping to get out of paying. An argument commenced, so they took the dispute to the local Iman at the mosque, who acted as a local court. He ruled in favour of Abdul's father, so the businessman had to pay up. A year later, Abdul continued, the businessman died.

Mike interrupted to ask Abdul whether he thought that the business man had been struck down by his God. Abdul laughed. "No," he said, and resumed the story. The house his father built for the businessman had collapsed on him.

At this point, Jack interjected to ask how this story helped Abdul through life.

"Well," Abdul explained, "it just showed me that even God and my parents could get things wrong. Just being right won't necessarily save you. Oh, and always take payment up front." Mike and Jack just shook their heads.

Chapter Forty-One

The Movement Grows

Anna and Joss had been very busy since the meeting in the park: Government Stock, as it had been dubbed, after Woodstock, the famous peaceful music gathering of the sixties. Although, Anna was quick to point out the lack of accompanying music. She made a mental note to put that right at the next gathering.

Social media numbers, following their website launch, were in the millions, from all over the world, and were rising. They had arranged to meet with a group from the University who they had quietly contacted, so as not to attract any undue attention. The local steak house was quiet during the day. It was the perfect venue. So they sat and ate lunch while they planned their next move. They had invited people who they knew had a genuine interest in Government Select or the proposition; they weren't sure what to call it yet. Anna and Joss were also looking for skills that could help them, as they didn't want to get caught unprepared, as they had done in the park.

The restaurant had a great reputation amongst students. Which meant they served big servings of great food, at a low cost.

There were plenty of seats, and, as they had envisaged, it was almost empty at that time of the day. The kitchen was one of those where you could look in. Always reassuring for those who were concerned about hygiene. This had the added benefit of tantalising smells to get the taste buds going.

It was dimly lit inside and the huge round tables near the kitchen were perfect for their purposes. They arrived early, and explained their needs to the waitress, a beautiful lady from

Romania. As it turned out she spoke passable English. Anna spoke to her and she sat them in a position where they could spot the others arriving.

Anna voiced her concerns to Joss. She was worried about the group of men they'd invited. Would they try and take over? She was, despite being a strong character, quite concerned. Especially as she'd been unable, despite some serious recruitment attempts, to bring females into the ranks. The simple requirement had been to find people with the background and knowledge they needed. She consoled herself with the fact that sticking by her criteria made her a better manager. Despite her misgivings, Anna decided she would have to live with her decisions.

A short while later, she spotted the others walking towards them. They were all fairly big men, which Anna noticed and commented on as they walked up. Joss explained they all played for the University rugby team. Perfect, she thought.

Tim and Andrew were both studying Business; Anthony and Paul were a few months away from their Law degrees. They also recruited Eddy and Jim, who were in advertising. The hope was that they could set up some sort of organisation, to give a voice to the people who wanted to give options or support to the idea. Anna spoke first.

"Hi guys, thanks for taking time out of your busy lives. I know you feel, as do Joss and I, that this idea is worth pursuing. So, if you have any ideas, we would love to hear them."

Andrew, usually a quiet man, spoke first.

"Thanks for inviting us, Anna, and you too, Joss."

Andy, as he was known to his friends, had a quiet but very sincere way of talking. He also had a very dry sense of humour, which was almost always followed by a cheeky smile, which made him popular with everyone who got to know him.

"One thing you want to establish up front, is your objectives.

It's okay to be just some sort of fan club, but if it's more, then you want to be clear on what you are looking to build."

Paul, who was also fairly quiet, took up the conversation.

"Andy's right, from a legal standpoint. It is imperative you set up the organisation in a manner that is appropriate for the goals you set today."

Anthony joined in. "On that subject, none of us are in a position to hijack the whole idea, not without approval from the authors of the proposition, at least."

"We don't know where they are," Anna answered, looking a little flummoxed.

"That may be, but you want to be careful with what you do or say on their behalf," Anthony cautioned.

"Good point," said Anna. "Thanks, Anthony!"

Not one to be left out, Eddie waded in. He had a strong character and cared a great deal for those around him, much more than he let on to the outside world.

"How about a name for the organisation? That would be a great starting point."

"Makes sense," Joss agreed.

"Do you have any ideas?"

"What do you think?"

"Any Ideas," said Jim.

"That's what I just asked," quipped Joss.

"No, that's my suggestion for a name. 'Any Ideas Inc.', or something like that."

"How about 'Any Ideas Welcome'?"

"Actually …" Joss agreed, "… that's not bad at all. It says it all."

"What I like is that it instantly conveys the message, 'don't dismiss any idea', which should, given the state the world is in, be a phrase every one associates with."

"Okay, let's go with that then."

And so it was agreed.

"It would have been presumptive to call ourselves 'Government Select', although, that it is quite catchy, too."

Anna and their new friends debated, swapped ideas and generally had a good time. She felt she had quite effectively put together a very impressive team, who looked like they could work together. One thing was certain, they were all equally enthusiastic. By the time they parted, they had put together a workable plan. As they all felt it very important to gain the permission from the original authors of the paper, Joss was given the job of finding the people behind the Government Select idea in the first place.

Chapter Forty-Two

To Err is Human

The Horse of the Seas crew spent the afternoon cleaning the boat. The glass doors had been repaired. Although, the man who'd been tasked with the repair had left a real mess, add that to the bill he handed Abdul, and it took a lot of diplomacy from Ellie and Mike to stop the poor man's fate closely resembling that of Henry's.

Abdul and the others were understandably nervous and acted like bored teenagers, pacing around, which is why Ellie put them to work, with the noted exception of Joan and Michael, who she felt were busy enough looking after the babies.

They refuelled without incident and left the port for Jersey. They could have gone direct to Southampton, but Michael and Joan wanted to see the island of Jersey. It was a small diversion and Abdul was happy to fulfil their wish, as long as they didn't stay the night. He was in a hurry to get to England and get the paperwork done for his family.

This time, the weather was much better, with good reports. The cold breeze, however, signified winter had well and truly arrived. The boat slowly passed the harbour. The children who were gathered around the harbour waved, and the crew waved back until they disappeared around the corner and out to sea. Fatima had prepared sandwiches. No one fancied a big meal as they were leaving, but, as usual, they turned out to be special: soft French cheese and razor cut garlic, with basil leafs and thin cut tomato. Mike mentioned Ambrosia while he ate. Noticing Abdul and Fatima's reaction to the word, Ellie pulled them aside and explained the compliment. Both emerged from the galley and went to hug Mike, surprising him. Ellie wondered whether she'd explained Mike's comment correctly but decided it had ended well. It was best to leave it there.

They played cards for the next few hours, which only served to prove just how mysterious Abdul was. He won every hand, which, over a period of time, was not only infuriating, but mathematically impossible. So, when he disappeared to the head, they took the opportunity to quiz his wife and son, who just raised their hands in a gesture that said they wouldn't tell, even if they did know.

Noting their reaction, Abir spoke in English.

"No, he really does always win with me and my mum. We looked to see how he does it, but if he cheats we couldn't catch him. But anyway, he always wins," Abir concluded with the same hand gesture: palms facing upwards, as if praying for the impossible.

Mike was almost certain Abir was being sincere. But, he reminded himself, so did most Arabs when they dealt with you. You just couldn't tell. Mike shook his head. One thing was for sure, he thought, he was determined to catch Abdul cheating before they reached Southampton.

The journey took several hours. Although they were eager to reach their destination, they were in no real hurry. When they finally approached Jersey, the tide had been on its way out for about an hour. The nicer weather had brought with it some fog, so Abdul took his speed down to a slow movement forward, or so he thought. After about thirty minutes, he started tapping the plotter screen. Mike, seeing the look of concern on Abdul's face, joined him at the wheel. Abdul explained that they weren't moving. Giving Mike the wheel, he went forward to check what was happening. What he saw surprised him. The wake from the boat's forward impetus was there, but he could see that it came from the tide, not their forward movement.

Abdul dashed back to the cabin and took the wheel from Mike.

"It's just the current. It's very fast here. We just need to power through."

Abdul pushed the two throttles forward together. The boat responded immediately and the front rose up, further restricting Abdul's view. He checked the plotter, and, sure enough, they had started to make headway. He could see the breakwater coming up and, just for moment, had doubts in his mind. He couldn't remember if he had to go to the port or starboard. Within his mind, electrons had started to dance, and not a good dance, more like a punk rock pogo.

If he had more experience, he would have known to back track or do nothing until he had a clear understanding of what he needed to do. Abdul chose poorly. A fifty per cent chance of being right is reasonable on a Vegas roulette table, but at sea, it's Russian roulette, with half the bullets in the chamber. Abdul pulled the trigger and went to port. This in itself would not necessarily have been a problem, but Abdul shouldn't have been there, anyway. On his first time into the harbour, had he called the harbour master, he would have been informed of Jersey's world record tide changes, of up to ten meters. Abdul was more used to a meter or two at most. The tide rush had caught many experienced skippers out. Jersey's demons in the fast water had no problem with Abdul.

The Horse of the Seas, with both engines on full, ran between two sharp rocks on the left, or port side, of Elizabeth Castle. Nothing Abdul did from that point onwards could help her now. The polished, thick white fibreglass, over two inches thick, split open like a log hit by a practised lumberjack, but on both sides. She scraped along for six meters, then swung forward and back, stuck fast between the two rocks.

At first Mike thought they were being attacked. Then, he looked over and saw Abdul's face contorted with stress. Abdul was turning the wheel back and forth in an effort to free them, while trying to restart the permanently stalled engines. Eerily, now without the engine noise, they were left with only the sound of the enormous tide sliding past the boat. It sounded like a panicking crowd running from a fire.

Ellie came up from below with Michael and Joan, each carrying a baby. Ellie helped them up first, then Fatima and Abir, before scrambling up the ever-moving stairs herself.

"We're taking on water at a hell of a rate. Abdul, get on the radio and call in an emergency."

Abdul was frozen. Mike slapped him to bring his senses back. Luckily, Abdul responded.

"Abdul sorry. It will be ok."

"No, Abdul, it won't," Mike said in a firm voice, looking straight into Abdul's eyes. Picking up the microphone, Mike called in the emergency.

"May Day, May Day. This is the Horse of the Seas. We are taking on water, fast, and sinking. We are a fifty-foot motor cruiser, run onto the rocks, directly next to Elizabeth Castle in Jersey. I have activated our digital distress beacon. We have ten souls on board. Over."

Mike repeated the message. A voice responded on his second attempt.

"The Horse of the Seas, we read you loud and clear. This is the Jersey coast guard. We are launching the St Helier in-shore life boat. We need you to be ready for immediate evacuation. The tide will not allow much time. Can you confirm the medical status of your crew and passengers, please? Over."

Mike pushed the transmitter button.

"All are well; two are infants under a year old. All are now putting on life jackets. Over."

"Horse of the Seas, this is the Jersey coastguard. Passing you off to the skipper of the life boat. Over and out."

Only minutes passed but to Mike it seemed like hours, then the radio came alive.

"Horse of the Seas, this is St Helier lifeboat. I have just launched. We will be with you in under two minutes. What is your situation? Over."

"St Helier life boat, this is the Horse of the Seas, we are taking on water fast, but are wedged between two rocks, and the tide is leaving us higher by the second. Over."

"Horse of the Seas, we have a visual of you, prepare to de-ship."

The lifeboat crew carried out their duties meticulously. They managed to get everyone off safely, but it took them three hours. Effectively, the group could have walked back to shore as the tide had gone out and the area where the boat had been wedged, was now dried out. It was only now that they noticed the extensive damage to the yacht. It had broken in two and dragged out by the strong currents. As they sat waiting, wrapped in blankets, they received the news and realised just how lucky they'd been. Everyone, but Abdul, realised the horrors of the situation they'd been in. But he had no insurance, and his beloved boat was gone. He was inconsolable. Mike had fought with him on board, and had lost the battle to stop Abdul going below to retrieve his bag of money. Mike had suspected it was of great value. How else had they got this far? He had a black eye from Abdul, but he still helped convince the lifeboat men that it had to come with them when they disembarked, which wasn't easy to do as the emergency team were focused on saving people, not their luggage and other possessions. Another ten minutes and they would have been too late. The lifeboat crew could have joined them in death. Mike thought they were the most incredible men he had ever met. The skipper, Tod Green, had spoken to him when they reached the shore. Mike had wanted to thank him. As he shook Tod's strong but freezing cold hands, he noticed that Tod was shaking, almost as much as they were. Mike suspected it wasn't just from the cold temperatures. Despite the fear and adrenalin, they'd left their families and dived into cold tides, which were just as dispassionate about killing Tod and his crew as it was them. He knew he would never forget them.

As a matter of routine, they were taken to hospital and given a check-up. Other than being shook up, they were fine. The hospital spent more time with the children, but when they learned of the refugees' history, they discharged everyone. They were put up in a bed and breakfast near the front, which was not busy at this time of the year. The owners were very caring and offered their best rooms.

Ellie had worked out that they, like the lifeboat crew, all had family connections with the lifeboat, especially being so close to the lifeboat's base. It wasn't so odd to assume that someone in their family was on the crew. After a night's rest, they drifted down for breakfast, Abdul was last in with his family. As he walked through the breakfast room, one by one, they stood and hugged him, then kissed him on the cheek. They sat and ate without a word. The gesture almost broke the proud man, who sat rubbing his eyes. Looking up, he wrapped his arms around his wife and son, and smiled at everyone. They had all said everything that needed saying regarding the night before, all without words. Abdul's wise old smile as a response was also as clear as crystal. Then it became too much for him and he addressed them all.

"My family, and you my friends, survived. That's what counts." There wasn't a dry eye in the room, including the landlady who was serving breakfast. Jack gave her a hug too, which was met with laughter.

After breakfast, John Summerville from the UN came to see them. He hugged Ellie, and gave his condolences for Bob.

He knew they had been close friends. They walked down to the harbour, where it was confirmed that the boat had broken up, and the strong currents had dragged it into deep water. Abdul said nothing, he just listened to the harbour master as he passed on the news. He already knew in his heart that his boat was gone.

John suggested they go for coffee to discuss their plans. The group went along, not unlike a tour group following a guide. The coffee was drinkable, but they missed the strong, dry small cups Fatima always made for them, but no one said anything. It was starting to dawn on the group that they were going to miss a lot of things, which was confirmed when John suggested they split up. Processing would take time for the seven without UK passports.

Their reaction was totally unexpected. As a whole, they jumped up from their seats and protested. Ellie explained that she had a large property in Southampton, and that everyone was welcome to stay with her until … at which point she hesitated … until whenever.

John said he would make some calls and that they were free to have a look around, meeting for dinner later in the evening. They agreed and went to walk around the town, after choosing the local tavern as their dinner venue.

The day was cold. Abdul took Michael and Joan shopping for clothes. They protested, but the logic was undeniable. The babies also needed a lot of things. They had lost everything with the yacht. Ellie and Jack went off and drew some cash, then headed into town.

Later that night, at dinner, they were all dressed in their new clothes. Ellie thought they must have of looked like a fashion parade, but with ruck sacks. No one had bought a lot. It was if they had a joint lesson in travelling light. John sat down at the large table the inn had put together for them. He started with small talk, admiring their new clothes, and then Ellie spoke. She needed to know things and couldn't join in the talk on fashion.

"John, we all just want to know what you have found out."

"Well, it's like this. The powers that be in the UN and the UK government, just want this to go smoothly. Frankly, and off the record, no one wants to be the bureaucrat getting in your way, despite you all being serious flight risks. Then again, heaven knows where you would go from here. So, tell me what you want. I'm your man."

"Oh," is all Ellie could say. She'd been ready for a fight. "So, what's the catch?"

"Well, Ellie, I'm sure there is one, but what it is, I've not been privy to. So, make the most of it, you don't have to tick the 'terms and conditions' box to move forward."

"Okay, flights to Southampton it is." She looked around, knowing everyone would agree with her. She nodded to John.

"I'm on it," John said smiling. "What would you like to do about the press, and you do know they're going to want to meet you? They're probably on their way here now."

"Oh really?" said Mike.

Jack muttered something that sounded rude and Abdul spoke in Arabic, getting an elbow from his wife. He looked at her in shock. So she clarified for him.

"Well, we're UK citizens now. I'm allowed to beat you up." Abdul didn't look like he knew whether to laugh or cry.

John explained about the coverage they were getting and the meeting in the park, which they told him they had seen on TV. He went on to explain that an organisation calling itself "Any Ideas Welcome" had emerged from Southampton University. Ellie was the first to comment.

"Well, I don't know about you, but my first impressions are good."

"I suppose," agreed Joan. "But really? An organisation? It's only been …" she struggled to continue.

"I think we have all lost track of time," Ellie said, agreeing.

"Well, this a big thing," said Abdul in his broken English. His sandpaper voice resonated across the table. "We got to face this … this. Whatever it is, we have to talk to press; and we have nothing to hide."

Jack agreed with him and, looking at the others, it seemed to be consent from them all.

John told them he would arrange something when they were settled at Ellie's. He also said he would arrange flight tickets, which they could pick up at the airport.

Chapter Forty-Three

Southampton at Last

Southampton airport was not large, despite its routes to Europe. It was easy for the group to clear customs here than if they had been at a larger airport, such as Gatwick. They were off the plane and in a taxi in under thirty minutes, which, bearing in mind their status, was in no small part due to high level calls being made to the Customs officers in charge that day.

No one had tracked them down yet, but they all knew it was just a matter of time before the media caught up with them.

Ellie lived in a small part of Southampton called Woolston. She had bought the place when she was young, and had never regretted the decision. The town had changed a lot since then. The Vosper Thornicroft ship builders used to be just down the road back then. She would hear noise from the hooters marking shifts, along with the smell of welding and the sound of hammers on metal. Now, it was all gone, replaced with blocks of flats and houses. The village had changed, too. The old Woolworth, which once dominated the small shopping mall, was now closed. The road had been revamped to the new style, a pedestrian friendly street, with very little parking. Ellie understood it was progress, but, as we all do as we age, we hanker for the way it used to be.

One good thing, she thought, was that the neighbourhood used to have a rough reputation, but that was now being replaced with a newer, friendlier atmosphere. The locals had come together and erected a giant sculpture of a feather, with glass inlays of all colours, along with seats and a small garden. The road to the water and Ellie's home used to have a ferry at the end, which took passengers across the water of the Itchen River to Southampton. Now, the Itchen Bridge took the traffic, for a charge. The rumour was that it was to be charge-free after a while, but that was some years ago. Now the locals were paying to go to visit their own city! It was a bone of contention amongst many of the Woolston community.

They arrived at Ellie's house and set about arranging who would sleep where. Fatima was relieved when Ellie showed her to the kitchen, offering for her to make herself at home. Fatima had been secretly worried about using another woman's kitchen. To her it was sort of territorial, a no-go area. She need not have worried; Ellie loved her cooking far too much to let it be an issue.

Michael and Joan took a walk with the children, although they had to carry them for the time being. They walked along the river, or as close as they could get to it. The area next to the bridge was lined with workshops and garages, covering everything from paint to cars, to even hovercrafts. Michael was fascinated at the diverse industry and the old setting. The innovation of the British businessman left him with no doubt as to why the UK had felt it was better going it alone, outside the European Union. The place was called Spitfire Quay. Michael later learned it was due to the Spitfire planes being manufactured there during the Second World War. He thought that was just perfect.

Abdul visited one or two local takeaway food places. He was also amazed at the diversity in such a small area. He counted three Chinese, at least three Fish & Chip shops, three Indian curry houses, a Hot Potato shop, a Thai restaurant and, not to mention, a number of Italian Pizza shops and two Polish supermarkets. He was sure he would find more, he'd only been walking for twenty minutes. Everyone was happy and impressed with their new surroundings.

The group waited patiently for Fatima to produce another marvel, this time with the two chickens they'd picked up. They had got into the habit of saying grace on a rotating basis, which, given their circumstances, seemed apt. As it turned out, they all looked forward to it. Although, when Abdul or Fatima's turn came around, only five really understood what was being said. Although, their voices made up for this. It had a calming effect on them before the meal and always seemed to bring them closer together.

Fatima did not let them down this time and no one spoke until their plates were empty. Once cleared away, they sat around chatting. The main topic of conversation was Southampton. Ellie was always working away and, having been born in a different city, she could not tell them too much, but the little she knew seemed to keep them satisfied. After a few hours, they called it a night. Their travels had exhausted them.

Their late morning sleep in was interrupted by the phone. Ellie answered. Mike, watching her answer, immediately noticed the change in her voice. Ellie was usually very confident, but talking to the press, as she was, had made her very nervous.

"I'm not sure." Mike heard Ellie say. "I will have to check with the others."

"No, I can't make a comment now.

"No, I don't want to give out any names right now. I would appreciate it if you just left a number." Ellie scribbled something down.

"Goodbye, yes I will be in touch. Goodbye." Ellie quickly ended the call.

"That sounded like fun," Mike said, smiling.

"Next time you talk to them, then," she said as she pushed past him. Mike was leaning back on his chair and lost his balance, falling backwards, and bumping his head as he did.

"Oh, I'm sorry, Mike." Ellie rushed over to help him up.

Abdul, who had now joined them, couldn't stop laughing as Mike got up, rubbed his head and glared at Ellie.

"Well, remind me not to get on your bad side again," he finally said, joining in with the laughter.

After breakfast, they decided to get the press conference out of the way. Mike phoned them back and arranged a meeting at the football ground, where, apparently, the press had rented a conference room. They also called John Summerville to let him know their plans. John was pleased they were going ahead and said he would get in touch with a young man called Joss from the "Any Ideas Welcome" organisation.

The Dell football stadium was a short drive away. It was an impressive structure, and was almost new. They managed to find the reception area, which was very much like a hotel. From there, they were directed to the lifts that led to the large conference rooms.

"I don't mind telling you that I am shitting myself. Abdul never do thing like this before."

"None of us have, so don't worry, Abdul. We do this together, don't answer any questions you don't like, just refer them to the proposal if they want any detailed information on something."

"Yes," agreed Ellie. "And, if you feel pressured or you want to leave, we all leave together." This suited the group just fine.

The lift stopped at their floor and the doors opened to flashes and a barrage of questions. So intense was the onslaught, Mike held them back and closed the lift doors. He took them up another two floors and dropped everyone off there.

"I will go and quieten things down. Stay here, it will be fine, I promise."

With that he closed the lift doors and went back down. As the doors were shutting, he saw that Joan and Michael were very upset, even the babies had started to cry, which was unusual of them. He was not happy. When he opened the doors to the press, the same barrage awaited him. Only this time, he was prepared and pushed his way through, knocking two reporters over in the process.

"Feels bad, doesn't it? Feels bad when someone's rude to you and doesn't respect your space. Did any of you notice the babies? I have a good mind to call things off today and arrange an exclusive with anyone who is not here right now. Would that suit you all?"

The hall went deadly quiet, followed by a muttering of apologies.

"Okay. Everyone back in the room you paid for. Make yourselves comfortable. When I bring the rest down, you will hold up your hands and wait until you're pointed at before you ask your question. We will try to get to everyone, and if we don't, live with it. You were probably too ugly to be noticed, anyway, and that's not my fault. If you want to moan, go moan to your ugly parents."

Mike didn't wait for a response. Luckily the lift opened, as if on cue, and he went to get the others.

They all filed in to an almost silent room and sat at a table where microphones had been set up.

"Okay," Mike said, gesturing for hands to be put down. "Before we start, we don't have press packs, so, for everyone's benefit, I will start with introductions and a basic outline of the sequence of events to date. After that, we will take questions, so get your pens out and don't ask me to spell names, I don't write for a living."

Mike did as he promised and introduced everyone. Then he briefly re-retold their story, deliberately leaving out the deaths and killings, which did not leave a lot to share. Then he handed over to the floor for questions, pointing at one journalist at the front.

"David Frogger, *The Times*. This all seems a little far-fetched.

Do you really expect us to believe that you put this proposition together over a few drinks? This has become a huge political debate. Is it not true that one of the political party is behind the whole thing?"

They all looked around. Ellie nodded.

"The fact is, and I think I speak for us all here, we don't give a sausage what you believe. But, for the first and last time, it is the truth. Secondly, why would any political party support their own demise."

Ellie pointed to another lady, who was desperately waving her arms.

"You please. The lady in the green top."

"Is it true that you're connected, in some way, to the spate of bombings in and around the Mediterranean?"

"No, that's the Russians and the Syrians." Ellie's fingers were crossed behind her back.

"So, you weren't near the boat that blew up in the harbour at Santander last week," the green-topped reporter persisted.

"We were close by, but it didn't affect us," Ellie answered as confidently as she could, but the room sensed blood and a flood of questions flowed almost simultaneously. Mike stood up.

"What did I say? One at a time, or goodbye." The room went quiet and several hands jumped into the air.

"You." Mike pointed at Joss, who seemed the calmest in the group.

"Thank you, my name is Joss Stern and I am part of the 'Any Ideas Welcome' group that supports your ideas. Can I just say … the country has had enough of politicians. In fact, from the feedback we've been getting, it's more like the world."

"Thank you for your support," Mike answered "Although, I have to say, we're all a little taken back by the growth and publicity this document saw. We never meant for it to be taken this seriously. I'm sorry, but Joss, did you have question?"

"Oh, yes, I do. How do you foresee the setup of this world committee, to choose this parliament of the people?"

"Good question." Ellie took over. "We have no idea, other than the world body we mention in the proposition. So maybe your 'Any Ideas Welcome' group can come up with some suggestions?"

Joss sat down, beaming. Ellie couldn't have said anything better to him. He would happily go back and pass that request on, he thought.

The conference went on for an hour. They were quizzed on everything, especially the bombs. But, with no real evidence, the press had to let that subject go. One or two pushed on the absurdity of the whole thing, to which they were told, emphatically, that the group didn't care. The movement was self-fuelling and propelling itself. It didn't need them. They called an end to the session, despite there being more questions. It was more than they could or were prepared to answer.

The journey back home was mostly quiet. Only Michael commented on the whole experience. He said it had been like getting caught in a fireworks factory with a raging fire. The conference had exhausted them all. When they arrived back at Ellie's home, they all went to their separate rooms to rest and sleep. No one wanted to talk anymore.

Chapter Forty-Four

Setting a Fuse

The meeting room adjacent to the main hall at the UN was occupied by the Secretary General and ten others who represented various departments. They had come together to discuss the proposition, which they referred to as Government Select.

The meeting was opened; the Secretary General spoke first.

"Ladies and gentleman, we at the UN have been the only world body with a mandate to keep the peace. If we are to do this well, we must be prepared to criticise ourselves if we are to succeed with this goal. So, let's look at our history and achievements. This is what I was asking myself as I was shaving this morning. The conclusion I came to is that I should buy an electric shaver. Why, you ask? Well, I will tell you. Then I wouldn't have to look at myself in the mirror every day. That, my esteemed colleagues, is getting harder and harder every week. We have in front of us, a proposal, which is marked Government Select. It can honestly be described, without any doubt in my mind, as one of the most naïve, idealistic proposals I have seen. At worse, it represents an attack on the nation's sovereignty, which, if I am not mistaken, could be read as being against our own Charter. At best, it is a popular representation of the simple truth, which, I am sure you will agree, has been lacking, not just for some time, but for all time.

A murmur of agreement went around the table.

"However," the Secretary General continued, "the fact of the matter is, we have no other or better proposals. In fact, we have no other workable proposals either, despite my request for some to be put forward as a balance to this one."

He sat down, giving the room space and time to reply.

Juan Almeries, the head of the DESA (Department of Economic and Social Affairs), cleared his throat.

"With respect, Secretary, the matter of sovereignty is not a small issue, we can't brush it aside. We are not a world government, and we do not have the mandate for this."

The Secretary looked over at Juan.

"Yes, you are right, we don't, which is why we need to get that mandate. I'm not suggesting we force the proposition forward, I'm suggesting we sell it. We have, for years, complained about the lack of resources, but this is just my opinion, because we keep trying to put out fires instead of preventing them, which, at the very least, is expensive. We have, over the years, become engaged in the worst type of crisis management. We react to wars, starvation and slavery. What we don't do is offer viable alternatives, and when we do, we are inevitably talking to corrupt or power seeking individuals, who have their own religious or greedy monetary agendas. This, ladies and gentlemen, has to stop. The only resource we need more of, and I say this with the greatest respect to those of you here, is intelligence and good ideas. So, does anyone have a better one?"

"Your point is well put, Secretary General," said Jannetta Sanchos, the head of the DPA (Department of Political Affairs).

"Why would any nation put this pre-formed Government Select on the ballot? They will simply point at Europe and the United States and ask why they don't have to do it."

The Secretary said nothing. He raised his significant eyebrows and stared at Juanita, smiling slightly.

"Are you suggesting …" Juanita stopped to think.

"… The US and Europe will never go for that. Why would they?"

"Because of public opinion, that's why," answered the Secretary. "They can't be seen not to support this. They may not see it straight away, but believe me they will. After all, it is still an instrument democracy. No one is forcing anyone to do anything. If you follow most of the electoral procedures in different countries, you'll find that they can put Government Select on the ballot anyway. Nationality may be a problem, but even that could be worked round."

Niska Hem, the Head of the OSS (Office on Special Adviser on Africa), was more positive.

"This would potentially reduce corruption, which is killing Africa quicker than AIDs. I know a lot of people who will love this, and only a few hundred who will fight it."

The Secretary spoke again.

"Thank you, Niska. This is not an exercise or an ad campaign. This is the difference between life and death, or enslavement for millions, and potentially a better world. I need all of you, including your departments, to sell this as a concept. It will take a little time, but if it works, it could save a country, or in certain circumstances, our world. You have all been around long enough to know that today's politicians make decisions for the next five years at most. Wisdom has left the world of governments, replaced by more and more skilled spin doctors. Look, to be perfectly honest with you all, I have no clue if this will work. All I know is that what we have now, doesn't. As this has never been tried, let's give it a chance."

The meeting didn't end there. It went on for several hours more, but the conclusion was that the proposition was accepted. All that was left was for them to sell it to the world's governments. Nobody left the room thinking that would be easy.

The days passed and the various departments busied themselves with the task at hand, which, to a large degree, involved dealing with negative reactions from staff, although these proved to be in the minority. They were very disruptive and slowed the process significantly. The following week, the follow up meeting took place. Everyone held their breath, waiting to see how the news would be received by the world.

The meeting was opened by the Secretary General again.

"The UN, was founded on the principle that democracy is the only governmental system that is worthy of support. So, as you are only too aware, we are going to have to get this proposal through a vote. Make no mistake, this could alter the destiny of millions, potentially billions. As such, I propose we start on an individual basis to take the shock value out of the equation, starting with the big players, the members of the UNSC (United Nations Security Council). If they fall in line, the others will, too.

The behind doors meetings took place over the following days. None of the UNSC would give their support but, as the Secretary envisaged, it had taken the sting out of the proposition. He decided to personally talk to the member states and their representatives. He knew if he could get the US and Russia to back the proposal, he had a chance; admittedly, a slim chance, though.

The first meeting was a video conference, which had not been easy to set up. The Secretary realised that, without Putin, he was dead in the water and so was Government Select. His strategy was simplicity itself. Let Putin feel it was his idea to put the proposition forward. The call came through on a large video screen.

"Vladimir, it is good to see you again."

"You too, Mr Secretary. How may I help you? I am usually better briefed, but not this time. I am asked to trust you. Why would I get such a request?"

"Nothing shady, Vladimir, I can assure you. You may have heard of this new form of Government proposition, which is floating around."

"Yes, I have," Putin replied, adding nothing more.

"We at the UN feel it could put an end to corruption and instability, in many smaller countries of the world."

"Really, that's interesting. So what do you want from me, Mr Secretary of the United Nations? What can Russia do for you?"

The Secretary was starting to feel this wasn't going his way. Even worse, it was showing on his face. He was starting to wish this had been an old-fashioned telephone call.

"Well, it's like this: Russia, is one of the most powerful nations ..."

Putin interrupted.

"Please, this façade has gone on long enough. I already know what you want, so relax, you can have it. I will vote to agree to this Government Select being put on Russian ballot paper, after all, they are not a threat to me. It will show the world that I am not an unreasonable person. The question is, can you get the others to agree?"

"That's incredible, thank you. At the risk of talking you out of your position, which I can assure you I don't want to, may I just ask why you are agreeing so easily to this proposition?"

"You may ask, Mr Secretary. As we are friends, the answer is that it affects my nation's security. I also like the idea. Do you understand me?"

"Yes, Mr President. I think I do." The call ended and the Secretary was left wondering what had just happened.

The following conversation with the US President took surprisingly longer to arrange, and did not go as smoothly. It was Obama's last few weeks in office before the President Elect, Donald Trump, took over. It had proved to be one of the most controversial elections and appointments in history. The meeting took place by video link again. The Secretary was a lot more nervous this time.

"Good morning, Mr President."

"Good morning, Mr Secretary," came back the usual respectful reply. He was one of the world's greatest diplomats.

The Secretary was under no illusions about how hard this would be. Obama was a lot of things, but he was no walk over.

"I expect you have been briefed on the upcoming vote on the Government Select proposition? We would appreciate US support."

"Well, yes, I have read the report. Although, it has its merits, I am not convinced that I can throw my weight at what is left of it."

The Secretary, thought for a moment.

"On another subject, in the near future, myself and my staff will have to deal with the President Elect, do you have any thoughts to share that might be useful?"

"My opinion is a matter of public record, Mr Secretary. What are you fishing for?"

"No, nothing like that, Mr President. It just occurred to me that, if a new president, any one I mean, not just this one, came into office and turned out to be less than palatable, or maybe erratic, the thought of competing with a government made up of geniuses, along with world renowned experts and trusted people, might calm him down a little. That is, if he was looking for another term."

"Okay, I see where you are going with this, but it won't work. In fact, that could be construed as an attempt by me to go against the will of the American people, which, despite my feelings, which you may have guessed correctly or not, I simply will not do."

"I see. As usual, sir, what you say and stand for is true. I apologise for taking that route. It was wrong of me."

"You're forgiven, Mr Secretary. So, let me help you out. You would be better just telling me why I should support this? Perhaps start by telling me why you support it."

The Secretary took a breath and wiped his forehead before answering.

"When this proposal came past my desk, I thought it was a joke at first. I even heard a rumour that it was never meant to get out as it did. Apparently, it was a genuine mistake. Then I read it again and again, and you know what? I can't disagree with it. I could, perhaps, debate certain parts of it, but you know what, if you did, you would have to be careful not to hurt it. It's like a living thing that breathes in bullshit and exhales wisdom. If that sounds cheesy, I apologise, but I could see it as a solution to conflict and hunger, mostly through eliminating corruption. While corruption reigns, the people are doomed. Anyway, that's how I saw it."

This time it was Obama's turn to hesitate. He played with his chin for a moment, then answered with a face that gave nothing away.

"Interesting. I will need to do some reading of my own. I will come back to you, Mr Secretary. You can take some relief in knowing you have done something few others have done over the last few years. You have turned me from a definite no to a maybe, so let's leave it at that."

The next few days were taken up with calls to the UK Prime Minister and the President of France, who had proved to be the toughest of them all. References to liberty and possible relief from the refuge crisis had turned the French and UK premiers around. One common theme ran through all the conversations the Secretary had. All of those who eventually agreed to vote for the proposition, did not themselves believe for a moment that it would affect them. They believed their decisions were ultimately for the good of the smaller nations that had nothing to do with their own. A number of European countries had voiced concerns but, eventually, Germany, Spain and the others followed suit.

The next and last call was to China. Before it had even been set up, it was denied and replaced with a simple release stating that China did not feel that the vote was relevant to them, so they would abstain from voting.

The sad truth was, thought the Secretary, that many countries would only support the proposition in order to follow the money they received in aid, or worse the country they were most threatened by or protected by. Such was world of politics. Hopefully, he thought, this may help change things.

Handing the file to his assistant, he decided to leave it at that and see how the vote went. He knew he and his staff had done all they could.

Chapter Forty-Five

Threats

The days passed by happily at Ellie's home; the days turned into weeks. The meeting with the press had, in everyone's opinion, cleared the air with the public if nothing else. They were still, however, hounded by the press, which they had begun to accept. They even had another meeting with their groupies, as Mike had amusingly called the "Any Ideas Welcome" organisation, which had grown in size to literally millions worldwide. They knew that the motives behind the newly formed organisation were pure and they genuinely believed in similar goals to those set out in their proposition, of which they were proud of.

Joan and Michael suggested they leave the questions and publicity to the "Any Ideas Welcome" team, so they could get a break. Joss and Anna had enthusiastically agreed. In fact, so had the others who were closely involved. This energy had shocked them all, but they were all relieved to be sharing their strange burden.

From what they had been reading in the press, the UN had indeed decided to get behind the ideas in the proposition. For Ellie and Mike especially, this seemed nothing short of a miracle, having in the past watched them take months to decide on the paint colour for vehicles that were meant to be going into Rwanda to try to prevent the attempted genocide there. As it turned out, they couldn't even decide whether to call it genocide. This was a giant leap for the organisation. Ellie had talked for hours with Mike about the reasons behind their change of heart. They could only assume that the recent atrocities in Syria and Jordan had pushed them too far. Also, the timing of the proposition becoming public would have played a crucial part, popular opinion was proving more powerful than ever before.

The other prominent story was the news that the so-called Government Select would be on every ballot within the next ten years, and that a world body led by the UN was being formed to put together the first Government Select committee. It would be on standby should it be called on. The speculation then turned to who would be invited to form this new Government, and how many would be needed. One leading newspaper decided to run a vote. Its readership had come up with two models and a soap star, which left Ellie furious. Jack had to calm her down, pointing out that those newspapers were always going to make fun of everything to sell papers. The argument that followed, though, made them realise how important this had become to them all.

Popular feelings across the world seemed to be gaining momentum. Then they were contacted to tell them an urgent matter had arisen and that John and a group from the government were to visit. They arrived in black SUV's and sat crowded together in Ellie's living room, looking a little out of place and passing around cups of tea and biscuits. Charles Perkins was introduced as a member of the security forces, which led to Ellie and the others asking a lot of questions. Eventually, everyone was settled down. The babies had been put down for a nap before the security team arrived. They had fallen asleep immediately.

The meeting was brought to order by Mike and John spoke first.

"I firstly wanted to say that everyone at the UN and the British government are very grateful for the open and honest way you have all handled this whole affair. However, the security forces have identified a number of potential threats directed at you, which we believe are credible."

"Is that from our government or some other place?" Mike interrupted.

"They deserve that, Mike, but no, this is very serious. We believe you have joined a very small prestigious list of people who are at high risk of being assassinated. This list includes the Prime Minister and the US President, among others."

Silence descended on the room, and everyone just looked at each other.

"Why?" asked Joan, who was holding onto Michael.

"Frankly, it's because your ideas threaten a lot of people's plans, from African dictators through to corrupt home grown politicians, which I'm sorry to say there are too many of. Even ISIS want you dead."

"So, what are you saying?" Mike asked. "We go into hiding for the rest of our lives?"

"I wish I could give you an answer, but I really don't know what the future holds. I do know that, right now, we have to move you."

"Where you move us?" Abdul asked. "My family and I just got UK passports."

"Which is one reason you are all getting the celebrity treatment," answered Charles. He said this in a voice that left no one in any doubt of how serious things had become.

"How long do we have to get ready?" Michael asked.

"You don't have any time. In fact, we're wasting time now."

"Oh," Michael said. "So where are we going?"

"Sorry, that's classified. It will be easier to chat when we get there. Please, there is one other thing … you will have to give up your phones and computers, basically anything that gives off a signal."

Jack gently moved past Michael.

"What about contact with the family, how will that happen?"

"It won't, Jack. I'm sorry."

"Then screw this. I am not giving up talking to my children and grandchildren because some idiot makes a threat, and that's final."

"Jack, this is serious, you could be killed," Ellie tried.

"I'm old, let them do their worst. Why kill me, anyway? I'm no threat to anyone."

"We can't force you, Jack," Charles said. "But, if you don't come with us now, you're on your own. We can't look after you out there in the open. Do you understand, Jack?"

Jack hesitated before responding quietly, but with conviction in his voice.

"Yes, I have only one life; I won't live it on the run."

With that, he left to pack. Ellie grabbed his hand as he passed her. She was crying.

"Please go and pack. We will have two cars outside in twenty minutes," Jack encouraged them with a look of urgency.

They filed out of the room looking stunned, and headed to their rooms.

Three, black four-wheel drive cars pulled up outside the house. They wasted no time getting in, all except Jack, who wandered up the road. Ellie was too upset to speak, but she knew how much her brother loved his kids, and that nothing would keep him away from them. He disappeared around the corner, so she said a prayer in her mind and wondered if she would see him again. He had been in her life longer than anyone alive.

The cars drove at speed on the short drive to the airport. The gates were opened and the cars drove right up to where they boarded a large helicopter, also black in colour. Mike made a spiteful joke about the lack of imagination with regards to their theme colours, which didn't get a smile from the security escort.

"Looks like black is the new black!"

Still no smiles from the security team. Mike gave up.

The flight was bumpy and Michael was sick. In their haste, they'd forgotten to pack the pills and were told to get some from the lady security officer who looked a little less serious than the rest, but she still turned out just like the others and had a very business-like approach, not at all motherly thought Michael.

Two and a half hours later, with travel sick passengers who were cold and miserable, they landed. As they got out, they were met with open fields, a farmhouse, some trees in the distance and the sound of a river. They made their way to the farmhouse and were let in by another security guard. He was over six foot five and broad shouldered. Mike, who was six foot himself, disappeared behind the man and, with his usual humour, asked if there was enough food. The big man bellowed with laughter, then stopped abruptly and looked at Mike as if he were a bug about to be swatted. Mike quickly made his way in.

The farmhouse was large and the kitchen had a large fire and a log burner, which, when in use together, filled the house with a pleasant, but smoky atmosphere. They were greeted by a lady and a man in their late sixties, who introduced themselves as the owners. Later, it came to light that the husband was ex-special forces and they were at a trusted safe house set up within the security community. The couple showed them their rooms, which couldn't have been cleaner or better equipped. Ellie and Joan, while checking the rooms, even noticed a book of jokes on a string next to the toilet, presumably to give the occupier something to read. It looked like everything had been well thought out, with the noted exception of a phone, which couldn't be found anywhere.

They settled in then went downstairs. At the table, the only one looking a little downtrodden was Fatima. Joan noticed it first, and as she went to say something, Abdul caught her gaze and shook his head furiously, telling her not to speak. The food was a dead giveaway to their current location: haggis and mashed potatoes with peas. Abdul said he had heard of it, but didn't know what it was. Mike offered to explain, much to everyone's amusement. He informed Abdul that they were lucky to be there while they were in season, and that it was likely they'd get the chance to hunt them. He warned Abdul to be careful, though, as they were dangerous little creatures. If you missed them, they ran up your trouser leg and bit off your balls. Abdul visibly jerked, but everyone else cracked up with laughter. It took a while, but Abdul finally got the joke. When they explained what haggis really was, it took the rest of the evening to persuade him that they still weren't joking. He did, however, enjoy the whisky that accompanied the old Scottish traditional meal.

They went to bed early that night and slept like bears. Breakfast had been a cholesterol-loaded, heart stopping feast of bacon and butteries, including local scones made with a lot of butter. The scones were loaded with bacon and eaten as a sandwich, still warm from the oven. In short, it tasted a little like heaven to the group.

For those who travel, the experience of Scottish meat was known as one of the greatest discoveries, especially when combined with their pastries. The group were now in a position to agree with that wholeheartedly.

Following breakfast, they sought permission to go for a walk. They were given Arctic camouflage jackets and trousers, socks, gloves and woolly hats, as well as combat boots, which, as it turned out, they needed. The outside temperature had dropped overnight to minus eight. Abdul and his family had experienced cold in the desert evenings, but somehow, that had felt different. He shivered as they left the farm.

"Now, I know why you come to Abdul's country," he said. Fatima and Abir voiced their agreement.

"Come on, Abdul," Ellie said gently, patting him on the back.

"It's refreshing, isn't it?"

"Ice in my vodka on a hot day is refreshing. This is place for bear of polar."

Ellie and the rest of them laughed. Abdul certainly had a way with words. The landscape was fairly flat, apart from a few hills far off in the distance, which, Mike thought, was probably why this place had been chosen as a good safe house location. They would easily see an attack coming across the open fields around them.

As they explored further, they heard a river flowing, about a hundred or so yards away. Out of curiosity, and without thinking, they headed towards the water. It turned out to be a small river, possibly ten meters across at its widest. It was, as they say in Scotland, in spate, which meant it had rained and the river was full. The river was beautiful, which is probably why we are drawn to them, thought Ellie. She and Joan walked arm in arm. To Ellie's amusement, Joan and Michael were playing like children with the freezing mist indicating their breath. She assumed they had never seen conditions like this, nor a river as beautiful.

Abir was throwing stones and breaking up the ice along the sides of the river. Every now and then, a piece would break of and drift swiftly down the river, breaking into smaller pieces as it smashed into small rocks. Abir's face lit up. Mike watched him playing, remembering the very different boy he'd first met, his face contorted as he fired his automatic rifle at the Russian mafia boss's yacht. It was hard to reconcile the two. In the past, a thought such as this would have just received a shrug from him. But now, it occurred to him that he may have helped do something to improve things. Suddenly, he felt less helpless and less useless. For the first time, he realised what a good feeling this was, so he smiled.

"You look like the cat that found the cream," Ellie remarked.

"Something like that," Mike replied, the smile still spread across his face. Ellie thought it was a long time, if ever, since she had seen Mike happy in this way. She decided not to spoil the moment with questions and just let him enjoy whatever it was.

A figure approached them from the farmhouse; he was unmistakably the huge security man. He approached methodically, in no apparent rush, but his face seemed even more serious than the first time they saw him on their arrival.

"Ellie Summers?" he said quietly, bowing his head a little. Ellie's face dropped. Her earlier cheerfulness was now replaced with caution.

"Yes, you know I am. What it is?"

"I have bad news. We believe there has been an accident."

"Who?" Ellie answered, knowing full well what was coming, but wanting, somehow, to delay the news.

"It's you brother, Jack Summers. He was in a car accident."

"Is he …?"

"I'm afraid so. He was found with another lady, his daughter we think, and a child. No one in the car survived, I'm afraid."

Mike caught Ellie as she started to fall. Everyone looked at each other, only to see a reflection of their own grief. Jack had become like family to them all, but to Ellie he was family. For reasons she couldn't explain, memories of them together as children flooded back. Ellie was younger; he was the big brother she would torment. Unlike most brothers, though, he doted on her. He was always willing to play with her. Over time, he became and always remained her best friend. Her thoughts went to her niece and her baby. At this point, it became too much for Ellie and she passed out. The giant security guard picked her up as if she was a child and carried her back to the farmhouse. The others followed. Suddenly, the cold didn't matter to them anymore. They filed back into the farmhouse and made their way to the living room where a fire was burning. They removed the cold weather gear and sat around in a circle on the large settee and armchairs. Ellie was now conscious. Joan tried to hold her hand, but Ellie withdrew it, smiling at Joan. Joan returned the smile, understanding Ellie's need to protect her personal space and not wanting to be touched. They sat like that for an hour, just absorbing the news. The security team left them alone. The elderly owners, who they were told just to call Fobe and Nellie, not their actual names, supplied hot drinks without a word.

Chapter Forty-Six

Grief and Fear

Ellie stayed in her room for two days before Joan and the others managed to persuade her to come down and join them. Everyone felt Jack's loss, but, as expected, none as hard as Ellie. When she joined them, everyone was shocked at her appearance. She was pale and withdrawn, a shadow of the strong confident woman she had been. The woman who had pulled them together and taken them through the events of the previous months. She sat near the fire. For a long while, no one spoke.

Abdul decided to break the silence. "You know what always helps me, Ellie?"

"No, Abdul. Does it involve alcohol?"

"No." Abdul seemed as though he'd been insulted. "I like to play cards."

"What?" Ellie said, turning to him in surprise.

"Cards, you know, trumps, rummy, snap."

"Well, snap sounds appropriate," Ellie said with a small smile forming.

The others took the cue and laughed, the kind of laugh that was cathartic, ending in tears of emotion.

"Well, do we have pack of cards?" Mike asked, looking around.

The week went better from that point onwards. A lingering question was emerging and the security detail pre-empted the need for them to ask. They requested a meeting and gathered in the living room, this being the only room big enough to hold them all. The team covering their security worked in three shifts, five days on and five days off. The men present today weren't familiar with the group. A dark-haired woman in trousers and a white roll-down polo neck, addressed them.

"My name is Sasha Moon and I am the head of the current security force. First, please accept my condolences for your loss. We weren't aware that the threat to you was so imminent. The police and MI6 are investigating the car crash. It does seem like foul play was involved, at a very sophisticated level. It was thought the brakes failed. However, further examination showed that the hydraulic oil had been tampered with. An additive, one we still don't fully understand, was poured into the car's break system, which in turn caused the breaks to malfunction. Other measures were taken to ensure the sabotage was a success, which I shan't go into now. But, I am assured they did not suffer. Again, I'm so sorry for your loss. The other reason we needed to talk to you is that, although we are as confident as we can be that your whereabouts is secure, it needs to remain undisclosed, to anybody. I can't emphasise how important that is. Ellie, I'm afraid that means you can't attend the funeral or see your relatives. I hope you understand why. This is not just a matter of your safety now, but, as we now know from the tragedy that just unfolded, it concerns the safety and lives of those around you, too. Are there any questions?"

"Do you have any idea who is behind this, and why?" Mike asked, looking deadly serious.

"No, we have some ideas, but the truth is it may be more than one group or government."

"Why, though?" asked Joan. "We only shared an idea."

"People die for less disruptive ideas every day. Yours ignited the world," answered another of the agents. He was a smart man in his late twenties, with short hair and eyes that ensured his presence was noted.

"But why kill us? We don't really have any further part in

this," Michael asked, throwing his arms in the air in frustration.

"I know it's hard to understand, but the governments you may have affected are, in most cases, corrupt. That means that they are mad at you. Generally speaking, they have access to near unlimited funds, so getting vengeance is simply a matter of a wink to an aid. After that, they probably won't give you a second thought." Sasha looked down at the floor, as if she couldn't comprehend the evil she had to deal with.

"So, basically, we're screwed," concluded Abdul. "Well, fuck that. If they come for me or my family, I'm going to make them wish they had stayed at home with a good book."

"We may have a better solution," Sasha said with a look of confidence. "We think it would better, and simpler, for everyone if you were to die."

The room went a little quiet, and then Mike spoke.

"I hope I understand what you mean."

"I think you do!" Sasha answered with a grin. "We have to fake your deaths. Although, that's easier said than done these days."

"How many of these have you done?" Joan asked, looking curiously at Sasha.

"Not that many, and not recently. The world is more visible now. We can see everyone from everywhere. We have DNA matching and photo recognition, so it's tough, but not impossible. The hardest part of the whole process is, and always has been, you."

"Because we can't talk to or see anyone we know again. Am I right?" Mike clarified for her.

"Yes, you're right. So, I will leave you all to talk. If one of you says no, it's a big fat no for you all. I could apologise, but won't. You can all figure out the logic behind that, can't you?"

Sasha left them to think. Ellie got up from her seat, and brushed off invisible dust from her clothes, her hands were shaking. Mike went over to comfort her, but she gently pushed him away.

"We all need time alone," she said. Ellie was still tearful but her old self was starting to return.

"If we make a decision like this as a group, someone may feel pressured into agreeing. This is far too big a life changing decision to be made that way. We must sleep on it at least, then do a blind vote tomorrow. Do you agree?"

They all muttered their agreement. As usual, the group felt Ellie made sense. They retired to their rooms. All, except Mike, who, stating he had made up his mind already, grabbed a bottle of beer and sat down with one of the security guys for a chat.

The next morning, the group were ready to vote. Ellie handed out pieces of paper instructing them to just write yes, opting for their fake elimination, or no, to go home. "It is that simple", she added, really. They all did as instructed and sat down at the dining table. Ellie asked them to fold their papers twice and place them in the middle of the table, un-named. When all the folded papers were in place, Ellie shuffled them into a pile and placed them into a plastic bag. Then, one by one, she picked them out and opened them. The first was a 'yes', so were the next few, until they came to the last one. Ellie opened it … it was a 'no'.

Everyone sat back in shock, looking from one to the other. Mike looked angry.

"I know you said this was supposed to be anonymous, but whoever decided this, has just about killed us all. I think we have a right to know who that was."

Ellie put up her hands.

"Okay, everyone calm down. It was up to everyone to make their choice. We are all more than friends, so I'm as surprised as the rest of you."

"Ah," said Mike. "So, it wasn't you."

"Look, that's not the point … shit, Mike, that's not fair."

"Well, I want to know. Who's so bloody stupid?" Abdul said, looking really pissed off.

They all looked at Joan and Michael, who had voted as a couple. Abdul had also voted as a family, so it had to be them.

"Why are you looking at us?" asked Joan. "We voted 'yes.'"

Everyone looked confused. Then Abdul spoke up.

"If you vote 'yes', you voted go home, not die in fake accident, yes?" he asked a little sheepishly.

"No, Abdul," Ellie sighed.

"Seriously, Abdul? You voted 'no'. Weren't you watching me open them? So, what do you want?"

"To die of course!" Abdul answered.

This brought on a good laugh, but the discussion then took on a darker side as they discussed the implications of the vote. All considerations were taken into account. Finally, when they were satisfied with their decision, Ellie went to tell Sasha, who gave her a little smile in return.

"I'm smiling because I know you have a better chance of life now," she said.

"How will this work?" Ellie enquired.

"The less you know, the safer you will be, and the more likely this will work."

Ellie left feeling like they were in good hands, but when she got back to the room, she could see the fear on everyone's faces. They had been through so much together.

"One good thing is that we will get to keep the babies, that formed a big part of our decision." Michael smiled at Joan.

Ellie and the others nodded. They all shared the same feeling. It was nice to be part of something nice, even if it wasn't your own.

Sasha came back into the room and took a seat.

"I have some more news for you and don't worry, no one's been hurt."

They all breathed a sigh of relief.

"So, Sasha, what's happened?"

"You may find this hard to believe, I know I did, but the member states of the UN just voted in your resolution."

They all looked at each other, a little confused.

"What exactly does that mean?" Joan asked.

"Well, from what I can tell, the nations of the world have agreed to put Government Select on their ballot papers, at least for the foreseeable future. They have formed an international body to put together a world body, who will select individuals to form the first Government Select."

Chapter Forty-Seven

To Die and Let Live

Anna and Joss were considering setting up a foundation. For some reason, without even asking, they had been receiving donations. Not the odd cheque, but thousands of them, along with piles of cash. There was so much, they'd spent most of their time just counting it all. Diligently, they recorded every penny and opened an account, with trustees to manage it.

The problem they seemed to have, at least in Joss's opinion, was a silly one. How would they spend it? A meeting at the steak house was arranged, where they discussed their options. They were on their third round of discussions, and the suggestions were getting less useful and more stupid. Anna was about to call it a day, when her mobile rang. It wasn't a number she recognised, but what the hell, she thought. The others carried on drinking and talking, until Anna asked them to keep the noise down. After a few yes's and no's, she thanked the person on the other end of the call and hung up.

"That was MI6; they want to meet us, something about another big event for the Government Select founders. Apparently, they would like to run it for charity and wanted some suggestions from us. Oh, and one more thing, she asked me if I'd heard! When I asked her what she was talking about, she told me to put the news on."

The restaurant didn't have a TV, so they moved to a bar nearby. After ordering there, they asked if the barman would switch to the news.

What followed was a celebration that lasted well into the night, having decided that a small proportion of the funds could be spared for entertainment. All the trustees were present so the vote, not surprisingly, passed without further debate. Had it not gone through, the student's rent would have been at risk. Luckily, Paul, their legal advisor was present.

The next day, to say the least, was a struggle for the founders of "Any Ideas Welcome" everyone was suffering severe hangovers from the night before. Ironically, but not surprisingly, the one thing in short supply was ideas, After several coffees, also paid for by the entertainment fund, with a vow that it would be their last but essential expense, the board passed the vote for the coffees with minimal fuss or noise.

Once caffeine had soaked into the young minds, Anna proposed that they review their options, although she struggled to recall much of the conversation she'd had with Sasha. Thankfully, she had downloaded a call recording app off the internet. She looked up the call and pushed play. As soon as her voice was heard, she cringed. She had always thought it was awful to hear yourself on a recording, but far worse when you were drunk, especially on a call with MI6. Anna had to sit and bear listening to herself talk while the others tried not to laugh, partly because they didn't want to add to her suffering, but mostly because it hurt to laugh.

"Never mind," Anthony patted her on the back. "It could have been worse."

"How?" Anna pleaded.

"It could have been me," Anthony joked, receiving a kick for his troubles.

"Seriously, she mentioned Wembley Stadium, and what's worse is that I think the woman was serious."

"Well, it makes sense," said Andy. "We can expect a large crowd. Hey, you know what? We can turn this into something like Live Aid."

"You are too young to remember Live Aid."

"Yes, but didn't you watch it on TV? We could invite stars, bands, anyone really."

"You can try but, according to Sasha, this has to take place in a month's time. We'd better get moving, or the only people turning up will be us."

The day was spent calling agents, who were very non-committal. The big surprise came when they called Wembley Stadium. The organisers there seemed to be expecting them. At least, that's how it felt to Joss. Also, their attitude was very cold, bordering on rude, especially when you considered this was for charity, Joss thought.

Everything was set for a Thursday, in three weeks' time. Although, they didn't have a band yet. Anna was starting to panic. She and the others from "Any Ideas Welcome" had gathered in a conference room in the University. Within three minutes, four of their phones were ringing. The agents they'd spoken to previously had changed their attitudes. Suddenly, a number of well-known stars were available to perform. When the last call ended, they looked at each other and screamed, which, given their actions the night before, turned out to be a mistake. Joss looked around the room, his face very serious.

"We aren't up to this. Look at us. Can we really pull this off by acting like a bunch of twelve-year-old girls at a One Direction concert?"

"Wait a minute. Joss, don't you think that was a bit harsh? We have all worked really hard on this, so what do you want us to do? Actually, what do you want to do?"

"The donations are for our cause. I just think it would be sensible to spend some of the donations on a professional. We may even get a discount, as it's for charity."

"Actually, that does make sense," Anna agreed, holding her head in both hands.

"We really have no clue about dealing with stars at this level, not to mention the lighting and crowd control."

"Okay, I get it. You have a good point," Andy capitulated.

"Given we are still the founders, we should have more time to plan the finer details."

"Anyone disagree? … Well, that's good." Anna picked up her bag and headed for the door.

"Where are you off to?" Tim asked.

"Bed." Anna replied.

The weeks flew by. The students were glad they had taken on an expert. A company director had mentioned, in passing to Anna, that he had gone to Live Aid. It was, he told her, the inspiration behind the setup of his own company. Since then, he had organised many of the big rock events all over the world. Sasha had stayed in touch with Anna throughout the planning stages. As they expected famous people at the gigs they'd organised previously, the company was not surprised to have to deal with government agencies. Although, they hadn't been told which one they'd be working with. The event had attracted politicians who were eager to show that they were now behind the Government Select ballot proposition, which had yet to be ratified by the UK government. The word in the halls of Whitehall was that it would fly through. Neither side of the houses wanted to appear concerned about the idea.

A splattering of royals were also expected to attend, as their charities would directly benefit. Anna and the other students realised that a number of charities would benefit, so, to distract from any talk of political bias, they decided to get more charities involved. Otherwise it would seem as though they were going against the fundamental message of the proposition. A large consignment of posters arrived from nowhere. Sasha explained that the posters had been organised by Ellie and the group, so the students welcomed them. Some were huge, with group and individual portraits of all of them. In some of the shots, they were holding scrolls, which the students thought were not very tasteful as they weren't too dissimilar to a graduation shot. Little did the organisers know, but the posters had been edited to prevent any one using them to find the group. Facial recognition software would have proved useless if someone tried to use the posters; it would just mislead them.

During the two days leading up to the event, sniffer dogs and police combed the area. Tickets had sold out in one day. Not even MI6 had expected the numbers they had reached. People were coming from all over the world to attend. From Anna's perspective: "They are coming to see and hear about the work a group of people, who had a few drinks, put together, and literally put the world to rights."

Anna confided only with Joss, who admitted he had similar thoughts. They were both worried about the actual Government Select getting in. There were so many variables that could go wrong. "Are we all just dreamers?" Anna had asked Joss. He had simply replied with, "It's possible we are, but good things do come from dreams. Idealism is only a bad word to a cynic."

The day of the event came. The programme was packed with six big acts, mostly from the sixties, but two were fairly new artists. Apparently, a few other modern day artists would have come if they had been given more notice. Wembley Stadium made it easier, everything was already setup. The band's roadies and their organisers had no issues.

In the background, Sasha and her agents were at work. Initially, they had planned to carry out a controlled explosion in front of the crowd, but when the number of attendees was known, the idea was quickly dropped. They realised the need for the public as witnesses to the incident, so the idea still factored in theirs plans. They would also need CCTV to capture the sequence of events, rather than just relying on the public's viewpoint. They also had to factor in panic. It would need to seem like a disaster, so CCTV was absolutely required. Sasha decided to go ahead with their plans after the event, but while the crowd was still contained. They would be informed by the PA system of when the area was safe, then evacuated.

The bands were warming up. Sasha and her team were transporting Ellie and the group by helicopter. A small row had erupted when security asked them to leave the babies behind. Michael and Joan had not been pleased at all. Ellie spent a while talking to them, hoping to reassure them that they would be reunited later and that the only reason the children could not join was because it was far too dangerous for them to be there. Michael had seen sense, but Joan was not happy. Ellie knew that sentiment wouldn't change until she was back with the babies.

They landed in a part of the car park that had been specially cordoned off. Amidst the noise from the blades and engine, they were roughly shuffled across the tarmac to the stadium. Joan started to realise why they'd left the babies behind.

As they walked through tunnels leading to the changing area and conference rooms that had been designated to them, they were confronted by an Indian man. He seemed too elderly to be working at Wembley Stadium. One of the security team rushed forward, seeming like he was about to tackle the old man. Seeing this, the man threw his hands up in the air. Sasha had her gun drawn in an instant, calling for calm. The old man seemed harmless, but Sasha was trained to be cautious, so she instructed her guards to keep their distance as he could be wearing a suicide vest. He was asked to stay very still. In the meantime, Ellie and the group were moved back into a concrete corner of the tunnel for safety. For a while, they could hear shouting and shuffling around, then silence.

After five minutes, Sasha appeared. "He's not armed, and he wants to talk to Joan. You don't have to, but he seems harmless. Says he has a message."

"From who?" Ellie asked.

"He won't say, but he is very insistent, in the nicest way. I would have a quick chat with him so we can get on, but it's up to you, Joan?"

"Okay, why not. I have an army to protect me, anyway." She smiled nervously.

The two of them disappeared around the corner. They were gone for longer than a minute, more like ten. A silent Joan and Sasha then made their way back.

Ellie, followed by the others, approached Joan tentatively.

"So, what did he want?" Ellie asked, looking eagerly at Joan.

"He just said, 'Thank you.'"

"For what?" Ellie pushed.

"Apparently for 'lifting the message from the dust and bringing it to the light', or something like that. Sasha thinks he's a little nutty, but I liked him. His voice was so soft and sincere, but I was edgy as hell when we got there. Now, I'm floating on a cloud. He really did seem to be a reflection of my thoughts. Meeting him was a very spiritual experience."

"Can I meet him?" Ellie asked Sasha. The others joined in the chorus. It seemed everyone wanted to meet him now.

"We're on a tight timescale, so be quick," Sasha said with authority in her voice.

They all rounded the corner of the tunnel a little quickly, surprising the security team as they came into sight, who all turned with their guns in hand. They relaxed when they saw the group and Sasha.

"Where's the old man?" asked Sasha.

The team looked around, but the old man was gone. That, in itself, wouldn't have been a surprise had the long tunnel had exits, but there were none, which left the security team scratching their heads.

"He was fitter than he looked," commented Mike.

They all followed Sasha quietly, trying to remember what the old man looked like. Strangely, their memory of the old man was full of holes. He was wearing everything from a one-piece kaftan, to a shirt and jeans. They all described him as old, but argued over his origin. Indian, Afghani and four or five other possibilities. The only thing Joan could recall was that she had understood him. But it worried her that she couldn't recall the language he'd spoken in. It was presumably English, as Sasha was able to understand him. The only other language she knew was school standard French and Arabic.

This incident would add to the weirdness factor the day was generating and formed the butt of many jokes, which mostly came from Mike.

The stadium was huge, but as none of them had been there before, to them it seemed even bigger. They all walked out on to the stage, but Joan wasn't paying much attention. Her mind was still on the old man. As she walked out beyond the curtain she glanced sideways. There in front of her was the vast stadium. Joan turned and let out a little scream and ran off the stage. The others and the security team laughed until they were close to tears.

"Well, you could have warned me," Joan scolded Michael, clearly embarrassed.

"Take your time coming out. Later on, you will look a lot more confident than you feel, and it will help you relax."

They did as they were advised. As it was just a rehearsal, Mike even gave a reasonable impression of Freddie Mercury at Live Aid. George Michael came over to introduce himself. He also remarked that he thought some other great names would have loved to have been there; only 2016 had taken so many of the greats: David Bowie and Prince, just to mention a couple. It was one of the saddest days when George Michael himself passed before the year ended. But there, on the stage that day, the great singer gave his time and experience to advise and settle the group. He was, they thought, a beautiful soul.

Their moment of fame was over for now and they went to get ready for the big finale. The security team briefed them as to the manner of their death: they were to be blown up and then shot at for good measure, or at least their stand-in would go through the motions of being killed. Then they would then be flown to a remote airfield out of the country. They repeatedly enquired about their new destination, but Sasha would only say it was somewhere nice.

The crowd started to fill the stadium. Ellie and Mike watched from a box overlooking the pitch.

"Well, Ellie, we'd better not suck!"

"I don't know what the hell they expect from us. We can't sing, or I can't anyway. You were a mean Freddy though," she said, holding Mike's hand.

"How did we get here, Ellie? How in God's name did we get here? This has to rank as a world first. Next, they will publish Top Gear as a new philosophy. They crucified that, too, didn't they?"

"Don't blasphemy. We need all the help we can get."

"Sorry, mum," Mike said, putting on his best 'child in trouble' face.

"Apparently, we come on in the middle, then we're rushed off to die. I'm looking forward to that bit. I have always wanted to know what's on the other side. The Muslims blowing themselves up for ISIS think they are getting a hundred virgins. I expect the Church of England equivalent are the calendar girls from the Women's Institute."

"Don't knock them, I was a member once," said Ellie.

"Did you ever, you know, 'get them out for the boys'?"

"No, I bloody didn't. They only came out for men," Ellie returned cheekily.

Mike laughed and they walked back to the executive box with the others. Sasha suggested they enjoy the show. A famous interviewer from a popular TV show had volunteered his services and they were told he was looking forward to interviewing them.

As there were seven of them, they would set up the stage as a TV set, where they could sit down on sofas and be questioned. The crowd would see them on a giant screen, as they did for all the big events now. Abdul asked for the other security team members to be informed that he and his family were not terrorists.

"Tell them not to shoot the talent," he said, which also got a laugh.

The show went on without a hitch. The acts came and went. Everything was being shown live across TV stations the world over. They had their own monitors, so the group were able to watch the performances with Anna and Joss, who had also joined them. Security hadn't let the others from 'Any Ideas Welcome' in. They had been sent to another box as they had not been completely cleared. The group barely got a few seconds to shake their hands and thank them for their efforts.

The time came for them to go on stage. A live feed from America was showing on the screen while the set was put together. The interviewer introduced himself and they did the same. Nerves were starting to set in and stiff drinks were handed out to calm nerves.

The roar from the crowd when they came on stage was deafening, but it died down as they all sat down.

"Well, it's great to finally meet you. Where have you been?"

"We could tell you, but then we would have to kill you," Abdul answered before anyone could stop him.

Seeing the reaction, he continued.

"Well, we were told it's a secret."

The interviewer laughed and made a face on a close-up camera shot, which had the stadium laughing.

"Okay, at the risk of getting shot, I'll go on. Mike, in your own words, what do you think of the proposal for Government Select? A lot of people are saying it's naïve and unrealistic, how would you answer that?"

"Well, try to imagine there are no countries."

From back stage, some quick-thinking guitarist took up the John Lennon tune.

"Very good, but seriously, how would you respond to that?"

"Seriously ..." Mike began. "Seriously, the world is messed up. What is amazing is that it's taken this long for someone to suggest this. Politicians who retire as multi-millionaires, from countries where their people are starving, is just not realistic and should not be allowed to continue. It's insane."

"Well said," the interviewer weakly laughed. He was here for the entertainment factor, not Hard Talk with the BBC.

"How about you, Ellie? Why do you support this proposition?"

"I am fed up of working for the UN and seeing children gassed and blown up, while the most powerful man in the world plays with red crayons on the floor, smiles, then looks sincerely upset, before nodding his head and doing nothing."

"Okay, who's next?"

By now the crowd were chanting: "Government Select, Government Select".

"Wow, your idea has really taken off. Why do you think it's popular, Joan?"

Joan looked a little shy. "I can't speak for them," she said, pointing to the crowd, "but for me, I want an end to killings. All killings, all murders. I have no specific name for this action. It encompasses all forms of killing human beings, not specifically 'execution', 'eradication', 'genocide', 'war' or 'collateral damage'.

It's just killing, period."

"Thank you. That's all we have time for today, but I would like everyone to say a big thank you to the charities for all the work they've done in preparation for today.

The crowd clapped and shouted as Ellie and the group left the stage, relieved it was over.

As soon as they were off the stage, the security team ushered them down into the depths of the stadium. The LED lights gave a very clinical, unreal feel to the place. Ellie and Mike looked at each other, then turned to Sasha.

"Sasha, where are we going?" Ellie asked.

"Sorry, I should have said. We deemed it too dangerous to have you actually involved. It is far simpler for you not to be there at all."

"But why down here, then?" Mike asked.

"If we take you out now, there is possibility you will be seen. So, we've decided to hide you here, for about twenty-four hours, and then move you."

"I suppose that makes sense, I was worried you were going to take us out, you know, kill us."

"No, we thought about it," said Sasha smiling. "If we were to kill you, we would have done it at the top of all these stairs. Otherwise, we would have had to carry you back."

"Good thinking," Ellie said, a little nervously.

They finally came to a room furnished with blow-up mattresses, a table and chairs, and a kitchenette.

Mike spoke up. "This is a staff room, isn't it?"

"Give the man a prize," said one of the security team.

They sat down where they could. To Abdul's delight, there were two packs of cards.

"Not this again," moaned Joan and Michael simultaneously.

"I used to love cards, but Abdul's taken the joy from it. Nobody wins every time!"

"He does," said Fatima, grumpily.

"But you get used to it. Just play for second place, it's what we do." Abir nodded with an ironic smile.

"Whatever," Mike said. "Someone deal."

Over two hundred hands later and an audience of security guards, who were deep in conversation over the impossibility of what they were witnessing, the group were out of ideas, so one of them suggested filming the game so they could study the moves.

"Do you mind?"

Abdul just shrugged as if to say, "why not". The others followed suit verbally. Mike even said he thought it would be a good idea.

Another fifty hands followed before the top spies in the country checked the footage. It only ended with six, extremely frustrated, MI6 officers. The final hand was played and they added up the scores.

"I won!" Mike exclaimed. The others nodded in agreement.

"Well done, Mike," said Joan.

"Well done what?" asked Sasha.

"He came second, he's the winner," explained Joan.

Michael backed her. "He is."

"I see," said Sasha. "But that's just sad."

"You play him then," Mike suggested, passing her the cards.

"No way, my mind is off course enough tonight. What with disappearing Svengalis or hotdog venders. By the way, we're still trying to work that one out."

They all agreed that it was time for lights out, which turned out to be creepy as no other light came through at all at this depth. It was pitch black. An experience few people had. All your senses came alive and you heard everything. For the group, it was the gentle hum of generators, which seemed to be below them. Another noise was heard much later, and much closer. It seemed to be the stereo sound of Mike and Abdul's snoring. Whilst initially annoying, it had everyone laughing eventually. Finally, when someone farted, even the security team burst out laughing, which woke Mike and Abdul, who were not happy at being woken at all, especially as they thought it was the middle of the night.

"What's wrong with you lot?" Mike coughed out as he woke up.

"Yes, you noisy buggers," Abdul joined in.

That was it for Sasha. She ordered the lights on and organised another room for Mike and Abdul, who couldn't understand why they were being moved. When they were told they snored, they argued against the claim, but went anyway.

Morning came and they started the long climb up to street level and real light. Two vans were waiting. They piled into the back. Joan cried out when she saw the babies there. Joan and Michael looked like they'd just won the lottery. They had become wonderful parents, Ellie thought. They were driven away towards the motorway, along the main road. The windows were covered. Sarah handed them some newspapers.

The headlines read:

Government Selected to Die.

Proposition Murder.

The news reported that three suicide bombers had shot at security before blowing themselves up in an attempt to kill the authors of the new Government Select proposition, just carried out by the UN last week. The papers went on to sing praises of the group, elevating them to near sainthood. They read the articles one by one. Mike looked at Sasha.

"So that's it, I'm dead."

"You're dead, deader than Mc Dead the master of Mc Dead land, as Black Adder may have said," she smiled. "Sorry, are you grieving?"

"Well, it's official," Mike boasted. "I, Mike Ian Lenard Farmer, am officially now a lifetime member of the non-tax paying fuck you HMRC club."

"Seriously, dude," one of the sharp guards commented. "Your initials are MILF?"

"Yes, and?"

"Have you never watched American Pie? Man, that's a classic."

Everyone had seen it, including Abdul. He said it was only one of five DVD's the previous owner of his bar had left behind.

The rest of their journey was quiet. No one wanted to discuss the details in the paper as they included separate pieces on Jack, and how his death was probably related. They came to a small airfield and drove into the hanger. The doors were closed before they were allowed to get out. A small private jet was the only plane in the hanger, which they boarded. It felt strange not having to go through passport control, not that they had passports anyway. The old ones had been burnt in Scotland, and new passports wouldn't be issued before the flight took off.

On board, it was fairly basic. "Where's all the wood and leather? You know we're used to better than this?" Ellie joked.

"Oh yes, you had a luxury yacht!" Sasha retaliated.

"Don't mention Abdul's boat, please," Abdul pleaded.

"Sorry," Sasha offered. "I wasn't thinking."

The hanger doors opened and the plane taxied out and down the runway. They were the only plane on the runway and the pilot already had clearance to take off. They took off at a very steep incline, then levelled out. The plane became relatively quiet, with just a small hum, sounding like a content bee hive. Sasha removed her belt and walked down the aisle. Mike was usually the first to talk, but before he could say anything, along the lines of "Oh stewardess", Sasha threw a packet of nuts at him.

"Got you!"

That brought on laughter from everyone.

Sasha handed each of them an envelope, with a number on it.

"You will notice that your names are not on the envelope. That is because you no longer exist. I mean this … this is as serious as having a heart attack and deadlier. If you mess up, call a relative, send flowers to a grave, or, heaven forbid, write a letter or email, you could, and probably would, kill everyone here. Now, here is the good bit. You are all going to Greenland." Sasha waited for reaction.

"What? You have to be kidding."

"As a matter of fact, I am, but I thought anything would seem good after that."

"Very funny. Now, where are we to see our lives out?"

"Canada. To be exact, a place called Placentia. It's a small community with a French history. They are a very proud people and we chose them partly because they are an honest community, one that has offered to take a small number of refugees from around the world. We have put together a story of you coming from different parts for different reasons. Mike and Ellie will remain as UN workers, but under different identities. You will have spent considerable time in transit together, so it will be expected that you have become close. There's no need to hide your friendship, which we thought would obviously be hard for you. I will leave you in peace to look at your identities."

None of them wanted to open their envelopes, so Mike went first.

"Wayne Dibley?" he said jokingly.

"Seriously, who are you?"

"Apparently, I am now Richard Swift."

"Okay. Not bad. I'm Jill Douglas. Really, Jill?"

"I don't know what you're complaining about, I'm Mohamed Jamar," Abdul said, rubbing his chin. "Oh, I suppose it could be worse. It could have been Mike."

Mike kicked out at Abdul playfully.

"Joan what about you four?"

"Well, we didn't release the babies' names so they feel they will be okay. I am to be Sara and Michael is ... oh I hope this is okay, Ellie ... they have named him Jack."

"That's beautiful, but is it Syrian?"

"Yes, as a matter of fact, we do use Jack in Syria."

"Well, now I think about it, that is perfect." Ellie smiled.

Fatima and Abir were now Yana and Yaman, which they seemed pleased with.

The plane journey was bumpy as they flew in. Again, when they landed, they were off-loaded in the hanger. This time there was no van waiting, just four vehicles ranging in age, style and colour. All were four-wheel drives, but one was a Jeep, meant for Mike. There was a Ford truck for Abdul, which he loved. A Land Rover Discovery with baby seats, for Michael and Joan, and the last was a Nissan Crossover for Ellie. They were given directions to their new homes. Thankfully, they wouldn't be far apart. The cases in the cars contained all they would need to start off with. Sasha said her goodbyes. Suddenly, everything seemed to be moving quickly. Sasha explained that this was the best way. Ellie and Mike, being the UN workers, would show them to their new homes. In time, if they wanted to move, there was a chance they could. Tears were shed as they disembarked from the plane and headed into their new cars and their new lives.

Chapter Forty-Eight

Pride Comes Before Truth

Their settlement in their new community had gone well. Six months had passed without incident. The babies had started to walk, and the 'guess their age' competition settled on them being nearly two years old, so their birthday was set to the day they were found, minus a year. Abdul started working as a manager in one of the few bars in town. Calling him Mohamed was troublesome for the group initially. Funnily enough, only his name seemed hard to remember. Mike, or Richard, as he was now known, had said he thought it was due to Abdul's huge personality.

The UN had contacted Ellie to say they wanted to meet them all, under the pretence that they had to review the refugees progress. They were meeting at the docks in the harbour master's building. An old face greeted them, John Summerville, who had been let in on their secret. Although, he was limited to phone contact, using a monitored phone with a delay, so if any of them let something slip, the call could be terminated. John was pleased to see them and they all sat down to coffee.

"Well, what's the news?" Mike asked.

"Actually, it's good. You may have heard of the small African state that turned out to be the first to vote in Government Select? Well, it's been running for two months now and they are a very happy country. They retained a small monarchy, and since the new government took over, it turned out that some of their own land, which was being controlled by the previous corrupt government, was being withheld for a good reason. There are diamonds there and emeralds, a lot of which are quite valuable. You might not think that is fantastic news but, and here's the thing, they now see their country forming a proper police force and industry. Money for health is now available and a deal is being put together to build new infrastructure. It's already at the planning stage. All good things, but that has had a knock-on effect on the newly re-instated monarchy and the way they view themselves. They want to be more like the UK monarchy, and want to buy some respect, even if they don't earn it."

"Get to the point," Mike prompted. "I'll read the book later."

"Okay, keep your hat on. They have given half the mines over to the government to be used for the benefit of the people. Not surprisingly, the people love them, and they in turn love you, despite the fact they think you're dead. They love your memory and legacy. Anyway, they gave gifts to the Government Select and, as they can't accept gifts, they gave them to us. We could have sold them, but they ended up here."

John walked through the warehouse and out towards the water, where a forty-foot motor cruiser was moored.

"This, Mohamed, is yours. A gift from the King. You all have something. Ellie, you have a Rolex, I'm told a bloody nice one. You, Mike, get a small ranch in Africa. It's up to you what you do with it. Michael and Joan, you have an education for the babies in the finest schools in Europe and accommodation nearby until they graduate. So, you will have to wait for yours."

A Zombie-like Abdul walked towards the yacht. He reached out with one hand and stroked it, like an owner strokes the winning horse at Ascot. Fatima and Abir joined him, as stunned as he was. It wasn't as big or as luxurious as the Horse of the Seas, but it was more suited to the Canadian coast. It was obvious Abdul loved it. After their initial shock wore off, they sat down to have a drink with John, who said he had to catch the next flight out. They sat and chatted with merriment as the babies practised their walking, to the amusement of them all. There had been no shortage of babysitters since the children had been in Canada. They had several aunties and uncles to thank for that. Truthfully, they had all helped raise them, and Joan was happy that they did. The children were healthy, despite what they had been through.

Mike raised his glass.

"To us, to what we achieved and to what we may yet achieve."

"Careful, Richard (Mike). We are all God's creatures. We succeed because of his grace," Joan said in a quiet voice.

"Maybe, but I believe in me, and us. I think we did pretty well."

"No," injected Ellie. "I can't believe that. We went through too much not to have had some help. It can't be all just coincidence and luck."

"Abdul, sorry Mohamed, think God needs help, we help."

Suddenly, Joan realised the babies had wandered off.

"The babies," she shouted.

"Don't panic," Ellie reassured her. "They can't have gone far."

There were only two exits. One was closed and the other one, the one they had just come through, was a little open. It led to the water front. Joan jumped up to run, but a shadow appeared in the doorway. It was an old man and he had both children by the hand, helping them walk back in. Joan froze.

"Thank you," she said walking up and taking the children.

The old man spoke to her, but he was too quiet for the others to hear. Joan turned to hand the babies to Michael. When she turned back to the old man, he was gone. She ran to the door and scanned up and down the dock. He was nowhere to be seen. The day was warm, but a strong gust came from the sea, pushing her gently back towards the warehouse.

Inside, Mike asked, "Did you find him?"

"No, he's gone."

"What did he say?"

"It's hard to remember, but, and I know it's crazy, but I think he's the same old man who was in the tunnel at Wembley Stadium."

"Seriously?" asked Michael

"That's not possible." As he said it, he ran his hands around Adara's little neck to get a better hold of her. His fingers felt something hard, like a chain. Immediately he looked closer and called out to Joan.

"Joan, look at this please."

Joan and the others quickly gathered around. Michael removed the chain, which looked like it was gold. It held a stone. On the stone was some small writing in Arabic, barley legible.

He read the words out loud:

"*From the Dust of Hate Comes Love*"

"Look," Ellie said. "Adnan has one, too. Does it say the same?"

Joan took this chain and read.

"*Only Love can Carry the Truth*"

They sat down, trying to absorb what they had read.

"We're not going to fall for this," Mike said, sounding nervous. "It's someone who knows who we are, and they're probably after something."

"I don't know," Ellie answered. "None of us would have met if it hadn't been for the children."

"That's true," said Abdul. "She's got a point."

"So, are we saying that it was all a miracle from God?" asked Michael.

"The truth is, I think that, like with all miracles, there is always another logical explanation if you choose to look for one. There is no need for faith, otherwise," Joan remarked.

The End

21611551R00166

Printed in Great Britain
by Amazon